Missing: Sweet Baby James

Dedicated to my family who inspire me, especially to my grandchildren who hold a special place in my heart: Daniel, Samantha - who read this story many times, Steven, Jillian, Chase, Tanner, Mackenzie and Austin. This story had many eyes on it as it grew into being.

Thanks to Elizabeth Vollstadt who was there from the start, to my faithful writer's group in Hocking Hills: Sherry Hartzler, Justine Wittich, Jill Sanders, Pam Gary, Mary Ellen Donovan, and Cindy Parker, who continue to encourage me.

Also, to the GC Writer's Group who took me in as one of their own when I moved back to town.

To my readers, a big thank you for your support. May God bless you.

Other books by Barbara A. Whittington:
Vada Faith
Ezra and Other Stories
Dear Anne: Love Letters from Nam

CHAPTER 1

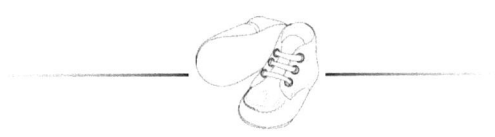

"DOREEN MOON, IF you don't hold still, I'm gonna hog-tie you to this chair!" Vada Faith whipped the pink salon chair around so she and Doreen were face to face. She shook her comb under Doreen's nose and the woman's eyes grew wide as china plates. "I'm a nervous wreck!" Vada Faith let out a long labored breath. "I've had six hair cuts since Joy Ruth left to take Mama to her doctor's appointment."

"Well, forgive me for living!" Doreen closed her tabloid ruffling the pages loudly.

"This day's been a disaster." Vada Faith swallowed hard, took a big breath, and blew her blond bangs off her forehead. "I'm sorry, Dorrie. The girls needed panty hose this morning for a school project. I had to wake up the baby and take him with us to the store." She smiled when she thought of James, who always woke up happy. "Then," she added, "I learned from a note in their book bag the girls had volunteered me to make pancakes this Friday, of all days! Fridays are crazy here!"

Vada Faith turned Doreen around so the woman could see herself in the mirror and started sectioning off her hair. "Their teacher, Miss Jenny, bought maple syrup at the farm they visited. Thus, the pancakes." She frowned at Doreen. "I dared them to volunteer me for anything else!" She shook her comb at Doreen's face in the mirror. "I'm done with that school."

"Calm down, honey." Doreen reached up and patted the beautician's arm.

Vada Faith breathed deeply as she wrapped another piece of gray hair around a roller.

"I'm sorry I can't sit still, honey." Doreen held up the tabloid. "It's this story. Someone has spotted an alien down on Bourbon Street. I hope it's moved on by the time they have that Mardi Gras in February. Imagine! An alien in the middle of that mess. Whew."

"That story isn't true, Doreen." Vada Faith glanced down at the tabloid. "Yep, that's the one. They make up stories and print them."

"This is *The Very Latest News.*" Doreen shook the magazine. "Aliens is everywhere. I saw it on TV." She shook her head. "Oops, I moved again, sorry. I hope your mama's tests are good. I heard over at the coffee shop that Helena had a doctor's appointment."

Vada Faith put in the last roller and settled Doreen under a pink dryer.

Thankfully, Doreen would soon be combed out and gone. The woman had the most stubborn gray hair and she never stopped talking. Vada Faith grabbed the broom and swept up the hair around her chair.

"When you see your mama," Doreen called, popping her head out from under the dryer, "tell her I'll put her on the prayer list over at the New Believer Baptist Church. It's where I go now." She opened the tabloid. "I switched my membership from Heavenly Tabernacle when they got rid of Brother Bo Shannon. They said he was a big flirt." Doreen grinned, and said above the roar of the dryer, "Well, he was not! He was real friendly is all. Besides too many young Democrats go there now. You know those liberals. Always wanting to change things up." She sighed. "Don't forget to tell your mama about the prayers." The woman's words trailed off as she pushed herself back under the dryer.

Vada Faith nodded. She wondered how someone over at the coffee shop knew her mama had a doctor's appointment. Shady Creek was a cauldron of gossip.

Just then Cindy Mahan, her baby sitter, pushed through the shop door pulling eight-month old James behind in his stroller.

"Well, look who's here." Vada Faith smiled and went to help Cindy guide the stroller inside. Her beautiful baby smiled at her. His little hands gripped the front of the stroller and his eyes sparkled.

"We got bored," Cindy said, plopping into the nearest pink chair. "Me and Sweet Baby James. We couldn't find a thing to do. He got tired of peek-a-boo and his ABC blocks. We thought we'd come and visit. Didn't we, James?" She ruffled his blond hair. James smiled up at her and batted his big blue eyes. He was a little flirt already.

He clapped his hands and drooled on himself. He leaned over the stroller and stared at his new blue tennis shoes. He wore his blue shirt with the yellow bulldozer that read, "Daddy's Little Man."

"Check out this little guy's new Levi's." Vada Faith patted the baby's leg. "They fit him perfectly."

"I know." Cindy leaned over and hugged James. "Little Fashion King of Shady Creek. Oh," she added, "James has an admirer. An old woman in front of the diner. She leaned down and patted him on the foot. He kicked and squealed. The more he squealed, the more she laughed. He reached out and grabbed the fringe of her ugly brown shawl. Ugh! She called him Robert twice. I gave her his correct name. She shook her head and grumbled. Then she took off down the street."

"Well, buddy, are you collecting girlfriends?" Vada Faith watched as James chewed on his fingers and clung to his brown bear. He hugged the bear, giving her a toothy smile. He put his hands over his eyes.

"Peek a boo!" His mother covered her eyes.

James squealed and kicked his feet. One of his little blue shoes fell to the floor.

Vada Faith's heart swelled. She leaned over, put on his shoe and tied the lace. She picked up the baby and squeezed him. He jabbered over her shoulder and pointed at the lights.

She carried him to the magazine rack on the wall and held up the new *Highlights* magazine with children on the cover. He chewed his fingers and kicked his legs. He was cutting more teeth.

Doreen waved at the baby and Vada Faith took him to see her. "Hey, little fellow," she said, pulling herself out from under the dryer to pat him on the arm. "He's a doll, Vada Faith."

"Thanks." James yawned as Vada Faith showed him around the rest of the shop. She put him back into his stroller and he promptly snuggled with his bear. "Time to go home, big boy." She kissed his cheek and smoothed down his blond hair. "Don't forget, Cindy, I'll be home early today."

Cindy nodded and buckled James into his seat. Vada Faith helped her get the stroller out onto the sidewalk and nodded as they turned to go toward home.

She waved them off and went to pour a cup of coffee. There was a lull in the shop so she picked up a magazine and leafed through it, thankful for the quiet.

When Doreen's dryer stopped, Vada Faith styled her hair and hugged her on her way out the door. Relieved the shop was finally empty, she drank from her bottle of water on the counter and added some items to her grocery list. She enjoyed going home early to be with James.

"Mama's feeling fine," Joy Ruth said, coming in the door. "She had blood work, a chest x-ray, and a mammogram." She slung her purse on the counter by her station. "Anyway, she'll have the results in a few days. I think she's just been tired. I'm doing her hair this afternoon."

"Great." Vada Faith grabbed her purse. "She can't be very sick if she wants her hair done. Well, I'm out of here. I need to hit the grocery then home to my boy."

"Sure. I'll stop by on my way home to see him."

Vada Faith headed for the door glad she'd be home soon. "See you later."

As she rushed out of the shop, she had no idea her world was about to change forever.

CHAPTER 2

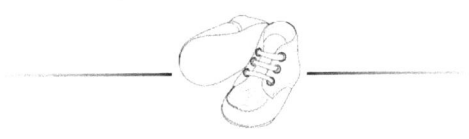

THE OLD WOMAN straightened her brown shawl around her shoulders. Her big sister had made the shawl for her. The baby in the stroller had jerked on it pulling it lopsided. He recognized Birdie. She smiled and walked down the street. The baby in the carriage was Robert, her baby brother, even if the girl said no. Birdie shook her head, trying to clear her thoughts. Where did the girl go in such a hurry? Why did she have Robert and wheel him away from her, his sister?

Her mind scrambled things like a mixer in a bowl of eggs. Like the directions to Sissy's house. Her mind had held the directions firmly in place until the minute she needed them. Then, poof, they disappeared, flying away to an inaccessible place in Birdie's head. Sissy instructed her to always ride the bus to her house. The swaying of the bus had lulled Birdie's tired body into a peaceful sleep. The directions to Sissy's house had taken flight.

Sissy reviewed the directions with Birdie each time she came to her house. However, this was a surprise visit. Birdie had left the home for crazy people in the middle of the night, with the key she'd stolen. There'd been no review of landmarks.

When the bus jostled to a stop and the driver called, "Shady Creek," Birdie woke with a start. Not knowing what to do, she disembarked with the other passengers. The streets went in every direction, baffling Birdie.

Her sister's warning rang in her ears. "Don't talk to anyone." So, she clamped her mouth shut for fear she might blurt out she was lost.

Scared, Birdie made her way past the Main Street sign with tears streaming down her cheeks and headed into a neighborhood lined with houses.

CHAPTER 3

AFTER AN EARLY lunch, Vada Faith leaned back in the front porch swing and pushed off with her bare foot. She smiled over at James sitting in his playpen sorting through his toys. She had changed his clothes putting him into his soft blue pants and matching Peter Rabbit shirt and bib. That little guy was the best thing that had happened to her since the birth of her twin girls eight years earlier, and helped with the heartbreak of the miscarriage she'd had a few years back.

Today the street was unusually quiet for such a sunny fall day. She liked the convenience of living a few streets from the center of town. Their old Victorian home, once owned by her husband's grandmother, Belle Waddell, now belonged to her family. As the town grew it encompassed the big home. It stood regally among a row of pastel bungalows, the perfect place to raise a family.

Vada Faith opened a magazine looking for new hair styles. A few of her customers wanted something different every week.

Just then the kitchen buzzer sounded through the open living room window. She closed the magazine and let the swing glide to a stop.

"Hey, buddy," she said to James, who chewed on his plastic duck. Her heart swelled at the sight of him. She patted the baby on his blond head as he pulled up to the side of the pen. He smiled, showing off his four front teeth.

"Mommy loves you, too." She bent and kissed him on the cheek. He dropped to his bottom to investigate the snaps on his pants. He was such fun to watch.

Earlier, he had tried to catch the shadows that fell over the teddy bear design of his play pen pad. He waved his arms in the air. When a butterfly landed on the play pen, he clapped his hands. "Mama," he said, looking straight at Vada Faith, his blue eyes crinkling in a grin.

He'd only said mama a time or two. Dada was what he said the most. She didn't mind. John's happiness when James said it was enough for her. He was a great dad.

As she opened the screen door to go inside, she turned and glanced back. She watched James roll onto his belly and start jabbering as a bug marched across the porch floor. A bottle of milk lay beside him.

She hummed as she took the apple pie from the oven and slipped it onto a mat on the counter. She turned off the oven. A meat loaf cooled beside the pie. The kitchen smelled wonderful. When she had pie later, James would have some fruit sauce his grandmother made.

Her mother, Helena Warfield, possibly the world's worst mother, was amazingly the world's best grandmother. She even made baby food for James, including teething biscuits from her own recipe.

Vada Faith's relationship with her mother had been on solid ground since the birth of James. Helena had left Vada Faith and Joy Ruth, her twin sister, with their father when they were toddlers. Delbert Waddell could've used a few parenting classes. It hadn't been easy but now she and Joy Ruth were adults and life was good.

With the arrival of James, Vada Faith became more tolerant and forgiving of her mother. There was something to be said for growing up. Maturing. Maybe it came with having a "last" baby.

Squeals of delight came through the front window as James made some new discovery on the porch floor.

"Coming, James," she called toward the hallway leading to the porch.

"I-love-you," she sang, opening the refrigerator door as Barney's theme song rolled off her tongue. "You-love-me, we're-a-hap-py-fam-i-ly!"

She grabbed a bottle of water for herself and a bottle of juice for James. She had to laugh as the jingle played over in her head.

She'd sworn never to watch Barney again when the girls outgrew him. Now she was playing the dvd's for James and singing along as he clapped. She was happy as a mother bird clucking over her brood. That was how James made her feel. Happy. Content. Her life was perfect.

The phone rang, interrupting her thoughts. The church secretary at Sunnyside Baptist needed two dozen cupcakes for the youth meeting on Saturday. Vada Faith found a scrap of paper and jotted a note to herself, leaving it on the counter as a reminder to bake the cupcakes. Then she hurried back to the porch and her baby boy.

CHAPTER 4

BIRDIE TURNED A corner and saw the street with houses lined like pastel candies in a lace box. Forgetting she was lost, she smiled as she trotted down the street.

She gasped with delight at the big Victorian home ahead. Could that be her childhood home? She rushed toward the tall white house.

"Mama's baking," she said, catching a whiff of spices. "I'll have pie and homemade bread and jam."

Wait, Mama was gone. Birdie stood still. Her big sister, Sissy, was in charge of her now. Why was mama's house here on this street? Where was her big sister?

Birdie shook her head. Then she saw the baby just ahead on the sidewalk. Her precious baby brother, Robert, was sitting right in front of her. Chewing on his bib. Drooling all over his light blue trousers. He must be cutting another tooth. She charged toward him her arms outstretched.

A skinny boy stared at Birdie from under a tree in the yard. She slowed her pace. The boy grabbed up the wire cage and hurried to stand over Robert. Birdie knew in that instant her baby brother was in trouble. A bird chirped at Birdie from the floor of the cage.

When the boy made the slightest move toward the baby, Birdie scooped him up. She positioned the child in her arms and wiped the drool off his chin with his bib. She hugged him to her. He held his plastic bottle of milk between his teeth. He looked up at Birdie with his big eyes. He took his bottle in his hand and said, "Ma."

Robert didn't know Ma was dead. Birdie wouldn't tell him. He would learn hurtful things when he was big, but he was only a baby now. She and Sissy would take care of him. They would keep their promise to Mama.

Birdie looked at the unfamiliar chairs on the porch, the bushes and trees in the yard. She knew it was urgent to get Robert away from this place that looked like Mama's house, but wasn't.

The boy was gauging her every move. She scurried away, looking over her shoulder as she went. Finally, she turned the corner and cuddled Robert to her. She would protect him just as Mama expected.

The baby felt warm in her arms. It was as though he'd been absent for ages. Now he felt so familiar. So good. "Well, look at you," Birdie said, glancing down at the child in her arms. "Aren't you something?" He was looking up at her expectantly, with his beautiful blue eyes exactly as he'd done when Mama had brought him into this world. It felt so good to hold her baby brother again. She'd never let him go. Not ever. She had to get him to Sissy's house.

CHAPTER 5

"HERE WE GO, Sweet Baby James." Pushing open the screen door with her toe, Vada Faith held the baby's juice bottle in mid air. The blinding sun made her blink a couple of times. She stumbled out the door, turning toward the play pen.

It was empty.

"James?" She shook her head to clear her vision. "James," she said. Then, she looked into the play pen and screamed, "Baby! James! Where are you?" She dropped the two bottles in a chair, and pushed aside the mound of toys in the pen. No baby boy.

"James!" She hurried across the front porch, looking in every corner. "James!"

She pulled her basket collection from under the long white church pew John had painted.

Her son wasn't there.

Her heart pounded.

She ran to the play pen. Where could he be? Could he have stood on the toys and climbed or fell out? She hadn't heard a cry. She'd heard only happy chatter.

She dashed into the front yard.

"James!"

Not one sound could be heard. Not even a dog barked.

She ran around the house, kicking through a pile of leaves the girls had left the day before. Back on the front porch, she gripped the sides of the empty play pen. Where was he? How could he be gone?

Her stomach knotted. Her breakfast threatened to come up. She walked to the sidewalk, her fists clenched at her sides.

Had her mother picked up the baby? No. Her sister? Never. Joy Ruth was doing their mother's hair at the beauty shop. Neither would take James without asking. They knew Vada Faith was paranoid about her children. She stared up and down the street.

Silence.

Suddenly, it came to her.

"Harriet," she screamed, tearing across the street towards Harriet Mitchell's house. She prayed Harriet had James. The woman had taken him from his pen a few months back wanting to show him the birds at her feeder.

That day, Vada Faith hadn't heard Harriet step onto the porch. She'd been planting flowers along the side of the house. Thankfully, she heard James squealing as the woman carried him to the sidewalk.

Now, she paused to get her breath. A For Sale sign loomed in front of Harriet's house. How could she have forgotten? Harriet was in a nursing facility and had been for weeks. Was she losing her mind like Harriet?

"My baby, James!" Vada Faith gasped as the dispatcher answered her 911 call. "He's missing!" She stood in the kitchen gripping the cell phone.

"James?" the woman repeated. "Missing?"

"Yes, my baby boy, James! One minute he was on the front porch in his play pen." She paced the kitchen. "The next minute he was gone. Please," she pleaded, "someone has to find my baby. He's only eight-months old. He was taken from my porch a minute ago. Vada Faith and John Waddell. The old Waddell home."

Tears ran down her face, dripping onto her new blouse. She had put it on with such care that morning while the baby crawled happily around her in circles. She wiped her tears with her free hand.

"Vada Faith Waddell! Oh, yes," the dispatcher responded, "Officer Cobb will be right there. Calling him now. He's at the gas station. You hang on, honey. He'll be there in a jiffy."

When Vada Faith put the phone down, she dropped into a kitchen chair, frozen with panic. She put her head on the table and wept.

CHAPTER 6

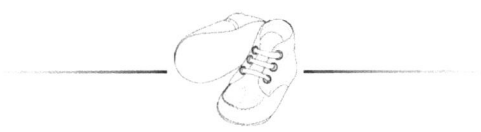

A NOISE MADE Birdie turn and look back, but it was the wind in the trees. She placed the baby inside her large tapestry bag that stood open at the top. He snuggled down on her flannel nightgown and smiled up at her. She felt a nip in the air and pulled her shawl tighter. Birdie grasped the leather handles of her satchel and moved on quickly.

She kept looking over her shoulder. The boy never appeared. If anything happened to Robert her sister would be mad as a wet hornet. Birdie got blamed for every mishap. She had to be careful.

Sissy would want to know their big white house was still there. It was different but it was there. The baby and the house had been waiting for her. A miracle, it was. Birdie's face crinkled in a smile.

CHAPTER 7

"VADA FAITH'S BEAUTY Bar," Joy Ruth answered on the first ring.

"James is gone!" Vada Faith paced the porch floor becoming increasingly panicked. How long could it take for the police officer to get there when his office was just a few streets away?

"Hey," her sister yelled over the din of the beauty salon. "I'm doing Mama's hair."

"James was taken from his play pen!" Please Lord, she prayed, let her son be okay.

"How do you like me now?" Toby Keith wailed from the shop radio.

"Hey, Vay," Joy Ruth shouted, "I can't hear you."

"Joy Ruth, listen! James is gone!"

"What? James is what?" Joy Ruth paused, then called out, "Juanita, take that walk-in."

Vada Faith jammed her finger on the button and ended the phone call. What did it matter if her twin heard the news now or in five minutes? She'd be heartbroken whenever she heard. She loved James like he was her own baby. "Please Heavenly Father," she prayed, "keep my baby, James, safe."

She called her husband's cell phone. There was no answer.

She looked down at her hands and wiped absently at blood on her thumb nail. She'd chewed off a piece of her nail without knowing it.

"Vada Faith, you're ruining a perfect manicure." She could hear her sister's familiar words. "Stop chewing those nails."

Well, who cared about nails? Who cared about anything? All she cared about was having her baby in her arms.

She went inside, passing the old oak chest in the hallway that her husband had refinished. Grandma Belle's black Bible was open on the top with a purple ribbon marking Psalm 23, her favorite verse. *"Yea, though I walk through the valley of the shadow of death, I shall fear no evil."*

The words chilled her.

Because she did fear evil.

She stepped back onto the porch.

She dug a tissue out of her pocket and wiped her nose. She started pacing again. She'd been far too smug lately. Was this her payback?

What if James was taken by a real kidnapper. He'd want money. She and her husband had money. John's business had really taken off. How much would the guy want? They'd get it somehow, no matter how much he wanted.

Did she have an enemy? Someone who thought she didn't deserve a baby. She'd been pregnant with a surrogate baby a few years back, and lost it which broke her heart. She had enemies. People with narrow minds who said she must be crazy to do that for anyone.

Someone may have come down the street and saw her baby boy in his pen. Nobody could resist him. He was so beautiful. Had they carried him off to another town? To another country? To another life? Oh, God, please no.

She put her hands over her ears to try to stop the horrible thoughts.

In the distance she heard the police siren. It wasn't long before the patrol car flew into her driveway, spewing gravel, and jerking to a stop.

She stood and watched as Officer Duke Cobb hopped out and slammed the car door. The tears rolled as she stumbled back to the empty play pen.

The officer nearly toppled a fern in a white wicker stand as he loped onto the porch like a big furry dog. He righted the plant and pulled a pencil and notebook from his pocket.

"Now," he said, coming to stand beside her, "what's this about your baby being missing?"

"James! He was in his play pen. I ran inside to take a pie out of the oven. When I came back he was gone!" She wrung her hands and tried to hold herself together.

"Slow down," he said, soothingly, "take your time and tell me what happened."

"James was playing with his toys. I went inside and took the pie out of the oven. I put it on the counter. I got his juice bottle and a bottle of water for me out of the refrigerator. I wasn't gone a minute or two. I answered a quick phone call from the church secretary about bringing cupcakes to the youth meeting on Saturday." She pointed again to the empty play pen where bears danced cheerfully across the pad. "James was right there. Minutes ago."

Trying to get her emotions in check, she breathed in and out deeply. "How can he be gone?"

"Hey, we'll find him." He scrawled something on his pad. "Don't you worry."

"I am worried." She struggled to draw air into her lungs. "I'm sick with worry. He's only eight-months old. He can't walk. He's a baby. He can crawl, that's it. You've got to find him!"

She dabbed at her eyes with her hand.

Duke Cobb stood there, unmoving, chewing on the end of his pencil the way he had back in high school. Vada Faith and her husband, John, had graduated from high school the same year as Duke.

"Let me have a look around." He stuck his pad and pencil in his pocket. He leaned over the play pen again. "I bet the little guy could get out of this pen."

"His legs are too short. He's tried. Over and over."

"Well, I'll search the premises first thing."

Vada Faith frowned at him. "Premises?"

He looked around him. "Premises. This whole place."

"I already checked the porch and yard. He was right here on this porch. Someone came and took him away." She wiped her eyes.

He poked around the wide porch. "Anything else happen this morning?" He turned and raised an eyebrow at her.

"No. I worked a couple of hours at the beauty shop. Cindy, our sitter, watched James. Mama usually watches him but she had an appointment for some tests."

"Anything unusual about Cindy?"

"No. She's a good kid. Lives down the street. She left when I got home, just before noon."

Duke made his way off the porch and around the house with her hurrying after him.

"He isn't in the yard. I was out here already." She gestured across the lawn. "He was in his pen on the porch." She ran her fingers through her short blond hair. "Oh, God!" She groaned. "What am I going to tell his daddy? You've got to find James. John will go nuts."

Back on the front porch, her heart nearly stopped at the sight of the empty play pen.

"Okay." He glanced at her. "I have to ask you a few questions."

"You're wasting time! Please, Duke, go find James!" She chewed on her lower lip until she tasted blood.

"Where did you say John was?" He flipped open his notebook.

"On a business trip." She fell into a porch rocker. "A woodworking conference. In Kentucky. He'll be back today." She sighed heavily. "I've tried calling his cell. He's not answering. He forgets to charge it. Sometimes he forgets to turn it on when he's working."

"Where's the rest of the family?"

"The twins, Charity and Hope, are in school. They're eight. In third grade. Joy Ruth is doing Mama's hair at the shop. I imagine John's mother is home, although she runs a lot."

Tears poured down her cheeks. She grabbed another tissue from the box on the wicker table.

The officer started toward her and stopped. He wasn't good at offering comfort, especially to her. Former cheerleader. Best looking girl in school. Stuck up. Anyway, he couldn't stop her tears from flowing like Niagara Falls. "Try to get hold of yourself. I need your help here."

"How would you act," she snapped, "if someone took your baby off your porch, Duke Cobb? Then, someone bullied you with questions?"

"I'm not bullying you. If someone took my baby, I'd be mad as hell. We'll find your baby, I promise." He walked across the porch, looking superior. "You can stop worrying."

Stupid man, Vada Faith thought. Duke Cobb didn't know one thing about finding a baby. God, where could her little guy be?

Her heart nearly stopped at the thoughts flitting through her head. The endless possibilities made her ill. She shook from head to toe. This nightmare could not be happening to her. She put her family in God's hands every morning. If God was truly holding them, how could this little one have slipped out?

BIRDIE CRISSCROSSED ALLEYS continuously looking over her shoulder. The boy with the cage was nowhere to be seen.

Confusion took over Birdie's mind. Why had she and Sissy moved from the big white house? Why was Sissy living alone out on the hill in the woods? Was Sissy still afraid of people?

Sissy never came to town. Never rode a bus. Never watched television. How awful she must feel to never do the things Birdie loved. Something else was puzzling. Why had she been living away in that crazy home with strangers? Mean people. They were not like Sissy who treated Birdie special. Sissy would work out this puzzle for her. If only she and Robert could get to Sissy's house.

In her mind's eye she could see the wooded road where her sister lived. She should have pulled the string on the bus and jumped off before the Shady Creek stop, the way she had last time.

"Keep off the main roads," Sissy always said. "Stay in the woods along the highway." That's what Birdie did.

Just as she stepped into the woods outside town, the directions to Sissy's came to her. Clear as a bell. Lone Oak Road and it wasn't too far.

CHAPTER 9

"I CALLED IN a detective from Charleston," Duke Cobb said, wiping his brow, "he'll be here soon. We don't have kidnappings in Shady Creek," he said, and coughed. "Uh, the truth is, we've never had a real crime here. I mean, you know. Small stuff. Stolen bikes. Fender benders. I think someone you know has your baby. They'll bring him back soon. Probably took him to the bakery for a cookie." He chewed his jaw. "Maybe John's mom picked him up."

"Never! Louise would never take James without asking."

Duke's phone rang and he turned away, holding a mumbled conversation and then said, "Thanks, Lefty." Putting his phone in his pocket he turned back to Vada Faith.

"Lefty Parr said James was taken off your porch once before." He moved a finger along the porch bannister. "Is that true?"

"A few months back Harriet Mitchell, a neighbor, took him out of his play pen." She sniffed and wiped her nose. "She wanted to show him the birds in her back yard. I was planting pansies in the side yard. I stopped her, of course. You remember the Mitchell's. We went to school with Donny."

"Yeah, I remember old Donny." He frowned and shrugged.

"Oh." She vaguely remembered Duke and Donny in a fight over Shirley Blossom, whose parents owned the local dairy.

"Well, let's move on," he said, opening his note pad again. "Why didn't you file a report on Harriet?" He jotted something on his pad.

"Why would I file a report? She's old and harmless." Vada Faith's heart pounded. She paced across the porch. Her sequined flip flops beat out a rhythm on the wooden planks. "I've known that family forever."

"How'd you stop her that day?"

"There wasn't much to stop, Duke. She shuffled along in old pink slippers, barely able to walk and carry James. The baby was waving his arms with excitement to be out of his pen. She told me how much she loved babies. Well, I told her I loved babies too, especially my own."

That day, James had buried his head in Vada Faith's shoulder when she'd taken him from Harriet. She could almost feel her warm baby against her now. She took a deep breath. "James patted my arm with his little hand when I took him."

As she thought of her baby's tiny hand patting her, she was chilled. James always did that when she picked him up. As if it were his job to console her instead of the other way around. Had he detected a neediness in her? She brushed away new tears.

"After I took James from her, Harriet stared down at her empty arms. It was as if I'd taken one of her own babies from her. I was furious. I told her never to come on my porch again. Soon after, the family took her to a nursing center. I feel bad now for being mean to her."

She looked up at Duke. "Do you know what Harriet said? She told me James said, 'Bird,' clear as crystal." She shook her head. "Oh, I know he probably didn't. He was only six months old. Still, I wouldn't be surprised. He's way ahead of babies his age." She glanced over at his note pad and said, "Write that down."

He shot her a puzzled look but made a notation on his pad.

"So, Harriet's in a care place. Whatever happened to old Donny?"

"I don't care about old Donny!" She threw a wad of tissues on the floor. "You need to find my son!"

"He'll be back before long. Don't worry." The man's voice grated on her nerves.

"He's been kidnapped, Duke Cobb!" She screeched. "Kidnapped!"

At his look of horror, she lowered her voice and measured out her words. "Someone took my baby boy off this porch. I don't know if they'll bring him back. You have to go out there and find him." She stood and poked her finger in the officer's chest. He backed up a foot.

"Lefty Parr has a large group of men out searching already," he said. "I should've told you. They're combing every corner of this entire town. I don't know what else to do, Vada Faith."

"You've got to do more, Duke Something quick!"

"Well," he chewed his bottom lip, "do you know Lefty?"

"Of course! Everyone knows Lefty Parr and his wife, Sandy." She sniffed and wiped more tears. "They had Little Hank dedicated at church the same Sunday we dedicated James. We all go to Sunnyside Baptist. James wore his tiny sailor suit and smiled all morning." She ran her fingers absently through her spiked hair. "He won everyone over. Poor Little Hank in his wrinkled jeans. He wailed the whole time. He's way behind James in everything."

"Lefty will put in every effort to find your baby. He's crazy about little Hank. All the guys will. We have good people in this town. Anything else about your son I should know?"

"He'll only eat certain foods." She tried to think of something that might help. Her mind had shifted into low gear, thanks to the Valium she'd found in the medicine cabinet after calling the police. A leftover from when the twins were toddlers. Thankfully, it still did the job.

She was not a pill person. She'd looked at the pink pill a good minute before popping it into her mouth. Anything was better than the nausea and pain she felt.

"James is special," she went on. "He's on sort of a special diet too." She thought of his baby hands reaching out for the Cheerios on his tray every morning and how he smacked down his grandmother's applesauce.

"A special diet? Is the kid sick?" Duke panicked, his voice sharper than he'd intended. Jeez. A missing kid was one thing. A missing sick kid was another. What was going on here anyway? He'd never had anyone in town kidnapped. Now, there was a sick one with special needs missing.

"He's not sick," she said, "we just think he's special. We believed we couldn't have more children when he came along. So we treat him, well, special."

"Whew," Duke said, relieved that the kid wasn't sick.

"Please," she pleaded, "do something. Anything."

"I will." He ran his finger around his tight collar, wondering what to do next. "I've got some ideas."

"The baby's name is John James Waddell," she said. "We call him Sweet Baby James. I used to be in love with the singer, James Taylor. I named the baby after his song. Do you know it? Sweet Baby James?"

"Uh, no. Don't think so." He'd listened to classical music growing up because every radio in the house was tuned to stations his mother liked. That and NPR for her daily news fix.

He walked down the porch steps quickly and into the yard. He didn't have a clue where to start. His job involved petty crimes, an occasional speeder, a few bar fights. This could be big. He pulled himself up to his full height. Here was his chance to prove to the Waddell family and to all of Shady Creek, Duke Cobb was capable of doing his job and doing it well. He was an officer any town would be proud to have on their force. Maybe even New York City. Well, he'd settle for Charleston or Huntington. If only he could figure out how to find Vada Faith's baby.

He'd stake his life there'd been no real kidnapping here. Someone would show up with the boy and a good explanation. Either a grandparent, an aunt, an uncle, or a neighbor.

Vada Faith would gush over her baby and forget, again, Duke Cobb ever existed. That was fine with him. He liked his life. Quiet. Peaceful. Devoid of women. Well, that part didn't make him happy, though nothing could be done about it. Every girl he liked was taken.

"Call the missing person squad, Duke Cobb, right now!" Vada Faith leapt from the swing, letting it bang against her legs.

"This is Shady Creek, not Chicago." He called over his shoulder. "All we have is me. You're lucky to have me, with the budget this town has. We don't get people disappearing around here."

"Someone has disappeared!" She screamed. "You need to find him! He's helpless and can't help himself! Oh, God, what am I going to do?" She pounded her fist on the side of the house.

Turning away, he put his phone to his ear.

She quit pounding and stared at her fists.

Standing under the big oak tree in the front yard, the officer didn't look competent enough to find a missing anything. Especially a baby. He wasn't professional, didn't seem in control.

Over the years Duke Cobb had existed on the outskirts of her life. Today, he was on the main screen, the person she needed most. Was he capable of finding James? The guy still lived with his mother. He'd never been out of the state. Had traveled no further than the police academy in Charleston as far as she knew.

"I want my baby," she wailed. "I want my son." Tears streamed down her face. Her arms ached for James. Where was he? How could he be gone?

Duke hurried back to the porch. He bent over her in the swing, patting her shoulder. "It'll be fine. Now, now, come on. Settle down. You'll make yourself sick."

It made him uncomfortable, trying to soothe her. She and her twin, Joy Ruth, had been at the top of everything that was important at Shady

Creek High School. At least where the guys were concerned. Vada Faith was the girl all of them fantasized about. The prettiest cheerleader, the homecoming queen. Oh, he'd dreamed about Joy Ruth, too, for a minute. She looked just like her sister. When he got to know her, he learned all similarity ended there. Vada Faith was soft and feminine. Joy Ruth was a drill sergeant, bossy as all get out. Vada Faith could melt your heart with one of her smiles. Joy Ruth could cut you in two with one of her looks. Forget that tongue of hers.

He cleared his throat. "That last call was from Lefty. He reported the guys have covered a large area already. They're working their way here." He cleared his throat. "That's good news, don't you think?"

"How can it be good news? They didn't find my baby!"

He walked over to the play pen, putting some distance between himself and the woman. He stared back at the porch steps. Who would come on the Waddell porch on this beautiful fall day and take their baby? Leaning over, he examined the play pen, hoping something would reveal itself to the human eye.

She moaned pitifully.

Not knowing what else to do, he pulled a Mountain Dew from his jacket pocket and uncapped it. He turned it up, taking a long swig. He was buying time. What came next? He was counting on the guy from Charleston to head the investigation. What was holding him up? Maybe traffic on the interstate. Roadwork. A wreck on I-64. Always something.

This was his first kidnapping, if it turned out to be the real thing. To his dismay, it involved Vada Faith Waddell and her husband, John, Shady Creek High's favorite football hero. He ran his fingers through his thick brown hair. It was going to be a long day.

"BIRDIE!" SISSY KAPP stared at her sister standing in the kitchen doorway. "You scared the daylights out of me!"

Birdie walked in, set a baby in the middle of the kitchen floor, and dropped her big satchel beside him. As always, her baby sister gave Sissy a big smile.

"Where'd you come from and where'd you get a baby?" Sissy turned to lower the heat under the tea kettle.

"It's Robert!" Birdie announced, still smiling. She leaned in for a hug. "Don't you recognize this little guy?"

"That's not Robert!" Sissy gasped, her face flushing. She pulled out a chair for Birdie. "That baby is not our brother Robert!"

"Is too!" Birdie dropped into the chair, exhausted. Robert was a load. When she'd arrived at Sissy's overgrown road, she'd lifted the baby out of her satchel. She'd hung onto him like a sack of potatoes. She gave him the rest of his bottle and he jabbered all the way to Sissy's.

Birdie remembered Sissy liked to pick fights. Being the oldest Sissy thought she knew everything. A know-it-all and a smart-aleck too. This baby was Robert. Sissy could go jump in the Kanawha River down the road.

The baby yawned, trying hard to keep his eyes open. Sissy took a quilt from one of the chairs and spread it on the floor. In minutes after she laid him on the quilt his eyes closed. He made sucking noises and smiled in his sleep.

"He was waving at me," Birdie said, sharply, "he even called me Ma. I picked him up from the sidewalk. When Mama died she said to look after Robert. Did you forget?"

"Robert died, Birdie. It's you who forgot." Sissy shook her head in disgust. She prayed Birdie wouldn't have one of her fits. When she didn't get her way she threw a tantrum, a scary one sometimes. "Our brother was three, honey, remember? That was a long time ago. Our little brother died in the house fire."

"Sissy," Birdie said, dismissing everything her sister had said, "you should've seen him waving at me."

"If I had a phone, Birdie Kapp, I'd call the police on you right now. You stole this baby."

"You would not, either, Sissy, you're too scared." Birdie's eyes narrowed. She was being mean and she didn't care. "I know it and you know it."

"No." Sissy sighed and spread the damp dish towel over the sink. "You're right, I wouldn't." Her mind churned. What could she do about this baby her sister brought home? It was evident Birdie was more addled than usual.

Birdie really didn't want to displease Sissy. However, she was happy with Robert sleeping at her feet. "I brought him home where he belongs. Don't you see? He's back." She leaned down and patted the sleeping baby. "He's back now and we'll take care of him. Just like we promised mama." Forever and ever Birdie said to herself.

CHAPTER 11

"WHAT WAS JAMES wearing when you last saw him?" The officer stared at Vada Faith sitting on the porch steps.

Oh, God, when she last saw him. Her mind was blank. Empty. She couldn't remember what her son was wearing thirty minutes earlier.

What had she chosen for him after lunch? He'd spilled peas on his shirt. She'd changed his diaper and his clothes. In his closet, she'd shuffled through the little outfits on the blue hangars. Some days she'd choose tiny jeans and a shirt with a train or a boat on front. Those times he resembled his daddy. She'd often select one of the new outfits her mother had bought.

She used to memorize what the twins wore when they first started to school in case one of them went missing. Today, she couldn't remember what she had for breakfast or anything else she'd done that morning.

"What was James wearing?" Duke repeated.

"He smelled like Johnson's baby lotion," she offered, buying time. "I kissed his cheek as I brought him onto the porch."

Then, just like that, she could see James clearly. "Peter Rabbit," she said. "Peter Rabbit, yes, his grandmother's favorite outfit. Light blue pants and the softest blue shirt ever. There was a big Peter Rabbit on the front."

"Umm," he said, writing on his pad.

"He has sensitive skin and likes soft shirts. Write that down."

Duke stared, as if he'd never heard of babies with sensitive skin. He wrote it down. He had a lot to learn about babies. Women, too, for that matter.

"White socks," she continued, visualizing the baby's little feet as she slipped his socks on. "His new blue tennis shoes. No jacket. It was sunny when we came out." Her voice trailed off. Happiness at remembering him in his Peter Rabbit outfit dissipated as she felt the chill in the air.

She shivered. The sun had disappeared behind the clouds. She was chilly. James wasn't wearing a jacket. Why hadn't she put him in a jacket? It was fall. The weather was changing. What was wrong with her? What mother didn't know when her child needed a jacket?

She put her face in her hands, numb with disbelief. How could her baby be gone so quickly?

James wasn't properly dressed and she'd put him in harm's way. She was guilty even if she wasn't blamed. She went over the details in her mind. What could she have done differently?

A few neighbors had gathered around the police car in the driveway. Duke nodded toward them. When the investigator showed up they'd all be interviewed.

"Vada Faith, let's go over the morning again, make sure you didn't forget anything." He wished she would stop crying. He'd like to go back to his office. He knew what to do there. Here, he wasn't so sure.

"You think I left out something important?" She stood and though she was shorter than Duke she seemed to loom over him. "You think because I couldn't remember what James was wearing, I left out something?" She pulled herself up to her full height.

"I didn't mean on purpose. I thought if we went over the details you'd remember something else." He downed the last of his Mountain Dew and screwed on the top, stuffing the plastic bottle into his jacket pocket. Though she acted big and mighty, she came only to his shoulder.

His cell phone rang and he walked out to the sidewalk to answer it. He put his head down as Herby Johnson, a community busybody, moved from the street to the yard. Duke waved the old man away.

Vada Faith sat down on the swing and punched in her husband's cell number. It rang and rang. She ended the call when the recording came on. Her news couldn't be delivered in a phone message. John always returned her calls, even when she didn't leave a message. He was always in touch. Was something wrong that he wasn't answering?

"George Buck!" The minute the name popped into her head she shot off the porch and ran toward Duke.

He saw her coming and ended his phone conversation. "What?"

"Carrie Buck's boy!" She gasped. "George. He was standing across the street when I went inside. There!" She pointed to where her neighbor Minnie Black stood now. "He was right there."

"Well, we have something to go on. Good." He wrote on his pad. "George Buck. See, you remembered something important." He looked up. "Is it true the kid can't talk since he was struck by lightening?"

"True, but his mother says there's no medical reason." She headed away from Duke. "I'm going to the Buck's. They live right behind us." She turned in the direction of the side yard. Her backyard adjoined the Buck's.

"No!" His voice was firm. "You're not going anywhere, Vada Faith." He softened his tone. "Someone could bring the baby home and he'll need you right here."

"Then you go! That kid might have James!"

"Before I go, I need to check the inside of the house." He nodded toward the front door.

She frowned. "What for? James was outside."

"The detective just instructed me to check the inside of the house. Now, not in ten minutes. This minute." He stared at her and shrugged. "Gotta do my job."

"James was taken from the porch!" She screamed. "You're crazy. My baby was in his play pen. Don't you listen? He might be at George's house this minute and you don't care!"

"Procedures, Vada Faith, I have to follow procedures." He walked to the porch.

"Screw your procedures! He's not inside the house!" Protesting, she followed close behind him. "Idiot," she muttered. What a blockhead he was. The detective on the phone, too. Whoever he was. Wherever he was. "James was taken from this porch." She stomped the porch floor so hard she hurt her foot.

He swung the front door open and stepped inside.

"THIS BABY IS not ours!" Sissy hissed at Birdie. "Did you hear me?"

Startled, Birdie dropped her head down on her chest and sucked on her lower lip. Her face mottled with anger. "I thought you'd want me to bring Robert home. You always know what to do."

"He's not Robert, Birdie, and I don't know what to do." Sissy tried not to frighten her sister. Although a good scare might do her good. Knock some sense into her. What a mess Birdie was in this time.

Birdie sniffed and wiped at her eyes with a handkerchief she'd pulled from her dress pocket.

"You've gone too far. Bringing a baby here. Wherever you got him, you must take him back!" Sissy turned off the heat under the steaming kettle. "Why are you here anyway? Does the administrator at the home know you left? Did you ride the bus?"

Birdie started to sob. Her whole body shook. "Yes, I rode the bus," she said shivering. "I didn't tell anyone. I stole a key." She wailed. "It was dark and I was scared." She wailed louder.

"Bird, stop it!" Sissy knew Birdie would do anything to wear her down. "I mean it! Right this second! You aren't helping matters!"

Birdie snuffled and sniffed, dabbing at her tears and then folding the damp handkerchief and stuffing it into her pocket. "I ran away," she said defiantly. "I'm not going back. They were mean. They smacked my cheeks. They took my Cinderella watch."

"Oh, dear." Sissy sighed. "I'm sorry, Little Bird. Don't cry."

Birdie smiled. When Sissy used her pet name, Birdie knew everything would be all right.

Seeing Little Bird suffer at a stranger's hand made Sissy see red. The girl had suffered enough. However, she'd gone too far this time. Way too far. She'd stolen dogs and cats. Now, a baby. Where had she found a baby? How would they get him back home? What if they couldn't? What would they do with him? They were too old to raise a child. They'd have to get rid of him, but how? She certainly didn't want to go to jail. Oh, the worries Birdie caused.

"Tell me where you found him." Sissy bustled around, getting out cups and saucers. She poured hot water over the mint tea bags. She hoped the tea would settle her stomach. Her heart pounded. Birdie had gotten them into a serious mess this time.

Birdie's eyes twinkled. She looked down at the sleeping baby, her anger at Sissy forgotten. She loved this baby and would never give him up. No matter what her sister said. Robert, her baby brother Robert, was hers for keeps.

"Where?" Sissy persisted as she sat opposite Birdie, dipping her tea bag up and down.

"He was at our big white house. Sitting on the sidewalk. You know, where we lived with mama. The wooden swing was on the porch. He pointed at me and said ma."

Birdie took the crock of honey offered by Sissy and dipped a spoon of it into her cup. "I picked him up. There was a mean boy on the sidewalk. I hurried here with the baby."

Sissy shook her head, hoping her sister would remember exactly where she'd found him. She knew it was unlikely. "There was a boy?" Sissy asked. "Was this house in town?"

"It was our big white house. With yellow flowers on the side. I used to swing on the porch. When we played, you were always the mother. I was the queen. Remember?"

Sissy took a sip of tea. Birdie had picked up the baby in town. Someone was looking for him. They had to get rid of him, but how? Where? She stirred her tea. Her mind twirled faster and faster until she couldn't think at all.

CHAPTER 13

FOLLOWING THE OFFICER inside the house, Vada Faith prayed that George Buck had James at his house. Why didn't Duke Cobb let her rush over to the Buck's?

He was peering around the hallway poking in every corner.

Vada Faith wondered if she'd blacked out and brought James inside or was she simply going crazy? She begged the Lord to send some answers.

The officer started toward the stairs.

"Bedrooms," she said following him up the stairs.

He stepped into the master bedroom. It was neat, the plush comforter smooth at every corner. She picked up a rubber teething ring from the carpet and stuffed it into the pocket of her capris.

"I'll take that," Duke said, slipping on gloves.

She held out the teething ring. "Why?"

"Evidence. Just drop it into this plastic bag." He'd magically produced gloves and a plastic bag from a black pouch clipped to his belt.

"Evidence?" She shuddered. "Evidence of what?" He ignored her and continued inspecting the room.

In the nursery, the smell of James was strong. Baby lotion and powder were mixed with the scent of freshly laundered clothes. Duke inspected the crib. "Okay." He walked into the hall.

"The girls' room," she said, opening the next door. Books were haphazardly placed in shelves, and the twin beds looked like little girls had made them.

"All right." He went to the guest room, glanced into the closet, and bathroom. "We're done here."

Downstairs, he headed to the kitchen. He glanced inside the sink, under the sink, inside the cabinets and drawers. He glanced into the laundry room. He went to the pantry off the kitchen and stared at the canned food. He stared inside the two hall closets, jammed with coats and jackets. He eyed her husband's new golf clubs. He even bent and checked the closet floor moving his hands through the tangle of shoes and boots.

"James isn't in the closet!" She wanted to pummel him. "Someone is running away with my baby while you're in here wasting time!" She blew her bangs out of her face and made herself back off. Breathe, she kept telling herself. Breathe.

He scrutinized the living room, the family room, and the office she shared with John. Not a paper out of place.

"Here." She handed the officer a framed photo of James she'd picked up from the living room table. "This was taken last month at Baby Talk Photo. Nancy, the photographer, has his photos all over her shop. She says he's the most photogenic baby. She thinks he should model."

The photograph showed her blue-eyed blond baby boy sitting on green grass with a backdrop of butterflies and daisies. His front teeth were shining. The photo captured him glancing sideways, showing off his cute baby profile.

"I'll take this with me," he said, indicating the photo, slipping it out of the frame. "I'll have some posters made up."

"Posters?" The blood drained from her face as she took the empty frame and placed it on a table.

"He'll be found before we need posters. It's protocol. I'll call Midgy Brown, ask her to distribute them. She volunteers at the office. You know Midgy?"

"Of course, did you forget we all went to school together?" She started crying again. Through gasps she said, "Please go to the Buck's. I'll call Midgy."

Duke Cobb didn't forget they all went through twelve years of school together. The young woman in front of him was clearly memorable, the prettiest girl in their class. Midgy, with her mass of curly red hair and kind disposition, couldn't be forgotten. She ran an accounting business from home and volunteered around town. Her personality endeared her to everyone she met.

"Yes, talk to Midgy. She'll make you'll feel better." Maybe Midgy could calm her down. He would rather try to rope a tornado than to deal with Vada Faith right now.

"I won't feel better, Duke Cobb, certainly not by talking to Midgy. I'll feel better when James is in my arms. Not until." She hugged her phone but didn't call Midgy.

He walked back to the porch. She followed, still crying. Her cheering in high school had left her with strong lungs.

"I'm headed to the Buck's." He went to his car and stuck the baby's photo inside. "I'll be back," he called. "Today's free cookie day at the bakery. Maybe someone took James for a cookie."

"You imbecile, he's not at the bakery," she screamed. She wanted to pound her head on the cement walk. That might make her feel better. Her baby wasn't at the bakery. How could this man be a law officer? He didn't have one clue about finding her baby.

"George takes care of injured animals," she called to him, sniffing. "He had his cage with him this morning in the street."

"Don't go anywhere." He yelled back, his voice fading as he went out of sight.

Where did he think she'd go? On vacation?

CHAPTER 14

"HE'S A QUIET baby," Sissy said, bending to stare at the little boy. She caught a whiff of baby powder and a clean smell. "Someone loves this little guy, I bet."

"Oh, he's good," Birdie clapped her hands hoping to change Sissy's frown to a smile. "He drank his bottle. Sucked every drop of milk on the way here. I had to sit on a big rock in the field to finish feeding him. He watched me with those big blue eyes, sometimes he'd smile up at me. He never cried. Not once. Robert is a fine baby."

"He's not Robert, Birdie. Do you understand? He's not our little brother."

"Yes, Sissy," Birdie nodded. "He's not Robert. Can I still call him Robert?"

"For now. Just for now. Why'd you leave the home, Bird? I thought you liked living there."

"Nope," the younger sister's mouth drew into a pout. "Not anymore. People came into my room in the night. Things were missing. My dresses disappeared. I want to stay here with you." She leaned back comfortably in her chair. "Please, Sissy, can I stay with you and Robert. Please? Do I have to go back?"

"You have to promise not to wander off. The baby's a problem though. We can't keep him. He's not ours." Her stern voice brought tears to Birdie's eyes and Birdie lowered her gray head.

How could Sissy make her understand the gravity of their situation? She didn't want to distress her. Birdie was fragile. "Now tell me," Sissy said, "do you remember the name of the street where you got the baby?"

"Oh, well, um, maybe." Birdie clapped her hands, happily, and sat up straighter in her chair. "The houses looked like cupcakes covered in pink and blue and yellow icing. Robert was sitting on the sidewalk in front of the big white house. He had his bottle. He waved." Birdie's brows furrowed. "I brought him home so we could take care of him the way our mama told us to."

"Do you remember the awful fire, Bird? Our big white farm house burned down years ago." Sissy frowned. "Poor Robert, he's gone too. You must remember? How the house went up fast? We never saw him again. We inherited this old place a long time ago from mama's cousin. You helped me cut weeds when we moved here. Then you went away to that home."

Birdie looked away. Sissy saw a tear trickle down her sister's weathered cheek.

"I wanted to fix things," Birdie whispered, her head turned from Sissy. "I wanted to bring Robert home so we could be a family."

"We are family. You and me. Robert is gone. We don't need a baby. There's just us. You can't pick up babies off the street and bring them home."

"I won't, Sissy. I promise. I put too much wood in the stove that day. I added those newspapers. You said not to but I wanted to get warm. It was so cold. I want to fix everything like it used to be."

"The fire wasn't your fault. There's nothing to fix, Bird. I shouldn't have let you near the stove. You weren't old enough to start the fire. I was caught up in listening to the radio music."

"I saved the radio," Birdie chirped. "I saved it for you. From the fire."

"Yes, you did." Sissy heaved a long sigh. "I don't listen to it anymore."

Birdie shook her head and wiped her tears on the hem of her dress.

"We're in a serious pickle with this baby." Sissy softened her tone at sight of Birdie's drooping shoulders. "You must recall the name of the street where you got him." She patted her sister's shoulder. "Come on, you think about it. Think real hard."

"I will," Birdie said, cheerful again, staring at the sleeping baby on the floor.

"Did anyone see you take the baby? You mentioned a boy."

"Well," Birdie said, drawing her eyes down, "I don't know. Maybe." She fidgeted in the chair and smoothed the skirt of her dress.

"Think!" Sissy demanded. "Was there a boy or not?"

"I don't remember." Birdie thought hard. "No, I don't think so." She was so tired. She'd ridden the bus from the home in the mountains to Shady Creek. The trip seemed to take forever. Then, she'd picked up Robert and walked a long way to Sissy's.

Sissy was mad again. Their mama used to laugh when Sissy got mad. She'd say Sissy could just get glad. If Birdie couldn't remember something, she couldn't remember.

Birdie smiled down at the baby. She was happy they were home.

CHAPTER 15

"NOBODY'S HOME AT the Buck's," the officer reported to Vada Faith as he came back to the porch. "Hey," he said coming toward her. "I looked inside the playhouse out back. Quite a place to play, a replica of this old Victorian house. You got some lucky kids."

"Yes, John built it." The officer didn't notice her body shaking. She didn't bother wiping her tears. "He can build anything with wood."

"Plenty of toys out there."

"Yes."

"Built well," he mused. "Saw the workshop too. Big place. John matched the white paint and green shutters to the house. Why's his workshop locked?" He shuffled his feet nervously.

"Because of his expensive woodworking tools. He keeps his furniture designs locked up too."

"Can you open it?"

"John has the key."

"You don't have a key?"

She ignored him.

"Hey, look, things are going to be okay." She was whiter than his mother's bleached sheets. "One of the guys took the baby's photo to Midgy at the senior center. They'll post the flyers and we'll find your little guy."

Vada Faith nodded.

Fifteen minutes later, with Duke engaged in a conversation on the street, she walked quietly toward the Buck's house."

She knocked loudly on the front door and rang the doorbell repeatedly. She wasn't leaving until she spoke to George Buck.

Finally, Carrie opened the door. "Come in," she said, patting Vada Faith on the arm. "The radio was so loud I didn't hear you."

"You know about James?" Vada Faith pressed her hands against her sides to keep them from shaking as Carrie went to the entertainment center and turned the radio off.

"Yes, it's awful. Any news?"

Vada Faith shook her head.

"I can't imagine. The dispatcher told my cousin who called me." Carrie wiped her hands on her apron. Her face carried a smudge of flour.

"George was on the sidewalk this morning," Vada Faith said fighting back tears. "He may know who took James."

"George," his mother called down the hallway. Turning to Vada Faith, she said, "He brought an injured bird home earlier and then we ran out to the store."

The boy walked into the room. When he saw Vada Faith he put his head down. A small gray bird was cupped in his hands.

"Did you know James was taken today?" Vada Faith asked.

He nodded keeping his head down. His mother said, "I told him."

Vada Faith trembled as she approached the boy. "I need your help, George. Did you come on the porch when you were outside this morning? Can you tell me what you saw?"

The boy raised his head. He opened his mouth but nothing came out. He tried again. Then he shook his head and turned toward his mother who put her arm around his shoulders.

"Honey, if you saw anything," she said, "you need to tell us. This is important. It's about the safety of baby James."

"Cage," he said, pulling away from his mother. He backed up against the wall and stroked the bird.

"Things have been tough lately." Carrie looked at her son. "He draws pictures when he wants to tell us something. Can you draw a picture of this morning for Vada Faith?"

He nodded.

"I'm desperate!" Vada Faith wiped her nose and stared at the boy who didn't move a muscle. "I need your help, George."

"I'll talk to him," Carrie said, taking Vada Faith's shaking hands as she started to turn away. "He'll draw a picture and I'll bring it over. He loves to draw. That's not a problem for him. He's just been through an unpleasant ordeal the last few months."

As she headed home, Vada Faith prayed this too would turn out to be nothing more than an unpleasant ordeal. She walked into her backyard biting on her lower lip until she tasted blood.

On the front porch, she sank into a wicker chair twisting the tissue she held. As she started to wipe her face a drop of blood fell onto the tissue and she dabbed at her bleeding lip.

CHAPTER 16

SISSY OPENED A drawer, and got out some soft cotton cloths. "Does his diaper need changing?"

"Oh!" Birdie jumped up. "I'll check." The baby didn't stir, just snuggled further into the quilt, his little mouth sucking in his sleep. "Can I change him, Sissy? Please? Can I feed him, huh?"

"Let him sleep. When he wakes we'll take care of him. Wonder how old he is? I saw some teeth. We can mash some canned vegetables for him. How's that sound?"

Birdie clapped her hands. "Oh goody. This will be such fun, Sissy. Like when we were girls watching the baby for Mama."

"You're taking this baby back, Bird."

"No, I'm not!" Birdie's face pinched with horror. "He's going to stay with me!"

"Did you forget what I said?" Sissy put the soft cloths on the table. Rage replaced Sissy's usual calm demeanor. "We are not keeping him!" She pointed a crooked finger at Birdie. "Get it out of your head. You'll take him back or you'll do something else with him." Sissy drew her eyes down. "Otherwise, I'll take care of it myself. Do you understand?"

Birdie nodded, her eyes growing wide. She knew exactly what Sissy meant.

It wasn't good. When Sissy got rid of things, like cats and dogs, they didn't come back.

CHAPTER 17

"I TALKED TO George Buck," Vada Faith said, when Officer Cobb stepped onto the porch. A breeze blew the swing back and forth with her. She had to stop it with her toes to keep it from hitting the officer in the knees.

"I told you not to go there. I'll handle that kid."

"My baby is missing. George knows something. I sensed it. He's drawing a picture of what he saw this morning. Carrie's bringing it over. George still isn't talking. He'd better start soon or John will make him talk when he gets home."

Duke scowled down at her. "You and John need to stay out of it."

She ignored his words. "George did say the word cage. Carrie said he's slowly starting to say single words."

"I'll let the detective know." He shrugged and walked away. He was beat and the day wasn't half over.

Vada Faith prayed James was found before his daddy arrived home. She'd tried calling John's cell again. No answer. She'd left a message for Midgy. Now she punched in the number of the Sunnyside Baptist Church, the worship center they attended. The phone rang and rang. She imagined the sound echoing down the long corridor of the new building.

"Sunnyside Baptist, Myrtie Streeter here." The old woman's voice boomed. "Available twenty-four-seven, just like our Lord and Savior."

"Myrtie! It's me."

"Why bless your heart, Vada Faith. How are you, honey?"

"James is gone, Myrtie! Kidnapped!" She took a deep breath. "Someone took baby James off our front porch."

"Well, thank the saints you called me! I'm pushing this red emergency button we just had installed. Pastor Pinwheel prays the second it buzzes in his office. Where'd you say the baby got took from? Let me get my pencil and pad, dearie. Sad fact is, I can't remember a thing. Can't hear well either."

"Someone took him from his play pen on the front porch. I went inside for one minute. When I returned he was gone, his play pen was empty!" Vada Faith wailed louder.

"Hang on, I'm scribbling. Baby James missing from porch of the old Waddell House. We'll use balloons, yes, and name tags."

"Balloons? Name tags?" Vada Faith caught her breath.

"We got supplies to use up from our membership drive. They're taking up space in my closet." Myrtie clicked her dentures. "No cost to you. We'll release balloons with information on James. We'll have a dinner and use up some of those name tags. Someone got carried away ordering. Now, did you know those Methodists jumped in and made our membership drive a big competition." She stopped to take a breath. "I heard they're raffling off gift cards!"

"Myrtie! Please!"

"Gift cards, Vada Faith! From the Donut Hole and Betty's Diner!"

"Myrtie!"

"Hang on, honey! I'm writing. Oh my. I'm sick over this. You know those Nazarenes? They're throwing a rap concert in the park Sunday afternoon, calling it gospel!"

"I need James on the prayer list, Myrtie. Right now! Call every church member! You hear me?"

"Why yes, soon as I hang up. I can't write as fast as I used too. I'll alert the women's Bread of Life prayer circle and the Christian

Soldiers Brigade. They all prayed over Ditzie Duncan. She got healed of a growth on her, well, never mind. Oh, and my Aunt Hazel Mitt got healed of shingles." She made a disgusting sound with her dentures and asked. "Do you know Ditzie?"

"Yes, but not well."

"Well, Ditzie will be in charge of the FIND JAMES COMMITTEE. She'll put on a dinner. Let me assure you, honey, your baby is safe. There're no kidnappers in Shady Creek. Nope. Sinners, yes. Kidnappers, no. Ditzie will make her potato chip chicken. If my Aunt Hazel Mitt brings her slaw Jell-O salad, do not touch it. She gets old cabbage from the Pick n Pack. Dear me! A kidnapped baby! It's like I saw on an episode of Murder She Wrote. What is this world coming to?"

Vada Faith took a deep breath while Myrtie talked. She wanted to scream for her to shut up. Yet, the woman offered a glimmer of hope and a small amount of comfort. She had to cling to every bit she could get.

"I'm sending our Retired Men's Brigade over to help search. They're here in the sanctuary praying. You can count on us at Sunnyside Baptist. Twenty-four-seven, dear girl."

"Thank you." Exhausted, Vada Faith ended the call.

Soon, the news of her missing baby would be all over town.

She walked to the play pen, wiping her swollen eyes. She'd find her son. Somehow. Some way. She'd give her life for that boy. She sat down in the wicker chair and picked up the phone.

The answering machine at St. Paul's Methodist Church informed her that they would be releasing 1000 scripture filled balloons at dawn Saturday as part of their membership drive. Staff was busy preparing scripture and filling helium balloons. Come and help. Free coffee and donuts.

It seemed every church in town had gone overboard during their search for new people to enlist in the Lord's service. Surely there were enough sinners to go around.

Vada Faith slammed the phone down on the wicker table and leaned her aching head on the cushioned chair.

Finally, she tried John's number. Still no answer. He used his phone for emergencies and business. Why wasn't he answering? Was something wrong or was he caught up in business decisions?

Where was her family? Her sister? Her mother?

This burden was too heavy for her to carry alone.

CHAPTER 18

"BIRD, YOU'RE RESPONSIBLE for this mess," Sissy heaved a huge sigh. "and you can fix it. I can't go into town or anywhere else. You know that. Midgy Brown from the center brings my groceries every week. It's why I never visited you in the home. Midgy mailed your Cinderella watch for your birthday."

Birdie ignored Sissy, who stood opening cans of vegetables at the counter and pouring them into a pan on the stove. "Do you still tape your own sounds, Sissy?" Birdie moved over to the tape recorder on the bookcase near the table. It made a clicking noise. It was time to turn the tape over. Dozens of audio tapes lined the book shelves.

"Yes, I do. Everyday."

Birdie stared at her.

"Don't look at me that way. I can't help my ways any more than you can help yours. Besides the tapes keep me company at night. I like to hear my hands at work during the day."

"You still sing?"

"Sometimes. At night I like to listen to myself singing or talking. Even washing my face, or washing clothes in the wash tub. Every sound is different. Hearing running water soothes me at night. I don't like the dark, anymore. The tapes are like having company. Only it's just me. I'm not scared of me."

"Why don't you turn on the television, Sissy?"

"Birdie! I don't have a television. Besides, I like to hear myself."

"I like television," Birdie said, defensively, "I watch television all the time. My friend in the home, Mildred Henshaw, says it's all reruns. I like reruns. Mildred told me that the home was for crazy people. Not good people, like you said, Sissy."

"Enough of that. You need to wash out the baby's bottle. After he eats we'll give him some milk. Get a can of Carnation from the cabinet. Mix half water and half milk. Use the water from the spring. It's that jug on the floor. We'll walk to the spring one day. After the baby's gone."

Birdie closed her ears to all talk of giving up her baby. "Oh, yes! I'll fix his bottle. It's like we're girls again." She smiled and scurried to do her big sister's bidding as she always had.

CHAPTER 19

WHEN VADA FAITH came back from the bathroom, a crowd had gathered in front of her house. Maggie Sims, another neighbor, pointed at Vada Faith. People gawked at her as though she had two heads. Elderly sisters from church, Betty and Winona Waybright, waved as Vada Faith leaned on the porch railing. She waved but couldn't return their smiles. People were talking and gesturing as if they knew exactly what was going on.

A news van from a Charleston television station pulled to the curb close by. News here spread like dandelion seeds. She wanted the news out, but if the wrong person found her baby, then what? Would he be in more danger? She wrung her hands at the thought and went to sit on the porch steps.

While she'd been inside she'd left an urgent message for John. "Help. Emergency." The same went to Joy Ruth and her mother. She'd asked Joy Ruth to call Louise, their mother-in-law. She prayed everyone would respond.

Officer Cobb stood in the yard frowning at the crowd that continued to grow. He walked over to the steps where Vada Faith sat.

Drained, she said to him, "I called the churches. They're sending more volunteers. I've been praying someone would bring James home." She clung stubbornly to the thought that her baby would be found any minute. Nothing else made sense.

"The church men are here already. Searching."

She stood up, stretched, and sat back down. Helplessness clung to her like wet wool.

When Duke went back to the street, a young couple shook his hand like he was a celebrity. The couple had moved here a while back. She couldn't remember their names. Could they have taken her baby for some unknown reason? She shook her head to clear the crazy thoughts.

James was gone. Her Sweet Baby James. The words kidnapped and abducted ran through her head. She sat on the steps deep in thought. When Carrie Buck appeared in front of her, she jumped. "Hey," Carrie said, handing her a drawing. "Any news?"

"Not yet." She stood and directed Carrie to the porch where they both sank into chairs.

"George is not himself today, Vada Faith. He knows something, I'm sure of it. I just don't know what. When I mention the police he's scared to death."

"He has to tell us, Carrie. He's our only hope. James may be in danger." She stared down at the picture. George had drawn a stick baby sitting in lime green grass beside a gray bird's nest. The baby had a mop of school-bus-yellow hair. A bottle of milk lay on the ground. A cage stood in the background. A round person stared down at the baby. The person wore dark boxy shoes and could be a male or a female. Long brown fringe circled the waist. Stringy gray hair came almost to the shoulders. Man, woman, or an alien from outer space? She couldn't tell as she studied the drawing and shuddered. Did this misshapen person have James? Would he or she bring him back? What if her baby boy never came home?

"George talked some after you left," Carrie's voice interrupted her thoughts. "He didn't say much. The doctor said the lighting strike was traumatic. It'll take time for him to recover."

"Did George lift James out of his pen?"

"I believe he's afraid to tell me, thinking he'll be in trouble. I tried to reassure him."

"The special investigator from Charleston will know how to talk to him." Vada Faith held tightly to the drawing. "He should have been here already."

"The news reported an accident on the interstate. Maybe that held him up." Carrie stood. "I'll go home and talk to George again. This time I'll be more firm."

"Thanks, Carrie." They left the porch together. Carried headed home and Vada Faith went to Duke Cobb who stood talking to a news reporter on the sidewalk.

She handed him George's drawing.

Duke stepped back from the reporter and stopped talking as he stared at the picture.

"You have to go talk to George," she said. "Carrie says he knows something. If you have to get rough with him, do it. We have to find James soon."

"I know, Vada Faith, I know. I'm calling the investigator again. See what the hold up is." He went to his car and climbed in.

She noticed he was sitting in his car a lot. It had to be the quietest place in the neighborhood right now.

She prayed, as she went toward the house that James would be found. Perhaps someone would bring him home with a good explanation for taking him. They could forget the explanation. If James was okay she'd forgive and forget. She would cuddle him, and smother him with kisses. She'd never let him go. Never. Her stupid job would be a thing of the past. She'd stay home with her children. She'd hold James and never let him go. At night he'd sleep between her and John where he'd be safe. Her three children would be her life. She'd wrap herself around them and never let go.

She went inside and slammed the front door. A lump formed in her throat. She got a drink at the kitchen sink and walked back to the front door and stared into the yard. A white SUV pulled into the driveway behind the patrol car. A man looking like a television detective got out and went toward the patrol car where Duke sat. The man stretched his hand out to the officer.

Duke jumped out of his car, excited as a puppy to see his master. "Hey!" He smiled and pumped the man's hand up and down.

She stepped outside as the two men came up the porch steps.

"This is Vada Faith Waddell." Duke said as she stepped outside.

She shook the man's hand.

"Vada Faith, this is Al Rook, the detective I was telling you about. He's retired. Lives in Jackson County. He's volunteered to help us out."

"Hello," the man said. "I'd have been here sooner but traffic was backed up. I'm sorry we have to meet under these circumstances. I'll do everything I can to find your son."

"Please," she said, "he's a baby, only eight months old." She swallowed down the nausea. "He was in his playpen when I went to the kitchen. When I came back a few minutes later he was gone."

"We'll find him." He walked to the play pen and studied every angle. He walked the length of the wraparound porch, observing every object.

He gestured to Duke. They walked to the driveway and huddled for a few minutes by the patrol car.

Then they stepped over to her car which was parked in front of Duke's. The detective opened the front passenger door.

"What're you doing?" She hurried to the driveway.

"Checking your car." The detective dropped his cigarette onto the graveled driveway and mashed it with the toe of his black shoe.

"Why?" Her voice quivered. "I haven't been in my car since I came from work. Before I brought James outside."

Suddenly, a chill ran through her. She hugged herself as goose-bumps popped up on her arms. He thought she had done something to harm James. Oh God. Dear God, how could he think such an awful thing? She put her aching head in her hands.

"Standard procedure." The man lit another cigarette and coughed.

Duke opened all the doors leaving them open. They both looked official with their gloves on.

"Someone took my baby from his play pen. It is there on the porch." She pointed to the porch. "Right there. That's where he was." Her voice came out scratchy and her throat hurt.

Duke Cobb ignored her and climbed into the front seat of her car.

"He isn't in there," she screamed as loud as she could, turning heads on the street. "Listen! John will kill you if you don't find our baby. I swear on my own life, Duke Cobb. I'll kill you myself if you don't get out of the car and go find my baby!"

"Calm down, Vada Faith." Duke spoke from her car. "We don't have a choice. We have to follow procedures. Just so you know, I don't think the baby is in your car." He opened the glove box. "My job is to do this while the volunteers comb the streets. Go inside. We're heading to Buck's to question the kid after we check out the car."

The detective nodded as he watched the exchange, smoking, as if he weren't a part of the scene. His eyes shifted in every direction.

She wondered if he could be trusted. Her arms started itching, thanks to her nerves. She backed up and gave the men some room. She scratched her arms until they were red.

Her mother's silver PT Cruiser shot into the driveway. Albert, her fiancee, was at the wheel. Helena jumped out and hurried toward her daughter. "Honey, we heard. Oh my God!"

Vada Faith ran to her mother as Joy Ruth's car swung in behind Helena's. Joy Ruth, Bruiser, and Louise spilled from the sports car. They came to form a circle around the women.

CHAPTER 20

Sissy twisted the knob of the old Philco radio seeking a station without static. She hadn't played the machine in years. It was a miracle it worked.

Birdie had dragged the cumbersome piece of furniture from the closet into the living room and demanded it be plugged in.

"Listen," Sissy said as a classical station came in clearly.

"It's mama's music." Birdie clapped.

"Yes, Papa bought the radio as a gift for her. Remember, back when electricity first crossed our land?"

Birdie rocked back and forth on the sofa in her own world.

While the baby played with wooden spoons on a quilt on the floor, Sissy cranked up the volume.

When a Beethoven piece started a smile crept across Birdie's face.

Sissy hummed as she sat in the old rocker and stitched the hem of a kitchen curtain.

Content, Birdie sat across from her, rocking, folding and unfolding the lace handkerchief in her lap.

Vada Faith stood at the front door, running her fingers through her hair for the thousandth time. She watched her mother come inside with the coffee cake she'd retrieved from the car.

"I'll make coffee," Joy Ruth said, taking the cake and heading to the kitchen.

Vada Faith could hear the family talking in hushed tones as if they were at a wake. She fell into Helena's open arms and buried her face in her mother's black blazer, comforted by the scent of her Lancome perfume.

"A stranger took James out of his play pen, Mama. I went inside for one minute. When I came back the baby was gone."

Her mother wiped her daughter's tears and petted her as if she were a child.

"How could this happen?" Vada Faith pushed out of her mother's arms. She wiped a tear with the back of her hand.

"Now, now, honey. He's going to be found."

"I should never have left James alone. I know that now. He was taken so fast, Mama. Fast as a firefly darting past."

"Come on. Dry those tears." Her mother took Vada Faith's hands in hers. "We'll find our boy. Let's go sit out on the porch and leave the others to their coffee."

The bond that had developed between them since the birth of James was amazing. It was almost as though her mother had never left the family. These days, she was concerned for her family's every need like mothers all over the globe. She, Joy Ruth, and her mother had become like sliced bread in a loaf, standing tall beside each other, pressing close and supporting one another.

Her mother glanced into the street as she pushed into the swing. "I wish this crowd would go home."

Vada Faith sank down next to her. "I know. Some of them are volunteers. Some are just gawkers."

Smoke from a neighbor's grill moved over the street. The smell of cooking food filled the air. "How can they grill?" Vada Faith shook her head. "Like it's a regular day."

"It is for them, honey. This isn't their tragedy."

"It's not a regular day. If it was, I'd be at the shop, standing next to Joy Ruth, cutting Marge Randolph's hair and listening to her complain about the mayor. Darla Hill would be in Joy Ruth's chair, adding her two cents."

Helena reached over and pushed a strand of her daughter's short hair away from her face as they swayed back and forth in the swing. "The mayor did promise them new storm drains, honey. It rains, their street floods. We knew when we voted him in, he's slippery as an eel and he slides out of every commitment."

"That's how I feel about Duke Cobb, Mama. He says he'll find James. I can't hang onto what he says because he hasn't found him yet. Oh, Lord, where can he be?"

"Someone around here knows something." Helena sniffed and continued, "I'd bet on it. They could be in that crowd out front right now." She examined her nails done at the shop by the new manicurist. Vada Faith hired the girl despite her multiple piercings and Joy Ruth's misgivings. "Our baby just can't be gone." Her mother put a tissue to her eyes.

"If someone out there knows something, why won't they come forward? People are searching. Duke Cobb is waving his arms like a traffic cop and keeps telling me not to worry."

"He's a good man and he means well, honey. Besides he has that seasoned detective guiding him."

The smell of food from the grill was making Vada Faith nauseous.

"Did they search all the yards nearby?" Helena put her arm around Vada Faith. "Jamie might have climbed out of his pen and crawled behind a bush. Our little Jamie could be asleep somewhere this minute."

"Mama!" Vada Faith brought the swing to a stop with her foot. "This is no game. James isn't in the bushes asleep and please don't call him Jamie. His name is James. How many times do I have to remind you?"

"Calm down, now, I just want our boy to be safe." The older woman ran her hands down her satiny slacks. "I thought, well, I don't know what I thought. I guess I want him to be nearby and safe."

"I do, too, but he's not in my yard under a bush. It's all my fault he's missing." She put her foot on the floor and pushed, letting the swing drift back and forth. "Leaving James alone by himself on the porch to take a silly pie out of the oven, ridiculous, stupid me."

"Stop it." The older woman spoke sternly. "You're making yourself sick." She touched her daughter's cheek. "You have to hold yourself together. James needs his mama. He needs all of us. We have to be strong."

"I'm not strong. I'm butter where James is concerned. I can't act like it's a normal day. It's the worst day of my life."

She stood and strode across the wooden floor kicking a wicker chair as she went. "There was a stranger here. On this porch. We should have moved years ago to a neighborhood where young people live. We have old people all around us. James might've been safe somewhere else."

"This is a great place to live. It's as safe as anywhere else. Listen, honey," her mother came to stand beside her, "someone we know could have James. Let's think positive. They may bring him home any minute. I heard Duke tell the investigator all stations are airing the story. If anyone knows anything at all, they'll call. We can't give up hope. It's all we have, hope."

Vada Faith paced the porch, her shoulders sagging from the weight of guilt. Her hands were tied. If only she could start the day over.

"I don't believe a stranger was here on this porch." Helena went to pick dead leaves off a hanging plant. "Something else happened. Children don't just disappear." She threw the dead leaves into the mulch below. Stopping at the porch railing, she stared at a man eating a brat on a bun as he stood on the sidewalk. Yes, people went on with their lives, especially when it was someone else's problem.

Vada Faith knew the kidnapper could be standing out in the crowd on the street. She watched the news every day. Someone could be watching her house at that moment.

"I feel in my gut someone will bring him home." Helena coughed. "You wait and see. James is safe." She wrapped her arms around Vada Faith.

"Oh, Mama." Vada Faith was weak from crying. "I'm losing my voice. I can't think. I don't know what to say or do." She wrung her hands.

"Wait. It's all we can do. Hang on to our sanity." She smiled at her daughter. "You do know Jamie, I mean James, feels like my own baby." Helena sank into the swing. "I love that boy."

"He loves you too." Vada Faith sat down in a chair beside the swing. Breathe she kept telling herself. In and out. Stay steady. Breathe.

"Where's John?" Her mother looked around the porch as if she'd just remembered him.

"At a woodworking show in Kentucky. He should be home soon." She was heartsick. John didn't know yet their son was gone. "I need him and he's not answering his cell. I left him a message to come home. There was an emergency."

"He'll go out of his mind when he hears James is missing."

"Yes," Vada Faith leaned her head back on the wicker chair, her arms feeling emptier than ever, "I know."

CHAPTER 22

"WE QUESTIONED GEORGE Buck," Duke said, coming into the living room where Vada Faith and her mother had gone to sit. The crowd outside made Vada Faith nervous, the way they stared at her.

"Mrs. Warfield," Duke walked over to Helena and took her hand. "I'm real sorry about your grandson. We're doing our best to locate him."

"I know, Duke. I appreciate it." Helena sat up straighter and touched her hair to see if she'd mussed it when she'd rested her head on the pillowed couch.

"Al sent me in to talk to you. He's making some calls."

"Please, Duke, sit." Vada Faith indicated the chair beside the sofa.

He sat down and cleared his throat. "George cried when he saw us. Maybe the uniforms. I gave him a pack of gum. He settled down eventually. Al showed the kid his drawing. When I pointed to the blob that could have been an adult he flinched. He pointed to the nest and to the bird he held in his hand. Al asked if the bird had fallen out of the nest? He nodded yes. I asked if the baby he drew was James. Another nod. He wouldn't look me in the eye. We already knew the baby was James."

"James doesn't have bright yellow hair."

"It's yellow where George is concerned," Duke said. "All we have to do is find the person with the boxy shoes and we'll have the kidnapper. I'm putting this drawing on some flyers. It might jog someone's memory."

After Duke excused himself, Helena headed to the kitchen for coffee. Vada Faith's thoughts were on George Buck. She wanted to scream at him to tell what he'd seen. How hard was that?

The ringing doorbell brought Joy Ruth stomping down the hallway. "Coming!"

Vada Faith could see her wiping her hands on her jeans as she passed the doorway to the living room.

Doreen Moon's voice echoed down the hall. "Hey, Joy Ruth! How's Vada Faith?"

Then, the woman popped into the living room and rushed to her side. "You okay, honey?"

"I'm not, not really, but come on in and sit." Vada Faith's voice caught in her throat.

"Oh, honey, I been praying for James and for you." Doreen bent to gather her friend in a hug. "I'm sorry. My prayer is someone finds him soon. This can't be a real kidnapping."

"That's my prayer too." Vada Faith leaned back and sighed.

"I'm here to help with whatever you need. I brought donuts from Betty's Bakery. I have six filled Long John's for you."

"I can't eat anything."

"I know honey. We'll save them for you." Doreen smiled and patted her friend's hand.

Joy Ruth came to pick up the two gallons of tea Doreen had left in the hall. "You can bring the donuts in here, Dorrie," she lowered her voice to a whisper, "we'll hide some in the pantry, for later."

"That's my plan." Doreen gave Joy Ruth a hug. "I might have one and a cup of that coffee I smell."

"This way." Joy Ruth lead the way into the kitchen with Doreen following.

"This is the first time I been here since the remodeling." Doreen's eyes were wide as she took in the large country kitchen.

"Look around. They did a great job. Just stay in the kitchen and dining room. Duke left orders most of the house is off limits. I don't know why." She shrugged her shoulders.

"Is my cousin doing a good job for you?"

Joy Ruth had forgotten Duke was Doreen's cousin. She didn't want to make any disparaging remarks about him. "Sure," she finally said. "I've been praying for Duke and the investigator from Charleston. The volunteers too. This is a nightmare. My stomach's in a turmoil. I don't want Vada Faith to know but I lost my lunch earlier."

She went to the coffee pot on the counter and poured a cup for Doreen and handed it to her. "The volunteers will be in soon for coffee and they'll empty the pot. Could you help me serve them? Mama and Louise are huddled in a corner of the dining room weeping." Joy Ruth glanced into the other room where the two women still consoled each other.

"Oh yes, indeed, I can help." Doreen beamed. She lived for serving others and for praying for needy people. She couldn't wait to get to Wednesday night meeting to tell her new pastor about James being kidnapped. She'd go to the altar to pray for him. Who knew when that little guy would be found or if he would. She refused to believe there had been a kidnapping, yet if there hadn't been, where was that little fellow?

Doreen took a donut from the box on the dining room table where Joy Ruth had placed it. She scooped up one of the yellow napkins. Sipping on her coffee, she scanned the room for a place to sit. A firefighter she knew beckoned her to an empty chair beside him. "I'll finish this coffee," she called to Joy Ruth who turned toward the kitchen, "and then I'll wash those mugs in the sink."

The firefighter smiled at her as she sat down.

CHAPTER 23

VADA FAITH WALKED out to the front porch.

John walked behind her. He'd been home a short time and already his face was frozen in shock. His mother had frustrated him more, trying to coax him to eat.

"Tell me again what happened." His words came out cold and stiff.

She repeated her story a dozen times. The baby had been gone nearly two hours now. So much had happened since she first found the empty play pen. Her heart skipped a beat every time she saw the play pen, empty without her precious baby boy.

John's presence soaked up what little energy she had, leaving her lightheaded and breathless. How could she help him understand when she didn't? His shock would soon turn to complete numbness as hers had.

It was her fault. Nobody had said it yet but she knew it.

"John, do you want me to say I left the baby outside on purpose?"

"No, honey, I don't." He stood and paced back and forth, his eyes full of questions. He looked over at the play pen and back at her, shaking his head as if trying to work out a puzzle.

Before John arrived, Duke and the detective had blocked off the play pen with yellow tape. Now the couple could only stare at the play pen from a distance.

John reached inside his pocket and pulled out a package of Tums, sliding one of the pink tablets into his mouth.

"I told you everything." She ran her fingers through her blond spiked hair, surprised she hadn't pulled it out by now. The frustration of not knowing where her baby was made her want to strangle everyone in sight. Why couldn't he be found? Where could he be? Why weren't the searchers running madly about town, looking in every crevice and cubby hole? Searching every home and business? How could this be happening? She felt as though her world had on cement shoes. Why was the search going so slow?

Her skin crawled at the thought of James being with a stranger. Who could have taken him? Was there a reason? She stopped. She wouldn't let herself go beyond the thought he was gone. It was unthinkable that anything bad might happen to her precious baby.

"Please," John turned from staring at the play pen, "think, Vay. Did you see anyone outside this morning? Do you remember anything else?"

John paced the wooden porch floor and stared at the play pen. He'd questioned her so many times she wanted to claw his eyes out. In the next minute, she was in his arms wailing.

Did he expect James to magically appear back in his pen? Did he think she'd suddenly remember leaving the baby at the grocery, and they'd run and pick him up? Was he as crazy as Duke Cobb or was she crazier than all of them?

All the questions nearly suffocated her.

She'd been interrogated by Duke and the detective, her sister, her mother, his mother, and Bruiser. Even Albert, her mama's boyfriend had asked how someone could come on the porch without her hearing them.

Now, John seemed to doubt her story. She put her hands over her ears. It didn't stop the questions circling inside her head.

She ran her fingers through her hair. Somehow the touch of hair brought her a small measure of comfort.

"I told you, George Buck was on the street. He drew a picture of what he saw."

"I can make that kid talk. He knows something he's not telling." John's face turned an unhealthy red.

"He didn't take James, honey. He would have brought him back. He cares about him."

"He knows who took James, I'd bet on it." John fell into a chair deflated.

"We might want to go over there and slap him around but we can't. He's a kid." Vada Faith willed away the scene in front of her, the empty play pen, her distraught husband, her baby's father.

Her mind began to wander, thanks to the nerve pill she'd taken. Medication had that effect on her. A small amount went a long way.

Her thoughts turned to hair. It had consumed her from the first pink comb and brush set she'd been given as a toddler. She's holding onto the little plastic set in the large Olin Mills photo hanging on her daddy's living room wall. Two little round faced girls, blue eyes, blond ringlets. Joy Ruth held her hands primly in her lap. Vada Faith held the pink comb and brush.

"Vay," John said, bringing her back to the porch. He didn't often use the nickname she'd gone by in high school.

She sat up straighter as he eased into the swing beside her, reaching for her hand. "I'm scared."

"Me too." His hand felt warm in hers.

He reached over and smoothed a wisp of hair away from her face.

"I'm a mess," she said, touching her hair.

She'd recently let Joy Ruth give her a short wispy cut. John had liked it when she came home but who cared now?

"You always look good." He relaxed against her.

"I'm glad you're home." She squeezed his hand. She felt his skin on hers and it brought an extra measure of comfort.

He covered her hand with both of his. "We'll get through this." He smiled at her with those big beautiful eyes of his. Her heart melted. It always did when he looked at her like that.

The warmth from his hands spread through her bones. Why didn't it reach her heart? It was shattered in a million pieces. Only James back in her arms could fix that.

Would their life ever be the same? Could they hold up under this kind of stress? She used to be able to read John's mind. Not today. What had happened to that period in their lives when they were in unison? When everything appeared perfect? When their hearts beat as one.

Would her husband ever forgive her for her negligence?

She eased her hands from John's. His eyes were closed. Not in sleep, she knew, but in thought. She went to sit on the porch steps.

"I fed James lunch." She started talking as she sat down on the first step. "I brought him outside to his play pen, to his stack of toys. Each day, he grins, and acts as if they're new. A few minutes later, I went back to the kitchen for his juice bottle and to take the pie out of the oven." She swallowed hard. "When I returned he was gone. Like that." She snapped her fingers.

She put her hand to her throat, feeling it tighten, wishing it would permanently close and end her pain. "That's what happened." She looked up at John. He'd come to stand behind her. His eyes were open, his face blank.

"I can't believe he's gone." He slammed his fist down on the wooden bannister. "Dammit." He pounded it again. "Dammit. Dammit."

John never swore. He'd quit when they had the twins. "How could someone do this?" He said. "It's crazy." He opened his fist and stared at his hand as if it belonged to someone else.

"John," Duke said, coming from a huddle of men in the front yard. He stopped at the steps where Vada Faith sat. "Some of the searchers have reported in. Still no sign of James. We won't give up, man. We'll find him. I doubt he's too far away."

John stood on the top step above Vada Faith.

"You don't think he's gone far?" John said, measuring his words. He went down a step edging closer to the officer. "The baby didn't go anywhere on his own, Duke. Did you forget? He can't walk."

"I didn't forget, John."

Fighting back tears, John pushed Vada Faith's hand away when she tried to stop him from moving closer to the officer.

"Hey, buddy," Duke said, putting his hand out as if to stop John from advancing. "A neighbor might have the baby. We have more houses to cover."

"Did you check for finger prints on the play pen?" John indicated the play pen enclosed with caution tape.

"It's going to the lab."

"Why did you wait so long?"

"Not my decision, John. This isn't television." The officer pulled himself to his full height, much like stretching out a tape measure. "We don't have a crime lab. Hard to believe, huh? You know why? We're lucky to have gas for the squad car. This is the first real crime in this town, if it is a crime." He turned and looked out at the people standing around in clumps. "I don't think it's a kidnapping. I bet a friend has James, that's what I'm thinking."

"You're thinking! You're thinking!" John went down the rest of the steps. "Here's what I'm thinking. I'm thinking you'd better get off your ass and find our son!"

Duke turned and walked to the middle of the yard with John close behind him. The crowd moved forward to stare at the two men.

"A friend wouldn't do this!" John shouted. "Never!" He edged closer to the officer with his fists clenched. "You better find him before dark. For your sake, Duke Cobb, you'd better." John choked on his words. "I'll call the governor! I'll have your job!" He placed his fist under Duke's chin and pushed it up, even though Duke was taller. "Don't you think I won't!"

"Hey!" The officer backed away, holding up his hands in surrender. "Call the governor. We're little people here, John. The governor doesn't write my checks. You need to control yourself." Duke turned and headed to the street. People moved out of his way. "I'm doing my job." He yelled back over his shoulder, "I'm doing a good job too. So don't you worry."

"You're the one who should worry!" John yelled even louder. He turned abruptly toward his wife, the veins in his forehead pulsing. He held his head for a minute, then looked at her. "Vada Faith," he stared at her, "where's the baby's blanket? I couldn't find it anywhere. I looked all over. Did he have it in the play pen this morning?"

John had changed gears so suddenly, she could only glare at him. "What?"

"The blue blanket," he said, frowning at her, "the one Joy Ruth made for James. Where is it?"

"I don't know." Her head ached. "Probably in his crib." She didn't want to think. She didn't want to feel. The effect of the pill had worn off and panic was setting in.

"James carries it everywhere." John raised his eyebrows. "Where is it?"

"Stop with the questions." If John didn't shut up she might slap him.

"His blanket, Vada Faith?"

"I don't know." Her stomach churned. She couldn't remember. She ran inside, and up the stairs with John on her heels.

In the nursery, the baby's Pooh bear sat in one corner of the crib staring down at the Pooh sheets James talked to every morning. If only she'd left James in his crib today he'd be jabbering to his toys now and this wouldn't have happened.

The scent of James hung in the air. The baby's favorite soft blue blanket wasn't in his crib. She checked his dressing table, his dresser. She fought back tears. "It's not here." Her shoulders slumped.

"Did he have it this morning? You know he always carries it." He looked at her, accusingly, his eyes narrowed. "Well," he said his voice stern. "Think, Vay. Think."

John moved around the room, pulling back the curtains to look out the window at the street below. "I wish those jerks would go home."

"You don't mean that, John. They're volunteers who don't have to do what they're doing. There's only a few here to be nosy. Most are serious about helping."

She rubbed her pounding head. "James did have his blanket this morning when we went downstairs. Yes," she said, nodding her head rapidly, "He held onto it as I carried him downstairs for breakfast."

"Where is it then?" He gave her an odd look.

"Stop! Are you Duke Cobb's assistant?"

"Have you checked to see if anything else is missing? Any of his clothes?"

"Nobody was inside this house." Tired of his games, she jerked open the dresser drawers. The baby's clothes were folded in neat stacks. Socks, pajamas, play clothes. Not a thing touched. All was in order, as sweet smelling as her baby boy. Only James was absent.

She opened the closet. His little outfits hung neatly in a row on the blue satin hangers. Everything in the room was in perfect order like always. Only things weren't as they always were. Her world had turned upside down like a snow globe. Would her life ever fall back into place like those bits of white plastic settling on the floor of the container?

"Look," he said, his voice softer, as he stood behind her staring into the closet, "we've got to keep it together. We have to support each other."

"Take your own advice, mister! I don't know what you are getting at. Nobody was up here. I was in the kitchen."

"Are you sure nothing else is gone?"

"I'm as sure as any mother can be with a child who has dozens of outfits and toys. Mama buys clothes for James every week. I wouldn't miss one outfit. Why don't you believe me?"

"I do, honey. I do." He pulled her to him and gave her a hug. "I just can't figure out who could have been that quick."

She pulled away from him and walked around the room looking at all the baby things they'd accumulated in the last eight months. Books, a wall filled with framed photos of James, a little red wagon and red trike waiting for when he was old enough to climb on. There were enough clothes and toys here for ten babies.

"If he has his blanket," John said, picking up a wooden block from the night stand, "it will keep him warm." He put the block back on the table, and went into the hall. "It's turning cold." His footsteps sounded heavy as he made his way down the stairs.

"Thanks," she muttered and sank into the white rocker by the crib.

She shook from head to toe, thinking it would be dark in a few hours.

She knew John was worried sick. Choked with emotion, he would put on a calm face before stepping through the front door. That was his way. Keeping his feelings bottled inside. Be strong. Be brave. This had put him over the edge. He was ready to blow. He'd already blown with Duke and with her. It wasn't in her husband's nature to blow up at her or to get angry. He'd never questioned her like this before.

As she sat alone in the baby's room, she was overcome by loneliness. She reached over and touched the empty crib. The Pooh light on the wall flickered on and off. It was one of those automatic night-lights. It would come on when a shadow fell over it. The girls thought the lights were magic when they were small. Magic. That was the way her life had been since James arrived. Now every bit of the magic was gone. In its place was a blackness that was seeping slowly into her soul.

After a brief walk around the yard to blow off steam she stomped inside and slung her jacket on a chair. She ran up the stairs and ducked into the closet in her bedroom. She closed the door behind her. She'd created a corner and called it her prayer closet where she could come and pray for her family. Sinking into Grandma Belle's rocking chair, Vada Faith pressed herself into the frayed fabric of what had once been red velvet. She tried to absorb the comfort of John's dear grandmother's body. The old woman had spent many hours rocking in that chair but any comfort she'd left was long gone. Vada Faith picked up the Bible John inherited from that old woman he'd loved. She turned the pages and read some of the words Belle underlined in red. *"Therefore I tell you, whatever you ask for in prayer, believe that you have received it, and it will be yours."* Mark 11:24.

Each time she picked up Grandma Belle's Bible she found passages highlighted that were perfect for the moment. It was as if she had left bread crumbs for her family to follow.

She knelt by the chair and prayed. Not her usual prayer of, "Oh, God, bring my son home and if you do, I'll never sin again." No. That one was no longer sufficient. Now, she prayed, *"Lord, thank you for giving up your son to save the world and thank you for giving us our son. I trust you to look after him, our precious baby boy, James, and thank you, Lord, for bringing him home. I praise your Holy name. Amen."* Very simple. Whether she'd get a miracle or not, she felt better.

John would think she'd gone crazy, thanking God for something that hadn't happened but if Grandma Belle believed she did too.

"VADA FAITH!" MINNIE Bright called from across the street. "Hello, over here." The woman waved her apron at the porch steps where Vada Faith stood.

She crossed the street toward her neighbor, weaving her way through the crowd.

Minnie had pulled lawn chairs from her garage right up to the street's edge where she could view the Waddell's yard. Others had joined Minnie with their chairs, hoping to be the first to learn the fate of baby James.

A news truck pulled into the curb and stopped near Minnie. Two men began unloading camera equipment right beside Vada Faith.

"Someone took James off the porch." Her voice caught in her throat as she approached Minnie. She had to put her hands up to shade her eyes from the sun.

"I heard, child, I heard." Minnie stood and wiped her hands on her apron. "I'm sick over it. I wanted to give you this." Minnie pulled a small black Bible from her apron pocket. "All the answer you need, honey." She tapped the small book. "It's right in here." She pressed the book into her hands. "God says he don't put more on us than we can bear. Just remember that, honey. Now, that baby will be back home. Mark my words. He's in the Lord's hands this minute. I prayed him there." She patted her arm. Vada Faith reached out and numbly took the Bible from the woman. "I did too, Minnie. I did too."

She held the little Bible to her breast. "Thank you." She leaned over and hugged the older woman.

"Now you go on," Minnie said. "I'll be along shortly with some cinnamon rolls. Fresh out of the oven." The woman turned to go. "It will be a long day. You look like you haven't had a bite to eat, child. You must eat."

"I'll eat when my baby comes home."

"Well, you'll have one of my rolls when I bring them over," Minnie said, firmly, and made her way toward her small gray bungalow. "Wait until you see 'em. My rolls will give you energy for when that baby gets home."

Vada Faith knew she'd be having one of Minnie's cinnamon rolls. The woman wouldn't take no when it came to her cinnamon rolls.

Standing at the edge of the crowd staring at everyone, Vada wondered what they were getting out of this. People acted as though a festival was about to begin. Her neighbors, mostly retired folks, stood around and gossiped while she stood there among them in shock. Her son was gone and they didn't seem to care. She was relieved they were ignoring her and giving her space. She wasn't up to talking. She just wanted James home. She wanted things to be the way they were that morning when life stretched before her as smooth and still as a ribbon of highway.

"Now folks," said one of the news reporters, "stand back. We're getting a shot of the porch and the play pen."

The media was having a bumper crop day. Nothing like this had ever happened in Shady Creek. The residents were standing in the middle of the street with the scent of Minnie's cinnamon rolls wafting through the air. It reminded her of opening day at the county fair when she was a kid.

The most sensational thing to ever happen here was the occasional stolen bike or Duke would give someone a speeding ticket. It would be the topic of conversation in the beauty salon for days. Her customers wore any new incident to a frazzle but this was unthinkable, her baby boy kidnapped, not a clue as to his whereabouts, and her street crowded with gawkers.

Mama was right. This street was the quietest in town. It was the most unlikely scene for a kidnapping. The most trouble they'd had on her street was a dog napping. An alleged dog napping. Anna Dudley, the town librarian, who lived at the far end of the street had filed a police report on Tommy Henson, a neighbor, accusing him of abducting her apricot poodle, Pixie.

Everyone knew Tommy had complained endlessly about Pixie's nocturnal barking but when the poodle went missing the man swore his innocence on his mother's Bible in front of Duke Cobb and Anna down at city hall. Everyone believed Tommy, everyone but Anna. When Pixie trotted home two days later with a male beagle on her heels an embarrassed Anna went to apologize to Tommy taking with her one of her Sugar Pies that always won a blue ribbon at the fair. Now the little dog sported a new rhinestone collar and a red leash compliments of Tommy who often accompanied Anna and Pixie on their daily walk.

James couldn't walk like Pixie. He couldn't return home. He could barely crawl. He didn't have the instinct a dog has to return home. He was a helpless little baby. He couldn't help himself. She shuddered and moved across her lawn.

"James! Hey, James!" Rowdy, Minnie's grandson, called out loudly as he walked down the street. "Hey, James! Where are you boy?" Like her baby would answer. What was wrong with these people?

She sat down on the porch steps and drew her knees up to her chest. She felt helpless. She closed her eyes and tried to wish herself to wherever James was. She'd comfort him, tell him how much she loved him, and that soon he'd be back home. However it didn't work. She was still sitting on her own porch steps when she opened her eyes and her baby's pen was still empty. She had the feeling, at that moment, that nothing would ever be right again.

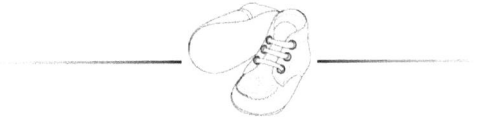

CHAPTER 25

SISSY ROSE FROM her chair to get them a glass of lemonade to enjoy while they listened to the radio. The baby smiled and hit the wooden spoons together making a sound similar to the beat of the song.

A man's voice burst out of the mahogany cabinet interrupting the piano piece. "There has been a kidnapping in Shady Creek."

Sissy lowered herself back into her chair. His next words paralyzed her.

"Volunteers are combing the area in and around the town, hoping to find the missing baby. Officer Duke Cobb reports there have been several breaks in the case. He vows to have the baby boy home by dark."

Sissy closed her eyes.

Birdie went to stand in front of radio. On the floor, the baby squealed and chewed on a big spoon.

Another bolt of static and Sissy shot to her feet. She took Birdie's shaking hands in her own.

"This could mean an arrest today," the man said. "Stand by. We'll keep you updated when anything else comes in."

Sissy snapped off the radio. "An arrest, Birdie. They're going to make an arrest. They know who took the baby. This is getting complicated. We have to get this baby out of here." She pressed her hands into her skirt. "If we don't, we'll be arrested. That means jail, Birdie. We'll be locked up."

Birdie shook her handkerchief and stuffed it into her skirt pocket.

"If they find the baby here, we're in big trouble." Sissy's breathing became labored. "Birdie, what have you gotten us into?"

"I'll take him away." Birdie kissed Sissy's stubby fingers. "You said I got us into this mess. I'll get us out. You said."

Sissy's face was as red as the Early Girl tomatoes their mama used to grow.

Birdie knew Sissy's heart was sick. She couldn't take any more worry. Birdie gathered her big sister in her arms. She wanted to cry but she had to take care of Sissy.

Sissy seemed as frail as a baby bird. Mama was right. She said someday Birdie might have to be in charge. Sissy was sick before mama died. The moment had come. Birdie was in charge. She had to fix things. That was all there was to it.

At that particular moment, though, she didn't know what it was she was supposed to fix.

As she stood in the middle of the room rocking Sissy back and forth, the baby on the blanket threw a wooden spoon and began to wail.

"See if he'll drink some more of his bottle, Birdie." Sissy pulled herself up straight.

"Oh yes." Birdie picked up the baby and settled in mama's old rocker. The baby grabbed his bottle greedily as if he hadn't already drank most of it.

Maybe Birdie could take Robert into the woods to live. They'd be a family. She loved the woods. They'd be like The Box Car Children. It was the only book they had and Sissy had read it many times to her. They'd find an abandoned shelter, maybe not a boxcar though. There were no railroads nearby. She'd decorate the place with twigs and berries. Mama had taught her about the woods and what she could eat. She'd teach Robert. They'd fly into the trees like birds. Birdie smiled at the idea of Robert flying alongside her through the air.

It might not be so easy living in the woods with a baby. Sissy wouldn't approve. The woods were too near her house.

Maybe if the police officer came he'd let her keep Robert. He might not be mean like Sissy said. He might take her to live in another place nicer than Sissy's.

Birdie's eyes fluttered closed. Maybe she'd wake up in Heaven. She'd be happy there.

The baby closed his eyes as the chair continued to rock gently back and forth.

CHAPTER 26

"HEY, JOHN WASPER," Duke said, using her husband's high school nickname, "let's talk about that workshop you attended." The officer had burst into the living room where John and Vada Faith sat in matching chairs. A table and tall lamp stood between them. "Where'd you say it was?"

"Kentucky."

"What city? Kentucky's a big state."

"Louisville."

"You spend the night?"

"Yep."

"Anyone with you?" The officer jotted something on his notepad.

"No."

"Did you meet anyone who'd remember you?"

"I'm not all that memorable. I talked to some buyers. Woodworkers. We traded information. Not sure they'd remember me."

"You talk to anyone else?"

"The desk clerk. She had a tongue ring and she had angel wings tattooed on both arms, in case you go looking for her. I have hotel and food receipts."

"All right." Duke wrote on his pad. He frowned at John, then wrote some more. "See anyone else?"

"It was a convention. I didn't write down every name. I'll unpack and get the names and receipts to you."

"Soon, you hear."

"Sure." He knew people at the event who would vouch for him. Duke didn't need to call them. They were his business associates and buyers, people who respected him. He didn't want Duke harassing them.

"That your truck out front?"

"Yep."

"You drive it on your trip?"

John nodded.

"Mind if I take a look?"

John fished the keys from his pocket and handed them to the officer.

"Don't you two go anywhere. I may have more questions."

"Where do you think we're going, Duke?" John asked. "James has been taken."

"Well, don't leave town." Duke snapped the note pad closed.

"That's a rotten thing to say." Her husband stood and faced the officer. "You think we'd go somewhere without our baby and the girls?" John yelled. "Do you think we had something to do with the disappearance of our son?"

Duke turned his back on them and moved to the hallway. He called over his shoulder, "I don't know what happened to your baby. Until I do know, I'm covering all my bases. Orders from headquarters. Got it?"

"You're crazy, have been since you were a kid." John's hands clenched into tight fists.

"Stop it!" Vada Faith jumped from her chair. "I'm tired of this bickering. It's old news you don't like each other. Who cares? My baby is what matters. Go find him, Duke Cobb! Don't come back until you do!"

John shoved past Duke and headed to the porch. He slammed the front door so hard Vada Faith thought it would fall off its hinges. She hurried after him with Duke behind her. John was kicking the wooden posts that held the bannister up. She'd never seen him act this way. One of the posts came loose and fell into the flower bed below the porch.

"I'll be in the workshop if you need me," he snapped, jumping off the porch steps and going toward the backyard and the safety of his shop.

Leaving Duke on the porch wide-eyed, Vada Faith went inside, padded up the stairs and locked the bathroom door behind her. In the mirror covering one wall, she saw her reflection. Who was this person with the shaggy blond hair, swollen eyes, and scratches on her arms? She sat on the side of the tub and cried. For James, for herself, and for her family. How on earth could she go on? She wiped her face and pulled a brush and comb from the cabinet. She sprayed some mousse on her fingers and worked it in. She had to pull herself together.

When she walked down the stairs, someone banged on the front door.

"I'm coming," she said, straightening her clothes. She'd changed into comfortable knit slacks and a tee shirt. The pounding continued until she pulled open the door.

Duke stepped inside. "Do you mind? I need to look around in here again."

"I don't care what you do." She shrugged.

She went to the porch and sat down in the swing, leaving Duke inside. She no longer cared. Her body felt numb. She pinched her arm hard enough to bring blood but didn't feel it. It was as if her body had been numbed with Novocain. She could see how people became cutters with emotions so out of balance they no longer felt pain. Not even when blood poured from their skin.

"Can you come inside?" Duke motioned from the doorway.

John stood on the lawn talking to some of his buddies.

"Now what?" Reluctantly she stood and the swing drifted slowly back and forth. "Did you find my fingerprints on the kitchen counter?"

"More than that." His voice sounded ominous.

Curious, she followed Duke down the hallway. He led her into the laundry room where he put his hand inside the washer and pulled out the baby's blue blanket.

"His blanket!" She cried, trying to take the damp blanket from him. He held on tight. "James spooned applesauce onto it this morning. I remember now. I threw it in with a load of his things. James likes it in his high chair when he eats breakfast. It has to go into the wash nearly every day. He never wants it at any other meal, just breakfast. Look." She reached for the blanket again, "It's showing wear." Duke wouldn't loosen his grip on the wet blanket. The look on his face told her something was wrong.

"What?" She stared at him. "What?"

He held the blanket out and inspected it. "Are you sure you didn't wash this blanket after James disappeared? Did it have something on it you wanted to wash off? Some kind of stain."

"It had applesauce on it, Duke. What do you mean? What kind of stain?" What was he talking about? "Why would I wash it after James disappeared? I haven't washed anything since he disappeared. I started the washer after breakfast. I forgot to dry the load. I try to keep his blanket clean. He loves it so much. Washing clothes is second nature to me. It's automatic. Not even something I think about."

He gave her a strange look.

"Why are you looking at me like that?"

He didn't say a word. Just stared at her and fingered the soft blanket.

"Applesauce doesn't stain," he said.

"I know." Vada Faith shook her head. "What?"

"Earlier, you told John you didn't know where the baby's blanket was."

"I didn't. How did you know what we were discussing?"

"I overheard you."

"You've lost your mind! You believe I hurt James and washed his blanket to cover it up!"

She knew now why Duke had closed the laundry room door behind them. Otherwise everyone in the kitchen and dining room would have overheard their conversation.

She felt her knees fold but didn't recall the floor rising up to meet her.

In the distance, she could hear John's voice. She felt his hand on her forehead, a damp cloth on her face. "Are you okay?" His face was etched with worry as she opened her eyes.

"My head hurts." She put her hand over his on her forehead. The coldness felt good. Then it came back to her. James was missing. Duke Cobb thought she was responsible. She sat up and grabbed her head. "Oh, it hurts."

Duke had his hands on his hips, staring down at her.

"I didn't hurt James." She looked at John. "Duke thinks I hurt our baby."

She was too weak to stand. Otherwise she'd have attacked Duke Cobb for thinking she harmed James.

"Let me help you up, honey." John reached down and pulled her up.

"Duke doesn't think that either, Vada Faith. Tell her Duke."

"All right." The officer stomped around the laundry room. "I don't think you hurt your baby or had anything to do with his disappearance. I know you both. So does everyone else in town."

His voice was the kindest it had been all day.

"I'm pissed," he said. "The county sheriff wants to take over the investigation. It's out of his jurisdiction. He's after more money for his department. He wants to solve this case and get all the accolades. He questioned my integrity and requested a list of everything I've done so far. Al sent me in to search again. "Maybe the sheriff's right," he sighed. "Maybe I'm not as good as I thought."

"Let them help you, Duke," John said, "we need more help, but stand up for yourself. You're still in charge."

"Let the sheriff help," Vada Faith said, still woozy, "and the park ranger and the game warden too. We need help." She collapsed in John arms.

"I'll be outside," Duke said and left shaking his head.

The slamming of the door reverberated down the hallway.

Vada Faith let John lead her up the stairs to their bedroom.

She crawled into bed like an old woman pulling the covers over her head. She pressed her face into her mama's quilt. As a kid she'd adopted the worn multicolored quilt, sleeping with it every night. She'd dragged it out of the closet earlier in the day and held it for a time hoping it would make her feel better. It hadn't. She tried to pull strength from the worn quilt. She needed something to carry her through the coming hours. She fingered the quilt's frayed edges, smelled its earthy smell. The old quilt, comforting as it was, did nothing to assuage her heartbreak.

"You okay," John asked, coming out of the bathroom. He leaned over her.

"I'll be okay when we have James back."

"I know." He pushed her hair away from her face. "I need to get back downstairs."

"Go," she said, and closed her eyes.

She listened to his receding footsteps.

She went to the dresser and pulled out the satin shoes bought for the surrogate baby. She crawled back into bed with them. She was heart broken when she lost that baby. The doctor said it was best, that it wouldn't be right. Right in whose eyes? She wasn't sure who losing a child was best for. Certainly not for the mother who loved it from its conception. Not the baby who didn't get a chance at life. While that child wasn't the child of the man she loved, John Waddell, it was her biological child and she'd loved it. The baby had been intended for a childless couple. That never happened. However, it was her baby, inside her body, and nothing anyone said made her feel any better after she lost it. Certainly not John. He hadn't understood. The pain had been buried deep inside her. Now, it came back in great waves. She held the tiny shoes tight. She'd never had the opportunity to hold the child she'd lost early in the pregnancy. She'd never rubbed its downy head or brushed its baby cheek with her lips. With James she had eight wonderful months. She loved him with all her heart and soul and mind. Without him her arms ached. Why had she been allowed to fall in love with James if he was going to be taken from her? She had to have him back. She could barely breathe without him. Why did she have to keep learning the same life lessons over? Nothing in life was certain and nothing could be counted on. Except God and she was wondering where He was in all this.

Was He punishing her for her selfish ways? She'd always wanted more than she had. Had someone taken James thinking she wasn't worthy of him? She breathed in and out deeply, trying to convince herself her baby was safe. She wiped her tears with her mama's soft quilt.

She dragged herself out of bed and returned the shoes to their special spot in the dresser drawer. In the bathroom she splashed cold water on her face.

She headed down the stairs toward the next step in this nightmare journey.

"YOU KIDS HAVE to eat." Louise handed her son a heavy paper plate. John stared at the plate in his hand. Turning to the buffet, Louise peeled a plate from the stack for her daughter-in-law.

"The food is delicious," she said to the couple. "Try a few bites anyway. We have to keep going for James."

There were ten chairs around the oversized dining room table. Volunteers and neighbors filled them. John had designed and built the table especially for his family.

Vada Faith glanced at the buffet and gagged. She couldn't eat. Down the hall, the tall grandfather clock chimed three, almost time to pick up Charity and Hope from school. Soon, it would be dinner time and then it would be dark. Her breath caught in her throat.

Darkness would come and they were no closer to finding James than when he first went missing. She choked on a sip of iced tea and started coughing.

"You okay, honey?" Louise rushed to her side with a napkin. "Here, I hope you aren't coming down with a cold. Come on, fill your plate."

"Any more of that macaroni and cheese?" Lefty Parr sat at one end of the table, nodding at Vada Faith. Louise rushed back to the kitchen for another casserole of the macaroni and cheese Myrtie Streeter had made.

A yellow linen cloth covered the oak table. On it were matching yellow flowered cups and napkins, leftovers from Louise's garden club luncheons. A huge ham rested on a platter in the center. It looked like a celebration but there was nothing to be celebrate. Not now. Maybe never.

At a card table in the corner, Minnie Bright poured coffee into a line of foam cups using the huge coffee urn she'd borrowed from the Methodist Church. She passed cups of steaming coffee to several men. Boxes of Kentucky fried chicken lined a library table against the wall.

The room had taken on a party air with the yellow floral dinnerware and the spirited conversation. Still, a few people huddled in small groups and whispered.

Vada Faith willed away the tears stinging the backs of her eyes. She tried focusing on the macaroni and cheese and the nachos on her plate. Finally, for something to do with her hands, she chose one of Minnie's cinnamon rolls from a blue metal platter by the coffee pot. She caught Minnie's eye and smiled. She took a small bite passing the roll to John who stood against the wall. The only thing on his plate was a spoonful of Louise's famous potato salad which he had stirred into swirls. As she slid the cinnamon roll onto his plate, he looked up. A thought passed between them. How had this happened? They were ordinary people leading simple lives. They weren't famous. There was no reason whatsoever for anyone to single them out and steal their baby boy.

Their home was crowded with people, many of whom they'd known all their lives, but who lived on the peripheral edge, never crossing their threshold until this day. Hoppy Carmichael was there from the car wash. He gave their car an extra chamois dry-off every week though it didn't come with the price of a wash. Emily, the teller from the bank, with every hair in place was sitting in their living room. She held an animated conversation with Hoppy while holding a large cup of McDonald's coffee.

A new phase of their lives had begun.

People brought gifts: flowers, gourmet coffee, a set of oversized red mugs, a soft stuffed dog for James, and a box of Whitman's chocolates. A large box of Whitman's chocolates. What was that about? It wasn't Christmas or Easter or any other holiday.

It was more than she could bear. Her baby gone. People walking around their home as if they were regular guests.

Even Mertie had shown up with her special macaroni and cheese and trays of Ditzie Duncan's potato chip chicken. Who could eat at a time like this?

A wave of grief washed over her. She slipped into the kitchen pushed her plate into a trash bag and headed to the back door. She needed to let go of the tears she was holding back.

She stepped between two men at the back door. She thought of pulling the loaded plates out of their hands and screaming, "Go find my baby!" Yet, they had given up time with their own families to help her and John. It wasn't their fault James was missing. It was hers. Hers. Hers.

Hurrying across the back yard, she slipped inside the door of her husband's workshop, relieved it was unlocked.

The scent of wood shavings and tung oil comforted her. She pulled a wooden stool from the work bench and slumped down on it.

Just as she dropped her head on the work bench, John stepped inside, locking the door behind him. His body shook with emotion.

She wiped her own tears and went to him, taking him in her arms.

"It's going to be okay, James is okay. He's going to be found." She kissed his tears and held onto him with all her strength. He pulled out his handkerchief and wiped his face, then he wiped her tears.

"This is a nightmare." He picked up an airplane from the work bench. He was building it for James. The plan was to hang it from the ceiling of the nursery. He wanted to do the baby's bedroom in airplanes for his first birthday, four months away.

"Vada Faith," Joy Ruth yelled, pounding on the shop door. "Open up, I've found something. Hurry! Open the door."

"What?" John unlocked the shop door stuffing his handkerchief into his back pocket.

"Does this belong to James?" Joy Ruth was breathless as she pushed a swatch of blue cloth toward them.

"What is it?" Vada Faith grabbed the item. "Oh my God! It's the baby's bib, John! His Peter Rabbit bib." She buried her face in its softness. It smelled of James. Of baby powder and lotion. It even bore his faint milky smell. "Where'd you find it?" Hope nearly lifted her off the ground.

"It was down at the corner. Come on, I'll show you."

The three of them hurried to the front of the house and raced to the sidewalk.

Vada Faith knew if she could hang on a little longer her baby would be in her arms. She just knew it. Her heart almost burst with gratitude at the sight of the baby's bib.

Joy Ruth reached the sidewalk and pointed. "It was down there just off the sidewalk in the grass." She touched Vada Faith's shoulder. "We'll have to give it to Duke. You know that, honey."

"I know." Vada Faith nodded holding the bib to her face. "James loves Peter Rabbit." She closed her eyes and held the bib tight as if it were James. Then she handed it to John.

He turned it over and stared at it as if it contained a secret message. He let out a deep breath. "Yeah, I'll give it to Duke." He walked toward the sidewalk where the officer stood with his arms folded and a Mountain Dew sticking out of his jacket pocket.

Vada Faith followed Joy Ruth down to the corner where she'd found the bib. She dropped to her knees and ran her fingers through the grass hoping to find a clue that would lead to her baby.

"Nothing," she mumbled, hopelessness pressing her down to the curb. She sat, pulled her knees up to her chin and hugged them.

"Hey, it's going to be okay." Joy Ruth sat down beside her and slipped her arm around her sister's shoulders. "It's hard, I know, Vay. We're going to find him. You'll see."

Vada Faith let herself be rocked. Her twin comforted her like no one else could, not even John.

"We have to have faith. Like your name, Faith. James will be fine. I feel it in my gut. I'm usually right. We just gotta hang in."

"I know." Vada Faith reached over and patted Joy Ruth's hand. "Your instincts are usually right. I'm hanging in."

"That's my sis." Joy Ruth glanced at her watch. "I need to get the girls from school now."

"The girls!" Vada Faith jumped up and brushed off her pants. "I forgot them. I'm the world's worst mother."

"Calm down. The girls are fine. Duke had the principal keep an eye on them this afternoon as a precaution." She nodded. "Duke Cobb's not as useless as we thought."

They walked back to the house arm in arm. "I'm going with you." Vada Faith turned to her sister. "I need to see my girls."

A white police van rounded the corner as they neared the driveway. Behind it came another cruiser.

Their eyes followed the vehicles as they parked on the street.

"It's okay, Vay." Joy Ruth watched her sister staring at the van from the lab. "You need to be here. I'll get the girls. Should I tell them about James?"

"It's up to you. Tell them he's okay. They're little worriers. They'll be upset. They love James. Dear Lord, how could I let this happen?" Her voice broke but somehow she kept the tears at bay. She had to start acting like the adult she was and stop blubbering all over everybody.

"I'll tell them." Joy Ruth squeezed her hand. "Honey, you didn't let this happen. It happened. It's one of those things. We don't know why bad things happen, they just do."

As Joy Ruth roared off in her sports car, Vada Faith knew the girls would be pleased. They loved riding in the car. They'd have a few minutes of enjoyment before arriving home to find it full of strangers.

CHAPTER 29

VADA FAITH WATCHED as two men put the play pen into the back of the white van. They didn't see her, standing behind the crowd as they shoved it roughly inside the back and slammed the doors. She wanted to beat on the van and scream. How could they shove her baby's play pen in that dark van and slam the doors on it? They didn't care about James. Of course they didn't. This was nothing to them, just a job. She moved away from the crowd.

She stood up straighter refusing to give the photographers another shot of her falling apart, beating on some object. She was on the news crying, disheveled, and screaming. It brought more curiosity seekers.

Duke stopped her as she walked across the lawn. He held up a plastic bag. "Could this belong to James?"

She fingered the clear bag with the white nipple cover inside. "It's a cover for a baby bottle."

"Did he have a bottle in his play pen this morning?" Duke scratched his head.

She nodded. "He had the cover off. He'd been chewing on the nipple. He can take it off and snap it back on."

Oh, God, she thought. The baby's bottle wasn't there either. It was in the play pen earlier. What else had she overlooked? It was further proof she'd failed James. In a nano second their lives were changed by her actions.

"They took his bottle," she said, terrified she'd be arrested for her negligence. Could they do such a thing? "Maybe there are fingerprints." Duke held the bag up and examined it.

"Where did you find it?" she asked, wondering how such a perfect day could have turned into such a nightmare?

"A dog had it a few streets over," he said. "Probably a hundred white caps like this in town. We'll check it out."

"Do you think whoever has James will take good care of him?" It was a stupid question. She needed hope and Duke obliged.

"Oh, sure," he said, giving her a compassionate nod, "the person had to be caring to take his bottle. Like I said, I haven't given up on this being an inside job."

"An inside job?" She stared at him in disbelief. She moved a few steps away from him. "You mean like someone in our family?"

"I mean inside this community. Someone on this street. I can't help but think this is a mistake. A gut feeling and my gut is usually right." He turned to look toward the street corner where a group of men stood.

"What's going on down there?" Several men were down on their knees.

"An expert came out from the city to make a mold of a footprint we found. This will be solved before long."

"Do you really think so?" She narrowed her eyes. Was he trying to make her feel better?

"I do," he said, quickly. "I do."

He was lying. She knew it. He walked away before she could comment.

If someone in the community had taken James, they would have brought him back. She prayed God would keep her baby safe. Wherever he was.

Who knew how it would end? Who knew these things? If God knew, why hadn't he stopped it at the beginning?

The pastor said to give every burden to the Lord. She'd done that. The minute James went missing, she'd prayed for God to watch over him, to bring him home safely.

How many prayers did He answer in a day. Did each person have a limit on how many answers he got? Were there more requests going up than answers coming down?

Something about the detective from Charleston reminded Vada Faith of her father, Delbert who lived in Alaska. He was planning a trip to see his grandson at Christmas. She couldn't bear to think that far ahead. His grandson might not be here at Christmas.

"Joy Ruth." The officer had spotted Vada Faith's twin on the porch. She'd made a snack for the children to take to their room while they watched a children's program on television.

It had taken Vada Faith awhile to answer their questions and assure them their little brother was all right. She tried to believe it herself.

Vada Faith stood behind a sprawling bush in the front yard where she could watch the activity without being seen.

"Joy Ruth!" Duke's voice carried a firmness it had lacked earlier.

Joy Ruth walked to face the officer who stood on the sidewalk. "What do you want?" Agitation was etched on her face.

"Where were you today?" The officer held his pad and pen.

"At work. Where do you think, Duke Cobb?"

"At your place of business?" He raised his eyebrows at her.

"Where else?" She stared at the detective across the way. She had no intention of letting her eyes meet his.

"Did you leave the shop at any time today?" His voice probed.

He was pushing her. She did not like to be pushed.

"Duke Cobb!" Joy Ruth moved close to him. She came up to the badge on his shirt, "I'm the baby's godmother. If anything happens to my sister and her husband, God forbid, I will raise James. I was with my sister when that baby was born." She paused for breath. "Stop wasting time asking me stupid questions. I didn't kidnap my nephew."

"You didn't answer my question." He snapped his notebook shut. "The question was, did you leave your shop at any time today."

"I know what you asked. I don't have to answer anything." Red faced, she stomped over to join a group of women who were searching the grass along the sidewalks.

They scattered out, scanning the yards as they went.

"We're not finished," he yelled toward Joy Ruth's back. Duke walked over to his car still in the driveway. Leaning on the door, he uncapped the Mountain Dew. The detective joined Duke at the car and lit a cigarette.

Vada Faith leaned into the prickly bush. The branches poked her through the thin shirt she wore. She thought of Jesus who'd worn a crown of thorns. He was nailed to a cross and died to give all his children eternal life. All they had to do was accept it. She couldn't imagine the kind of physical torture he'd gone through or the pain God had gone through giving up His only son. The pain she felt was unbearable enough.

CHAPTER 30

DARKNESS HAD MOVED quickly into City Park that night. A damp mist fell over the area where the candlelight vigil would take place. Vada Faith arrived with John and Joy Ruth holding on to her as though she were a fragile china doll whose legs and arms might fall off at any minute.

"It's going to be okay, honey." Midgy Brown wrapped her arms around the distraught woman. "It's going to be okay." She patted Vada Faith's arm.

"Here," Midgy said, digging into the basket on her arm. She handed them each a white candle, lighting them with a cigarette lighter. "We're going to find James, honey. I promise. Just keep on being brave."

When Midgy turned to continue handing out candles, Vada Faith slipped into one of the folding chairs and wiped her sore eyes.

"She's worked hard to put this together so quickly," Joy Ruth whispered to John. "Bruiser and the firefighters set up the chairs an hour ago. Hauled them from the Catholic Church. Myrtie Streeter is serving sandwiches at Sunnyside Baptist afterward if anyone's hungry. She keeps talking about having a big fund raiser for James, featuring a potato chip chicken dinner. I told her no. Not now."

Joy Ruth and John took a seat on each side of Vada Faith, leaning into her as if she might fall over and they'd have to catch her. Maybe they thought she'd run away if they didn't wedge her in. She'd thought about that more than once. Running away to stop the pain.

If she could get far enough away, the day might evaporate and maybe she'd get a do-over.

The dreary weather hadn't deterred people from showing up at the park. Most were seated, talking in hushed tones. Officer Cobb sat in the middle of a few volunteers on the front row.

Vada Faith clutched a flyer featuring a smiling James. Thanks to Midgy, flyers had been made and posted all over town. She folded the flyer and put it into her jeans pocket. Staring at it caused her stomach to turn over.

Midge patted her red hair and made her way up to the makeshift stage in front of the gazebo. She gave the mike a sharp thump and it made a screeching sound.

Vada Faith spotted her old high school rival, Paris Holiday standing at the side of the gazebo. She was known as Paris Huckendorf until she legally changed her name after graduation. Her blond head was bent, her candle's light reflected a scowling face. What was she doing in town? She'd heard Paris made commercials in New York City. She knew for certain the girl didn't come to support her. She hated Vada Faith.

The priest from the Catholic Church went forward and tapped the mike sending out another screech. Holding his candle high, he said, "Let's pray."

With bowed head Vada Faith listened but kept her eyes open and watched the people.

Suddenly, she punched her husband's arm.

"Ouch!" He rubbed his elbow. "Why'd you do that?"

"Did you hear that priest?" She wrung her hands. "He's praying for the soul of the kidnapper! No wonder Mary Conway quit the Catholics and became a Baptist."

She fumed as John drew his eyebrows down. "Don't punch me again!"

Well, excuse me, she thought. She couldn't summon one kind thought for the kidnapper. His soul could rot in Hell after he brought James home. She knew her attitude wasn't Christian. She didn't feel Christian at the moment, not since James was taken.

Then came Pastor Pinwheel, not known for his speaking abilities, from Sunnyside Baptist.

"Father, God," he cried, looking up at the heavens, "if you know where baby James Waddell is, please just send him home." He cleared his throat. "Not our Heavenly home, Father, but you know what I mean." He coughed. "To his home in Shady Creek. Be with the search, Lord, and the searchers. Let us find James safe and healthy. Comfort his family. We ask it in the precious name of your son, Jesus."

What was wrong with that man? The Christian leaders in her community had all gone bonkers. Right along with whoever had taken her baby. Asking God if he knew where James was. Of course, God knew. He was God. If the pastor knew anything at all he'd know God knew where her baby was. She didn't care if the minister was right out of seminary. He needed another lesson in public speaking.

What was the world coming to? She vowed then to become a better person, the person she'd always intended to be. She'd change, devote her life to God, when her baby was back. She'd study her Bible until it fell to shreds. She'd know more than the morons up front. She'd become another Joyce Meyers. She'd even work on becoming less judgmental, her biggest flaw to date. Who knew what heights she might rise to? It gave her something to contemplate as she wiped the tears that hadn't stopped falling since her baby went missing. The rest of the evening passed in a blur. Speakers came and went offering prayers and kind words.

"Thank you for coming," Vada Faith managed to utter, when Midgy summoned her to the front. "I love you all for being here. God bless you for searching for our baby boy." She broke down and sobbed, nearly falling when John guided her back to her seat.

Reporters with their cameras swooped down on the couple as they walked through the crowd. Cameras flashed before Duke Cobb and his men corralled the reporters to the sidelines.

"Duke Cobb has a few words to say," Midgy said, waving Duke to her side.

"The search is going well," he announced into the mike. "We've covered nearly all the houses in town. We won't stop searching until the Waddell baby is found."

From her seat, Vada Faith wanted to scream that Duke Cobb had failed in his search but nausea kept her clinging to John's arm.

In Duke Cobb's opinion they were right on target. Ha, Vada Faith thought. Just because volunteers had covered the community with flyers and knocked on doors.

Sure, everyone wanted James home but it wasn't happening.

"I want to remind the women," Midgy said, when Duke returned to his seat, "we're meeting at daylight at the Community Hall at Sunnyside Baptist. We'll plan our strategy. Duke will give us a list of the outlying areas not yet searched. Okay," she said, clapping for quiet, "let's sing a song. This is just for baby James. It's a variation of an old song. Listen a minute and you can follow my words."

"This little light of mine, I'm gonna let it shine," Midgy sang loudly, as she looked out over the crowd. "This little light of mine, I'm gonna let it shine. I'm gonna let it shine for sweet-baby-James, for sweet-little-baby-James, let it shine, let it shine."

Suddenly, the crowd followed Midgy's lead, singing exuberantly, their candles held high.

Vada Faith couldn't utter a word. Tears had left her face raw and it hurt to touch her eyes. She wiped her hand gently across her face.

Midgy ended the song and joined the crowd cheering and clapping.

"Oh, one more item," Midgy said, coughing, "I almost forgot. Charity and Hope, sisters of baby James, have asked to speak. Here you go, girls. Come on up here." The two girls stepped to the front smiling. "This is the Waddell twins." Midgy clapped.

Vada Faith's heart flew to her throat. She couldn't believe her eight-year old girls had asked to speak. They were sitting a few rows behind her with her mother, Helena, and John's mother, Louise. Well, they were growing up, getting more independent, especially with their brother missing. They adored that little boy.

"We just want to say that we love our little brother," Charity, always the leader, spoke first as they stepped together toward the mike. "We want that mean person to bring our baby home. We love you, James."

Vada Faith moved closer to John. He put his arms around her. The girls gave her hope.

Charity turned shy, now that the crowd's attention was on her. She continued in a softer voice. "We want him home. We miss him. A whole bunch."

"Your turn, Hope." Charity poked Hope in the ribs and whispered into the mike, "Speak up, loud."

"Well," Hope said, sniffing, "We sure miss our buddy boy. We want him to come home and we want mommy to stop crying." She was breathless. "We don't want our daddy to be sad anymore."

Tears rolled down John's face. He turned to Vada Faith and buried his head in her shoulder. Her heart went out to him. The girls were ready to burst into tears.

Charity pushed Hope and whispered, "Don't mention mommy and daddy again."

"Mostly," Hope pushed her sister back and went on bravely, "we just want James home. That's all we have to say."

"Thank you, Charity and Hope." Midgy nodded at the girls and the crowd applauded.

Thunder rumbled in the distance and then a hard rain started to fall.

By then, Vada Faith and John were in each other's arms crying. They opened their arms to the girls who ran to them and burst into tears. The four of them stood hugging while rain poured down their faces.

"Don't forget," Midgy called as she turned to run to her car. "Daylight. Sunnyside Baptist. Oh, and Miss Myrtie is serving sandwiches and coffee at the church right now if anyone is hungry. I'm headed there now."

Lightening zigzagged across the sky.

Vada Faith passed out tissues and helped the girls wipe their tears. John hugged them both tight.

The crowd ran in every direction, brightly colored umbrellas appeared, bobbing up and down like horses on a carousel. It reminded Vada Faith of that long ago rainy night at the county fair when John first kissed her. She had floated on air, knowing right then they were for keeps.

Only there was no festivity in the air this night.

The girls hurried off with Joy Ruth when she appeared with their hooded jackets.

Vada Faith and John walked slowly through the rain, heading home, hanging onto each other. He held his golf umbrella over their heads but rain pelted them sideways. It didn't matter. They kept on walking, bent over and broken, out of tears and out of words.

It was a relief and a burden that Charity and Hope wouldn't be home. Vada Faith wanted them with her. She just didn't know what to do with them. She'd never seen them so restless and whiny. They were agitated with each other. They couldn't settle down to anything with

James gone. She couldn't settle down to anything either. Mostly she walked the floor.

She was planning to keep the girls out of school the next day until she realized they needed to go to keep busy. Otherwise, they'd be at her side worrying.

The rain pelted them harder. They didn't care. Nothing mattered.

John wore a frown, not noticing the rain. Vada Faith stepped high to avoid puddles. She felt as though she were stepping from one black cloud to another. Her mind was as muddled as the puddles. What did it matter if she got wet? Got soaked? Ruined her good shoes? With her son gone, what else on earth mattered? She let herself sink ankle deep into the next puddle and muddy water went up past her ankles, over the leather boots she'd loved so much the week before and now loathed.

"I don't blame you," Vada Faith cried later that night as she talked to God. She looked up at the spot in the dark sky where she thought He might be hanging out.

The storm had cleared out, leaving the night black as ink.

John decided to take a walk, cutting through their back yard to the next block where there were no reporters or news trucks. Worried, Vada Faith stood on the deck watching for him.

She felt God was listening to her. He had his own time table, she knew that. He didn't owe her any favors either.

She wasn't the nicest person in the world. Often, she was the meanest. God forgave all sins, she knew that, but what if she'd racked up so many he didn't have the time to forgive each one. Maybe they were piled up beside his desk. A stack of papers with her every sin listed. She wondered if there was a sin limit?

"You are so doggone mean spirited, Vay," Joy Ruth said each time she gossiped about Midgy Brown. "Midgy has such a good heart. You shouldn't let her wild hair get the best of you."

"It's not just her hair," Vada Faith had answered. "It's Midgy's praise. She tells other customers I can work hair miracles. It puts stress on me to stretch beyond my capabilities. I have to keep outdoing myself."

"That's good for you," Joy Ruth said, and always added, "good for our business too." That's what Joy Ruth cared about, anything that would increase their business.

Vada Faith lowered herself to the back porch step. She wished John would return. She drew her knees up and hugged them tight letting the cold air wash over her face as she studied the sky.

As far as answered prayer was concerned, God had answered her biggest prayer request of all time. He had brought her mama back into her life when she thought she might never see her again. She didn't hold it against Him that He took His time doing it. The pastor says the God's timing isn't our own. His is impeccable. So the man upstairs had waited until she was an adult and could appreciate a mother. Her question still remained. How many answers did God allow in one lifetime?

Her baby was a different story. She was responsible for him being gone. She wasn't sure the Lord had any sympathy for her on that count. Maybe not one iota. She was humbled and sorrier than she'd ever been about anything in her entire life.

"Please," she prayed, "I'm sorry I left James on the porch alone. I can't rewind the tape." She wiped at gathering tears, cold on her cheeks. "You know the way the girls used to rewind their old Barney video." She sniffed. "I'm rattling on, sorry. You have more important fish to fry than listening to me. If you'll just keep James safe, I'll change my life. I'll volunteer in the church nursery Sunday mornings. You know how they can't seem to get anyone to help since Iris Dudley started bringing her two-year old triplets. Now the little girl is good but those boys need a leash. All right, maybe they aren't that bad. I will sacrifice my peaceful Sunday and watch them whether I like it or not. I'll make some dinners for Iris. When my twins were born I appreciated meals carried in by my Sunday school class. I won't complain anymore about getting up early for church or about what I'll wear. I'll bake for every church function. I'll work at the clothes drive for the cancer society and bring more canned goods to the food bank than anyone else."

She nearly strangled on her list of promises. However, if it meant James would be returned, she'd do anything. She'd even bungee jump off the New River Bridge if she had to, and the Lord knew she was petrified of heights.

"Like the Bible says, I have fallen short of the glory of God." She wasn't sure where the verse was located. She just knew it was there. What was wrong with her for not knowing where every scripture could be found? "Lord, I'm such a dumb ass. Forgive me, and help me control my runaway mouth. At least many Bible verses are stuck in my head. There's a bunch there from vacation Bible school. Most of the stuff I learned at Bible school is biblical. JESUS WEPT is the only verse I can recite without screwing it up. Sad, huh? It's the shortest verse in the Bible." Why was she telling God things he already knew?

She pulled her sweater tight. It had turned chilly. Fall was in the air along with the scent of burning leaves.

She'd been far too smug since James was born. She'd grown too content. Things had come too easily. She'd let her guard down. Now look what had happened.

"Lord," she found herself bargaining again. "if you bring James home safe, I'll be so good you won't know it's me. My whole family will be on the front row at Sunnyside Baptist every service. I'll even drag Mama. The girls will be in youth group every Wednesday. I will do all the things I've fallen down on. I'll even keep up with tithing. I'll give more than ten percent. Please God, bring our little man home safe. In the name of the Father, Son, and Holy Ghost. Amen."

She saw her husband in the distance and the red glow of a cigarette bobbing along with him as he walked. When he was upset he smoked a cigarette. Thankfully he would only smoke one.

Vada Faith hurried inside before he saw her spying on him.

CHAPTER 31

"THIS JUST IN," the young reporter said. He stood on the Waddell's front lawn at daylight. "A ransom note was found by a jogger in City Park early today." The reporter shivered in the damp morning air. "The note concerns the kidnapping yesterday of eight-month old James Waddell, from his porch in Shady Creek."

"A ransom note was found!" Vada Faith screamed, turning the television volume as loud as it would go. "A note from the kidnapper, John! Everyone! Get in here!"

"What?" Her husband hurried into the room, sloshing coffee from his cup onto the wood floor. He stopped in front of the screen.

Bruiser came behind his brother with a towel wiping the liquid from the recently polished floor. Since he and Joy Ruth had bought a new home, he was obsessed with floor cleanliness.

Vada Faith didn't care about floors or cleanliness or anything else. All that mattered was the safety of her baby boy.

"James is the son of Vada Faith and John Waddell," the reporter continued. "Mr. Waddell owns Master Wood Crafting and Mrs. Waddell is owner of Vada Faith's Beauty Salon in Shady Creek."

A misty fog rose up around the young reporter, threatening to swallow him and his crew. "For those of you just joining us," he said, "this is an update on the kidnapping yesterday of baby James Waddell. If you have information regarding this child, call the number on the screen." The photo of her baby boy flashed across the screen. James was smiling, sitting in front of a backdrop of daisies.

A shot of the Waddell home followed, the old Victorian place thickly shrouded in fog.

"Officer Cobb reports he has the ransom note in his possession. It'll be sent to the lab here in Charleston. We'll have more on this story," the young man said, "after this break."

"Thank you, Jesus." Vada Faith dropped backward onto the sofa, feeling a glimmer of hope.

She'd spent a sleepless night. Though it was just past dawn now, news trucks lined the street.

John cleared his throat and turned to her. "What do you think, Vay? About this note?"

She put her fingers to her lips as the reporter appeared on the screen again.

"The officer will not confirm the authenticity of the note. Could this be a hoax? We don't know. However, Officer Cobb says the note is being taken seriously. We'll be here all day bringing you the latest news on little eight-month old James Waddell. The minute we hear anything, we'll report it. Stay with us." He smiled broadly for his viewers. "You can see it's foggy and cold this morning. Let's go back to the station and our weather man, Jim, for his seven day forecast. Doug Pierce signing off from the Waddell's home where the baby has been missing almost eighteen hours."

Vada Faith stood, put her hands in the pockets of her jeans for warmth, and went to stare out the window. The reporter looked like a kid. He should still be in school. Going to parties. Not on her front lawn delivering devastating news about her missing baby.

John sat down on the sofa and ran his fingers through his hair. He stared blankly at the television screen.

Vada Faith turned from the window to watch the television as a pat of butter ran through the middle of a warm muffin melting down its sides, reminding her of the way her baby boy melted her heart the first time she'd laid eyes on him.

She'd had a caesarean with James and when the nurse pressed the baby into her arms for the first time, he was awake staring up at her with his daddy's big eyes. His thick blond hair was plastered to his little head and his eyes solemnly followed her as she counted his fingers and toes. Then, he had smiled up at her. From that moment, she was in love and the happiest mother alive. She had two precious little girls and a perfect baby boy.

As she stood at the window looking out, she was chilled to the bone even in a heavy sweat shirt and jeans. A cluster of reporters with note pads and microphones positioned themselves on the sidewalk. Her neighbors were already gathering outside at this early hour.

Heavy fog rolled in from the Kanawha River nearby. The temperature was dropping. The yellow tape around the porch and driveway struggled against the wind.

The tape was ridiculous. Before the tape went up the porch had been contaminated. It was all a pretense. Duke Cobb pretending to be a real police officer when he wasn't.

Anna, her neighbor with the poodle, stood with the early morning gawkers. The small-statured librarian pulled her heavy jacket around her and waited for a turn at the mike. Steam rose from the mug she carried.

If Anna knew something, why hadn't she spoken up yesterday? Why wait until James had been gone overnight? Was everyone but Vada Faith and John crazy? Were they the only ones who wanted this nightmare over? The community was turning the kidnapping into a circus. They seemed to be entertained by the media in front of her house.

John sat on the couch, a desperate man, not knowing what to do next. He kept running his fingers through his hair, distracted and disheveled. Usually he was a decisive man, going from A to B in exact order when creating his beautiful furniture. Precise like her when she created a new hairstyle for a show. They were methodical people. They went by the book. They did things the right way. Here, they were in uncharted territory and floundering.

She drifted over to a chair and sat down.

She hadn't closed her eyes all night on the sofa covered by a throw, listening to the muted sounds from outside. A few people had stood out there all night. Keeping vigil in case James was found. Each time her husband came into the room to check on her, she closed her eyes. She wanted him to think she was sleeping.

He'd finally gone upstairs and paced the floor. Sometime later he came down to the kitchen where his brothers, Bobby Joe and Bruiser, were on cell phones organizing volunteers for the day. She heard him say he'd be in his shop working. He closed the door quietly when he left and she never heard him return. She wasn't sure he'd been to bed.

Finally, he had come in for coffee with the first group of the day, mostly firefighters from Bruiser's station, when they returned at daybreak. She'd heard them in the kitchen talking.

Vada Faith prayed for her son as she sat there, her head in her hands. She put him in the Lord's hands. It was all she could do. If he wasn't found soon, she'd go crazy.

When someone banged loudly on the front door, Vada Faith jumped.

Duke Cobb walked in as John opened the front door, a man wearing a trench coat followed close behind Duke.

"Jim Herringbone," the man said, shaking John's hand, then Vada Faith's.

Duke said, "Jim is a retiree from law enforcement. Moved here from LA. He's got experience in abductions. He has a farm over in Jackson County. He's agreed to lead our investigation. I'll be helping him and the sheriff's offered back up."

Vada Faith struggled to breathe. Tension had absorbed all the oxygen in the room. She could only nod.

"We need the help," John said, exhaustion showing in his face.

"Here's the note we found in City Park." Duke extended a plastic bag toward John with the note sealed inside. "We don't know yet if it's a hoax."

"All right." John read it silently and handed it to Vada Faith.

Duke reached to steady John who looked as if he might fall over. The animosity between the two had evaporated. However, John ignored Duke's hand and steadied himself by leaning against the wall.

Vada Faith read the note which was scrawled in blue crayon. "Your baby is alive. We want five-thousand in cash. Stay tuned."

Bruiser and Bobby Joe, their faces grim, looked over Vada Faith's shoulders to read the note.

"What's stay tuned mean?" Bruiser asked.

Vada Faith shook her head and handed the note back to Duke.

"Guess it means he'll be back in touch." Duke shrugged.

"We have the money." Vada Faith said. "I have five-thousand in my own account. We'll give the kidnapper anything he wants. He must have an accomplice. He said we, John."

Her husband gave her a puzzled look. "You have an account?"

"It was to be a surprise," she said, moving toward him. He put his arm around her thin shoulders. "For a Disney trip next spring. It doesn't matter now. Nothing matters but finding James." John tightened his arms around her. She buried her head in his chest.

Bruiser spoke up, his face beet-red, "Me and Joy Ruth have money. Plenty." He glanced at John. "Money multiplies in my wife's hands. You can have every penny we got. Probably well over fifty-thousand."

Vada Faith wiped her tears. She reached over and patted her brother-in-law's arm.

"Thanks, Bro," John spoke, "I'm not worried about money." He looked hard at Duke. "When will we know if this note is real?"

"It's going to the lab right now. We'll know soon." Jim Herringbone nodded. "We can't start passing out money. We wait until we hear from him again. Unless it's a hoax, he'll contact us. It may be someone wanting money or notoriety. It could be a prank. Some jokester. We can't get sidetracked by the note. We're following several leads."

"The minute you hear anything," Vada Faith said, facing Duke and the investigator, "I want to know. I don't want to hear it on the news. You could have called us about the note, Duke."

"The reporters knew it before I did. You know how the press is." He acted as if dealing with the press was a daily occurrence for him.

"I do have some news." Duke beamed and rocked back and forth on his feet. "The lab found the baby's plastic bottle cover wedged under the play pen pad. The one the dog had on the street didn't belong to James."

"I don't want his nipple cover, Duke! I want my baby." She shivered and reached for the throw on the sofa, draping it around her body.

"I know, I know. The lab did report nothing of significance was found on the play pen."

Vada Faith wiped her eyes with the edge of the soft blue throw her mother had crocheted for her last Christmas. She'd cried when Helena gave it to her. It was the first thing her mother had ever made for her.

"Don't worry," the investigator said. "We're getting closer."

"Why would someone leave a ransom note in City Park?" She sunk into a chair. "It was so windy last night. Why didn't it blow away?"

"The note was found by an early morning jogger. I doubt it was there long. It was on a bench, held down by a brick from the flower bed."

The investigator turned to the couple. "I don't believe this note is from the kidnapper. I don't want you to get discouraged." He smiled. "I want to find your baby as much as you do. It's a hard thing to go through." He frowned. "My nephew was kidnapped."

"Did your nephew ever come home?" Vada Faith pulled the throw tighter around her.

The man looked away for a moment. "He did. Yes, he did. He finally came home."

He walked out of the room with Duke following him.

Vada Faith and John trailed after them through the front door and outside to the porch.

"Was he okay?" She asked. "Your nephew. Was he okay?" A blast of cold air hit her in the face.

The investigator paused on the porch and stared out at the spectators in the street.

He nodded, without turning around. He went down the steps, his shoulders slightly drooped.

She knew then. His nephew had come home but he wasn't all right.

CHAPTER 32

LATER THAT MORNING, Vada Faith and John, along with Officer Cobb, appeared on a Charleston talk show to plead for the return of James.

"Please, bring my baby home," Vada Faith said. She sat between Duke and John. "You won't be punished. You bring my baby back and we won't even press charges. I'll give you every cent we have. Just bring James home." Her voice broke and she put her head in her hands.

"You can't promise that!" Duke hissed at her and turned to the camera and spoke loudly, "The sooner you bring that baby home, buddy, the easier we'll go on you. If you wait, I'm not promising anything." He frowned and cracked his knuckles.

"You can have anything you want," Vada Faith wailed, "if you bring my baby home. I mean anything!" She ignored the police officer's frantic motions. Duke Cobb was an impediment to the investigation as far as she was concerned. He reminded her of a big furry dog who fell over his own feet. "I mean anything," she added, flashing a look of contempt at Duke.

The officer shook his head in defeat and frowned at her.

"Bring James home," John pleaded, "please." He was bleary-eyed from no sleep and unhappy to be on live television.

Vada Faith pictured the kidnapper, an unsavory man, sitting in a run-down motel room watching a small screen television. She shuddered at the thought of her baby being in that room, maybe even sleeping on the bed. In her mind the kidnapper was an unkempt man, ugly and mean. A woman would never steal a baby, not any women she knew anyway.

"It's been almost twenty four-hours." She wiped tears from her face.

Maddie Magill, the show's host, motioned for Vada Faith to continue.

"James misses his family." She looked down at the soft pink shirt she wore. James loved to touch it. Though he could hold his own bottle, she often held him while he drank it. He'd nestle into her, patting his bottle, pausing to say, "Baba." Milk would dribble down his chin and he'd smile up at her. Thinking of her baby broke her heart into a million pieces.

"He misses Blue Baby." She held up the shaggy blue dog James slept with. She held back tears and hugged the stuffed dog. Unable to go on, she folded into the chair.

"That's right," John spoke up, his face blotchy red. "We want our baby home! Now, you hear?"

"Don't threaten him!" Vada Faith narrowed her eyes at John."We want our son home safe."

"If you have our baby," John said, ignoring his wife, "or know where he is, call us or bring him home!" His voice broke.

"The number is running across the bottom of the screen," Maddie Magill announced, "and it's a direct line to Officer Cobb. If you know anything about yesterday's kidnapping, please call. For those of you just joining us," Maddie moved into the audience, "we're talking to the Waddell family and Officer Duke Cobb of Shady Creek police department. Eight-month old James Waddell was kidnapped yesterday around noon from the front porch of the family home. Blond hair and blue eyes. That's his picture on the screen now. If you have any information, please contact Officer Cobb. All right, we'll take questions from the audience."

"This is for the mother." A wiry gray-haired woman hopped to her feet and spoke into the microphone. "How long was your baby alone on the porch?" She stretched out her next words, "Exactly, how long?"

"Seconds." Vada Faith answered, her heart pumping wildly. She wasn't sure how long she'd been inside. Yesterday it seemed seconds. Today, she wasn't sure.

"Huh." The woman sat down.

"I should have taken him inside, I know that now." Vada Faith shifted uncomfortably in her seat. "James loves being outdoors." Her words sounded like flimsy excuses.

"You must have been gone more than seconds." A shout came from the back of the audience. Maddie turned but nobody stood up.

"If she says it was seconds," Joy Ruth yelled from the front row of the audience, "it was seconds. That's the thing about my sister. She's honest. Ask anyone."

"Joy Ruth is the aunt of James," Maddie explained, "but let's not get caught up in blame. Does anyone have anything to add? Did any of you see anything? Yes, you in the green dress."

The girl stood, rolling her heavily made up green eyes. "I'm not here to throw stones, but, people, listen up. Do you know Vada Faith Waddell? Really know her?" Paris Holiday held her head high. "If you do, you know she covets the spotlight. It's a sickness with her."

Murmurs rose from the crowd.

"What?" Maddie made her way to the girl.

Vada Faith gasped. Paris Holiday, a.k.a. Huckendorf, her nightmare all through school, was in the audience. They were in competition since Vada Faith won the fourth grade spelling bee, leaving Paris with the second place ribbon.

Paris continued, "Vada Faith was voted Homecoming Queen beating me out of that crown our senior year. Then she married Mr.

Football Star, John Waddell. When I stepped onto that train headed for New York City, I thought I was leaving those two behind. Ha! They might as well have been sitting on my lap, thanks to the Shaky Creek News. Oh, the hoopla when they had twin girls. Seems they were the first set of twin girls in the last fifty years in Shady Creek. Well, drum roll. And the photos. I have pictures of those babies at nearly every stage of their lives. If that's not enough, she's now featured on the front page winning awards for her hair art. Hair art, I mean, really, folks."

John tried to stand but Vada Faith pushed him back into his seat. She didn't need him to strangle Paris Holiday on live television. It wouldn't solve anything and it wouldn't bring James home.

"I'm sorry that you believe I would do such a thing to get publicity, Paris," Vada Faith said. "Sure, I loved being on top when I was a kid but we're adults now. We're talking about the safety of my son. A little boy, Paris. I have my faults, and I'm not proud of everything I've done in my life but I love my children and my husband. I would never do anything to harm them."

"Sure! You're sorry now," she said, finally lowering herself into her chair. "You weren't sorry when you were wearing that crown, and hurting me. I wanted that crown. I deserved it."

"You can have it," Vada Faith yelled. "It's in the attic. Come over and I'll personally crown you. It's brought me nothing but bad luck."

"Let's move on!" Maddie clapped her hands, furiously. She'd lost control of her show.

"I landed in Charleston yesterday," Paris yelled even louder, "there's Vada Faith crying her eyes out on TV in the airport lobby. Her baby is gone. Has anyone asked Vada Faith where her baby is?"

The show cut to a station break.

Duke moved closer to Vada Faith, whose face had lost all color, and patted her on the shoulder. Red-faced, John sat clenching his fists.

During the break, Maddie Magill handed out bottles of water to her guests on stage and tried to quieten the audience.

Paris gathered her things and left after a bodyguard chatted with her. As she exited, she gave the audience an innocent smile as though she were the wronged one.

CHAPTER 33

EARLY THAT MORNING, James opened his eyes and stared at the unfamiliar room. He kicked his chubby legs until they came free of the covers. He pulled one foot toward him and examined each toe.

Tiring of his toes, he flipped onto his stomach. After several attempts, he made it up onto his knees and rocked back and forth, making loud gurgling noises. He liked the sounds and by straining he was able to make them last longer. He smiled. A string of drool fell onto the cover beneath him. He wanted to be lifted from the damp bed. When his mama heard his noises, she hurried to see him. When he caught sight of her he waved his arms and legs in the air. She would pick him up and lift him over her head. Sweet Baby James, she always said, I love you.

This morning there weren't any of the usual sounds. His two sisters weren't poking at him through the bars of his crib, or pulling on his arms, trying to hoist him over the rails. He would press himself into the far side of his crib when they pulled on him.

Eventually, they'd give up and go to his toy box. They would hang over his crib with a bunny or his soft airplane and make silly faces at him through the crib bars. He'd smile and wave his arms but he didn't move closer to them.

Charity and Hope would tire of his toys and take themselves back to their own room or go clattering down the stairs.

James waited contentedly for his mama. He liked to be lifted from his crib by his daddy's big arms too, but his daddy didn't come to him in the mornings. Sometimes James would be in his crib at night when he heard the roar of his daddy's truck and then his whistling as he came through the door. He knew his father stopped to see his mother. He heard them talking. James could smell his daddy before he saw him. He smelled faintly of his mother's scent and the smell of his shop when he came to see James.

Wood, his mama would say. All your daddy cares about is wood. James often went with her to see his father in his shop and there were stacks of wood and other objects to investigate. He'd sit on a big pad his mother made for him and he'd play with the wooden train his father built.

Now, strange noises came from the next room. It wasn't his mama. It was Birdie, who had carried him here. He rocked back and forth harder, eager to move from the wet bed on the floor. He liked the way Birdie scooped him up into her softness and folded him into her arms.

He missed his mama, his daddy, and his sisters too.

James tired of rocking on his knees. More noises drifted in and he started to cry. He wanted his mama. He wanted the cereal to eat with his fingers. He wanted the Barney show. He wanted to be dry. He wanted to hear his mama talk to him.

It was not his mama who lifted him from his makeshift bed and he wailed louder and louder. Soon the taste of warm milk was on his tongue. He drank greedily from the familiar bottle.

He patted Birdie's hand as she rocked him back and forth in her arms. She wiped his tears with her hand. He said, "Baba." Birdie kissed his head. He smiled and milk drooled out of his mouth.

CHAPTER 34

AFTER BIRDIE FED James a bowl of canned fruit, she handed him to Sissy, who was feeling better, to tend while she went to spread bread crumbs on the porch for the birds. Mama gave her the name Bird in honor of the birds on their farm. It was Sissy who'd dubbed her Birdie, saying her little sister was flighty as a baby birdie.

Earlier, the two women had argued over the baby. Again. Birdie still begged to keep the child.

"Sissy," Birdie called, excitedly, from the porch, "there's a present out here."

"A package? Well, bring it in." Sissy wiped the baby's face with a warm wash cloth, cleaning the food off his face.

Birdie hugged the cardboard box as she opened the screen door and came inside.

The baby fussed and wiggled until Sissy set him on the floor. He began chewing on the plastic measuring spoons she handed him.

"A package from Midgy Brown," Sissy said. "She brings me things every week. She won't always take pay." Sissy examined the box and picked up her scissors. She slit the tape around the lid.

Birdie made a silly face at the baby on the floor. He gave her a half-smile and banged the spoons on the floor. Birdie leaned over and picked him up, smoothing down his blond hair. The little guy put his head on Birdie's ample shoulder.

"A small ham," Sissy said, unwrapping one of the parcels from the box. "New audio tapes. Cans of tuna and salmon, oh, and canned chicken." Sissy smoothed out a newspaper that was tucked into the side of the box. Her eyes grew fearful as she stared down at the Shady Creek News.

She held the paper at arm's length. "Oh, Bird!"

Birdie shifted the baby in her arms and leaned over her sister's shoulder to squint at the paper. "You have to read it to me, Sissy."

"Baby Missing in Shady Creek," her sister read, using the half glasses dangling on a cord from her neck. "James John Waddell, the eight-month old son of Vada Faith and John Waddell, was taken from his playpen on the front porch of their home around noon yesterday. If you have any information, contact Officer Duke Cobb at the Shady Creek Police Department. A special investigator specializing in missing children is on the case."

Sissy pointed to the phone number and to the picture of the kidnapped baby. The little boy sitting in a field of daisies on the newspaper was the baby in Birdie's arms this minute, chewing on measuring spoons, and drooling onto her dress.

Sissy pointed to the boy. "He's James Waddell. You took him from his front porch. What were you thinking?" She let the paper drop to the floor and clutched her heart. "What're we going to do?"

Birdie looked at the baby. His blue eyes flashed and his dark lashes curled down onto this cheeks. Birdie dropped into a chair with him.

"You went onto their porch, Bird?"

"No. He was on the sidewalk. He called me mama. He was chewing on his bottle."

"Well, you're taking him back. Now!" Sissy scooped up the newspaper and stuffed it back into the box. She opened the screen door, shoved the box onto the porch, and slammed the door.

Birdie cooed at the baby. He batted his eyes and blew spit bubbles onto his chin.

"Stop playing with him, Birdie! You're taking him home. Eat some toast and get ready. The police will comb these woods today. I can't let them inside my house. You know that. Don't you, Bird?"

"I know." Birdie rocked the baby back and forth. "I don't want to take Robert back. Please, Sissy, don't make me."

"He's not Robert, sister. He's James Waddell. If you don't take him back, they'll find you with him and lock you in jail. Do you want to go to jail, Little Bird? You're in big trouble. Do you understand?"

Birdie ignored her. She started humming as she rocked the baby in her arms.

"Did you hear me?" Sissy bent over her sister and took her by the shoulders. "You must listen. We have to get rid of him. Before men come tromping around here, asking questions. I'm scared of people. Do you hear me? Do you?"

"Yes, yes, I hear." She put her finger over her lips to shush her sister. The baby was nodding. He was ready for his morning nap.

Birdie gently carried him to the clean quilt on the floor in the next room. She kissed him on the cheek and settled a soft blanket around him. She'd hide her little brother. She wasn't giving him up. He was Robert. No matter what Sissy said. She knew that in her heart.

While eating peanut butter and jelly sandwiches, Sissy racked her brain, trying to figure out a way to help Birdie. She had to protect her addled sister. Somehow. From jail and from herself. Birdie was in big trouble this time but what could she do? She was scared of everyone. She couldn't even leave her own house.

CHAPTER 35

VADA FAITH WAS no longer speaking to John. He'd been rude to her last night when she was getting ready for bed. It was the second night without their baby boy. Neither one of them had slept more than an hour since James had disappeared.

She'd pulled her favorite pillow from the bed, contemplating a rough night. Earlier she hauled their huge comforter to the sofa downstairs.

"Do you have to take everything we own to the living room?" He asked, trailing behind her down the stairs. Without turning around, she knew his face was red and he was glowering at her back.

"Can't you be happy with the pillow and throw we keep downstairs?"

What was wrong with him? Did he resent her trying to be comfortable? Well, she was grief-stricken too. She knew she wouldn't sleep a wink. Having things around to comfort her helped. Why did it distress John if she carried everything they owned downstairs? She hadn't asked for his help with the heavy comforter.

"You're never happy." He said, walking into the living room behind her. "You always have to have your own way. Why is that?"

"You're an idiot." She spread the comforter on the sofa and flopped down on it.

"Shame on you. I heard you praying for James, then you call me idiot. I don't call you an idiot. Now, you fall on the sofa. Are you comfortable enough?"

"Kiss my a-s-s, John Waddell." Oh dear, where had that come from? She never said that to him. Well, not for a long time. She thought it but hadn't said it. Her breath caught in her throat, and she whispered into her pillow, "God, forgive me and please connect the wires in my brain to my mouth. I love this man but he can be mean as a bull. Forgive us both for these stupid sins our mouths keep committing." Recently she heard the minister speak about the sinful tongue. She needed to be more aware of hers. She needed to think before she spoke. Instead, her mouth took off like a car on the Indy Speedway when the flag went down. Her brain simply couldn't keep up. Maybe because she had a tiny brain and a big mouth.

John marched across the hall to the family room to the plush sectional he preferred, carrying his own ragged pillow. It was years old and he refused to let her replace it.

She snuggled down into her own pillow and cried.

Soon John's breathing sounded even. She suspected he was asleep. Exhaustion must have overcome him.

She went to the window to stare out at the stars, thinking the same stars were shining down on her baby boy, wherever he was. A light flickered in the street as a volunteer lit a cigarette. Why did people smoke when they knew it was bad for their health? Why did she do things that were bad for her? She ate fast food when she was in a hurry because it was fast. Did she derive comfort from doing things not good for her? Another question without an answer.

Finally, she snuggled into the comforter and pretended her baby boy was tucked safely in her arms. She woke a few hours later to learn John had gone to his workshop. It was just as well since they weren't speaking. She was shocked she'd slept. She wondered why her husband was working in his shop instead of pacing the floor with her. She would never understand men, that one in particular.

Pots and pans were being banged together in the kitchen. She could smell coffee. Louise's loud voice penetrated the house.

She hurried upstairs to shower. Pulling on jeans and a shirt, she wanted out of the house. Her life was disjointed without the baby. She didn't know what to do or say to anyone. She planned to head outside and search for her baby. Maybe she'd find something everyone else had missed.

"I'm going out," she said to Louise as she walked into the kitchen. The older woman stood at the stove frying eggs. The smell of bacon filled the room. "I've got to get some exercise. I plan to stop at the beauty shop to talk to Joy Ruth and check on the girls."

"Oh, honey, are you sure?" Her mother-in-law stood poised with her white apron on, spatula held in the air. Several pancakes sizzled in an iron skillet on the back burner.

"I don't have a choice," she said, "I'm going nuts." She poured a cup of coffee into a foam cup and snapped on a lid. She took a sip as Louise turned back to the stove to flip the pancakes.

"Can you eat something? How about it? Some of the volunteers will be coming in soon. How about a pancake?" She smiled at her daughter-in-law.

Vada Faith noted the worry lines on Louise's face along with the dark circles under her eyes.

"Nothing to eat, thanks." Bile gathered in her throat at the thought of eating. "I'll see you later." She slipped on a lightweight jacket. It was supposed to be 60 degrees later but the morning air was chilly.

Where was James, she wondered as she pulled her jacket tighter and walked to the back door? She knew God knew where her baby was. Why didn't he let her know?

"What a friend we have in Jesus," Louise sang as Vada Faith closed the kitchen door.

Louise had been a fixture in the house since James had disappeared. She was getting on Vada Faith's nerves. If she wasn't chattering incessantly, she was humming, or whistling. Ordinarily, the woman didn't bother her. However, she'd never spent this much time with Louise Waddell.

She had to stop herself from lashing out at the woman over every incident. Louise was either wanting her to eat, or to read, or exercise.

Vada Faith kicked the exercise bike every time she passed it in the family room. Louise hauled it from the garage the afternoon James disappeared. She said Vada Faith needed something constructive to do. Did Louise think she was out of shape? She might not be a size two but she certainly wasn't out of shape. She figured kicking the bike several times a day not only brought her comfort but provided all the exercise she needed until James was home. Then she would get her exercise. She would walk that baby around the world if he wanted to go. She'd push his stroller to the moon and back to make him happy.

The day before Louise had brought a dozen gardening books from home for Vada Faith to read. More than once she mentioned that her daughter-in-law might want to fill the empty photo albums on the desk where a stack of photos waited. How could the woman expect her to look at pictures of James? She couldn't get past his photo hanging on the wall in the stairway without falling apart.

As she walked she cut through several alleys, her eyes scanned every pebble and blade of grass. Had the kidnapper brought James this way? She put her hands in her jacket pockets as the wind whipped around her. She caught a whiff of burning leaves.

She should be grateful Louise came every day at dawn and stayed until dusk. She was angry instead. It was irrational. She knew that. It was having someone at her side every second that was difficult. Family and friends came in and out of the house, searching, organizing, and strategizing. It was a small price to pay for what they were giving her in return. Hang in, that's what everyone kept telling her. How long could she hang in?

Main Street was quiet as she opened the door of the beauty salon. She stood and let the smells and sounds of the shop gather in her pores. A strange comfort moved over her as she breathed in the scent of shampoos, conditioners, and apple cinnamon potpourri on the counter. It made her momentarily high.

She turned, put her coffee cup on the counter, and picked up a pink smock.

"Oh, my goodness, Vada Faith!" Daphne Dillard, a deacon at Sunnyside Baptist, rushed to gather her in a bear hug. Daphne wore large purple rollers. Yellow wax covered her chin and eyebrows.

"Vay," Joy Ruth said, grabbing her next and holding on the longest. "Let me do your hair and maybe give you a facial. How about it? It will help you relax. I'll be done with Coon's perm in a few minutes."

Vada Faith glanced at Coon Higginbotham's salt and pepper hair and shook her head. Fifty was too old for a man to perm his hair.

"Nope, I've come to work." Vada Faith slipped into her smock. "Let's see if I really can perform hair miracles as Midgy thinks." She spun her pink chair around. "Who's first?" She looked at several women sitting along the wall in the waiting area.

Her plan was to stay so busy she would not shed one tear all day. As a reward for not crying, James would be home by dinnertime. She'd made herself that promise. The thought would get her through the day, that and the pill she'd taken before leaving home.

"You sure you want to work, honey?" Marge Randolph sidled up to her, eager to jump into the pink chair, but hesitant until the beautician nodded.

"Absolutely. I have to get my mind busy. If I don't, I'm going to do something crazy like slap my mother-in-law." She looked around to make sure none of Louise's friends were in the shop. "She's on my last nerve. I talked to the Lord and promised to change my ways if he let James come home. Now look at me. I've blown it with my mouth."

She looked upward toward the ceiling fan, twirling aimlessly above her head. "I'm sorry. Again." She was thankful she had an inside line to the Lord. She'd become aware of it after becoming a Christian at youth camp. She had used that line off and on all her life, but especially in the last few days.

She blew her bangs out of her eyes. She needed a trim herself. The short hair cut Joy Ruth had given her was growing out. She put the comb in Marge's thick hair and started combing.

"I'm not talking to John," she announced to no one in particular as she combed Marge's hair. She gave a long sigh. "He's on my last nerve. He snapped at me last night."

Several women in the room stopped what they were doing to listen.

"What was it he said?" Joy Ruth asked, as she put another roller in Coon's head.

"He said I have to be right, always. That's not true. I don't have to be right all the time. His note this morning said he had to work in the shop. He should've stayed with me. Oh no. He never listens. If one more day goes by without James," she sniffed and waved the comb in the air, "I won't be responsible for what I do. I'll punch someone. Maybe John. Maybe his mother." She put the comb on the pink counter, and turned to her sister. "Louise has been nothing but kind. There's something wrong with me. Am I a monster? Have I cracked up, girls, and don't know it?"

Several of the women hurried to surround Vada Faith in a circle of hugs.

"Everything's going to be all right, honey," Joy Ruth said, hugging her. "Yes," someone else murmured.

"Shush, now," Joy Ruth said, breaking away from the hug, "you go ahead and feel what you're feeling, Vay. You're entitled. We're all praying James is found soon. You and John and Louise need each other. You can't break down now. You don't want to make an enemy of Louise."

"I know. She's been a big help. I'm just a wreck, but Joy Ruth you don't understand. You're still in the honeymoon phase. Things get complicated in a marriage after that. Just wait. John's been working in his workshop since James was taken. Why can't he stay with me? He could be more of a comfort. Our baby boy is missing and he's sculpting a piece of wood in his shop."

"All right," Joy Ruth turned back to her customer. "We all need to concentrate on our work. Let's get busy, come on." She reached out and patted her sister's arm.

"Will do," Vada Faith said, giving her sister a smile. "What is it to-day, Marge?" The woman had settled back in the pink chair and smiled at herself in the mirror. "How about a warm brown to cover those grays," the beautician suggested. "I'll add some soft highlights. It'll take the age off you."

"Oh, you think so?" Marge, Helena's best friend, fingered her gray hair. "Ralph might not mind me looking younger. My life has sure spiced up since I been dating Ralph. If you make me look younger than your mom, she might be mad."

"I can handle my mama. Now, are you up for a new hair do?" Vada Faith smiled down at Marge.

"Let's do it!" Marge blushed. "Is it real expensive? I have to watch every penny now I'm a senior. Did you know McDonald's coffee went up? I'd get a senior coffee but Anna from the library is always in there. I don't want her to tell it around town that I'm cheap."

Marge paused and nodded to herself in the mirror as Vada Faith checked through the woman's gray hair, deciding she needed a conditioner after the color. On the house. Marge was a senior. That's what she'd tell her anyway. She had a large surplus of the stuff.

"Give me the works, honey." Marge grinned. "I'll look even better than your mama and speaking of Helena, how's she doing? I haven't seen her much since I started dating Ralph."

"She's busy with Albert."

"I heard she'd had some tests recently."

"She did." How did the townspeople know every thing about every resident? "I'm happy to say they all came back negative. The doctor gave her a vitamin B shot. She's doing great now."

"I'm relieved." Marge fidgeted. "I'm praying real hard for baby James, honey."

"Thanks, Marge," Vada Faith said and headed to the back room to mix the color.

As she prepared the color she pretended James was at her mother's house taking his morning nap. The sun shone through the big shop window just as it did in the bedroom where he slept at Helena's. She visualized him there, his fist curled in his mouth, his beautiful brown lashes fluttering slightly as he slept.

She looked around the shop as she came out of the back room realizing her children weren't there. "The twins, Joy Ruth! Where are they? I thought you were bringing them with you to work today."

"Calm down. They didn't want to come in again, honey. They begged to go to school. I went in and talked to the principal. The school's locked. I had to be buzzed in. They're safe and they're happy." Joy Ruth frowned. "Stop worrying, honey. They're okay. They were bored to tears yesterday evening when I brought them in here."

Vada Faith sighed. She sectioned Marge's hair, and started swabbing strands of hair with color, rolling each in a strip of foil.

She knew the girls were better off at school where they could play and stay busy. They shouldn't be at home worrying about James. She and John had been wrapped up in their own misery and hadn't given the girls much attention. After school she'd make it up to them. It seemed she was a failure all the way around.

The shop door swung open and Paris Holiday stepped inside, her head wrapped in a red silk scarf.

"Hello." Paris spoke softly as she unwrapped the scarf. Her blond hair sprung in every direction. "I need help." She sighed. "I would've went somewhere else," she paused and looked around the shop, "but I hear this is the best place to go when you screw up your hair."

"What happened?" Vada Faith asked, wrapping another strip of foil around Marge's hair.

"I tried to spiral perm it myself." She fell into the pink chair nearest Vada Faith.

"Didn't work?" Vada Faith raised her eyebrows.

Paris made a face. "No, it didn't work. I was trying to save money by doing it myself. We don't all have tons of money, you know."

"I'm not sure I have time to work you in," Joy Ruth said, patting her customer's head for emphasis. "How about you Vay? You have time for Paris?"

"Not really," Vada Faith shook her head and continued working on Marge. "We don't ordinarily turn customers away. I'm thinking Paris could be our first. What do you think Joy? Should Paris be the first?"

"Why not?" Joy Ruth directed her customer to a dryer.

"Or should we be good Samaritans and help her out?" Vada Faith asked, feeling suddenly giddy. The piece of nerve pill she'd taken in the back room was working its magic. She felt almost normal, except for being unsteady on her feet.

"Oh, I'll work you in, Paris," Joy Ruth said as she straightened her work station and swept up the hair around her chair. "After my next appointment."

"Great," Paris murmured. "I appreciate it." She picked up a magazine from the table beside her chair.

"After the accusations you made, Paris, I shouldn't let you inside our door." Vada Faith directed Marge to a dryer and turned on the heat. "You said horrible things at the television show."

"I'm sorry. I swear. I don't know what got into me. I feel bad about your baby. Honest." She turned the pages of the magazine, glancing up periodically to watch Vada Faith. "I do need help. Desperately."

"I thought you had a favorite shop in Charleston?" Vada Faith asked, going back to her chair.

Paris blushed. "I didn't have enough money. They charge so much more. Anyway, I didn't trust them with this mess." She ran her fingers through her tight curls.

"And, you trust us, Paris?"

"I do trust you." She nodded, her face redder than ever. "I know your reputation, Vada Faith. You both do excellent work."

Joy Ruth checked her watch and signaled to Paris. "My appointment's late. I'll do your cut now."

Paris closed her eyes for a minute after arranging herself in Joy Ruth's chair. "Can you really fix this mess, Joy?" She opened her eyes and lifted up a few strands of her curly hair. She stared hard at her pale reflection in the mirror. "At the time, I didn't care how it looked. I could have ripped my head off."

"Well, you might have been better off." Joy Ruth ran a pink comb through the tangle of hair. "I'll give you a shorter layered cut. That'll help. Why would you want to rip your head off?"

"If you had my life you'd rip your head off."

"I doubt it." Joy Ruth picked up her scissors and started measuring hair.

The shop door opened and Midgy Brown walked in. Her eyes lit up when she saw Vada Faith. "Louise said you might be here." She folded her hands in prayer and looked upward. "Thank you, Lord." She smiled as she took off her jacket and hung it on a coat rack by the door. "I can't believe it."

"Didn't I just give you a trim, girl?" Joy Ruth pointed her scissions at Midgy. "What are you doing in here? You didn't like what I did?"

"It doesn't have anything to do with you, honey. I love what you did." She ran her fingers through her red curls. "It's just, Vada Faith does something special after she cuts my hair. Like this." She snipped the air quickly with her fingers. "She tames it down. She's magic. I know you understand." She slid humbly into Vada Faith's chair. "Vada Faith chips it. Isn't that what it's called, Vada Faith?"

"Yes, honey, that's it."

"Midgy Brown," Joy Ruth said, "I know all about chipping. You're like an old faithful dog to my sister. You could have told me what you wanted."

"I couldn't remember what it was called, Joy. Your sister just knows my hair a tad better."

"Give me a minute," Vada Faith said, heading over to Marge whose face was bright red.

"Is that dryer too hot?" She turned the dryer down. Marge nodded and fanned herself.

Walking back to her chair, she noticed the designer jacket Paris wore had some age on it. Not something the old Paris would have been worn. She looked pathetic. Worn down and rough at the edges.

"If you want to come by the house," Vada Faith said to her, "I have that homecoming crown for you." She swept the hair from around her chair into a dust pan. "I had to do some digging," she said, turning to empty the hair into the trash. "but I found it in the attic. It looks new. Still in the box."

"I know you think I'm crazy." Paris looked over at Vada Faith who was running her fingers through Midgy's hair. "I don't care. I need that crown." The girl checked to see if anyone was listening. All eyes were on the television in the corner where Rachael Ray chopped vegetables.

"I don't think you're crazy, Paris. I'm not thinking at all." It was the truth. Vada Faith's mind was blank. She was thinking nothing. She massaged Midgy's scalp and let her thoughts roam.

Yesterday, John visited their family doctor and requested medication for his wife's nerves. He'd seen the outdated prescription bottle and thrown it away. The doctor had given her a miracle drug. Half of the pink pill enabled her to go about life, dull and uncaring. She hoped the pills would last until James was safe at home, or for as long as she needed them to get from one day to the next.

She hadn't screamed for James once today. She hadn't kicked anything. She hadn't broken anything. The pieces of two bedroom lamps were in the garage trash can. Her red toaster sat in the utility room damaged from a run in with a butter knife at one a.m that morning when she'd made toast. A shattered glass rested in the bottom of the stainless steel bin in the kitchen. She'd knocked it off the counter purposely to see how many pieces it would shatter into. She wanted it shattered like her heart. Her behavior now reminded her of how she'd reacted after miscarrying the surrogate baby. The broken household items then filled the trash can and went unmentioned. Nobody paid any attention. Just like now.

"Okay, Midgy," Vada Faith resurfaced, "what'll it be?"

"Just chip the ends. It looks so good when you do that."

Vada Faith ran her fingers through the girl's hair. Midgy let out a contented sigh.

"How much you want off," Vada Faith asked.

"You be the judge. I trust you, honey."

Midgy watched in the mirror as the hairdresser toyed with the wavy strands of red hair, moving it this way and that. "I got 200 flyers out," she said, "and I hope they help find the baby soon."

"Me too," Vada Faith said. "Me too." She dropped Midgy's hair as quickly as she dropped the subject of James. "I'll trim this," she said, holding up a piece of hair that was uneven. "Your hair must grow a foot a day."

She picked up her scissors and started sectioning off hair, clipping one side back.

Midgy relaxed as Vada Faith started cutting. The scissors moved with a rhythmic motion.

"How's this?" The beautician asked, a few minutes later. She twirled Midgy around in the pink chair and handed her a pink mirror to see the back. "We got rid of some bulk. You should feel much lighter."

"Oh, I do!" Midgy tossed her head about. Her hair lay in soft waves around her face. "What a difference. How do you do it, girl?" Midgy smiled at her reflection in the mirror. "I feel awesome."

"You look awesome." Vada Faith laughed. She picked up the broom and started to sway to the music of an oldies tune as she swept hair into a dust pan.

Midgy jumped up and brushed off her slacks.

"Joy Ruth will take care of you, Midgy," Vada Faith said, her voice dreamy as the redhead stuffed a ten dollar bill in her pocket. Joy Ruth and Paris were up front by the glass case where her sister was showing Paris the product she'd used on her hair.

"Come on over, Marge. I'm ready for you," Vada Faith called. "Let's get you ready for that hot date with Ralph."

Vada Faith was back home in another hour, wishing vehemently she hadn't taken that last pill. Two cups of strong coffee and the fuzziness of the morning was fading. She had a headache to top all headaches. Thankfully, the house was quiet, the kitchen spotless. A note said Louise had run home for her mail. The front doorbell sounded as she poured half and half into her third cup of coffee.

When she approached the front door, Paris yanked it open and stepped inside.

"Don't those cops ever go home?" the girl asked, pointing back at the street. "I thought they were going to arrest me, the way they acted."

"They're not interested in you, Paris." Vada Faith shook her head at the girl's puzzled look. "It's hard to believe, I know. They've been camped here since James has been gone."

"Cool place." Paris looked around the entryway, and rubbed her hand along the top of the oak secretary John had refinished. "Where'd you get this beauty?"

"John's grandmother gave it to us as a gift. She had some lovely pieces."

"Is that really Eleanor Roosevelt?" Paris asked, pointing to a gilded frame above the cabinet. "Is that John's Grandma Belle with her? I can't imagine knowing that much of my history."

"Yes, that's Eleanor with Grandma Belle." Anyone who'd ever seen a photograph of Eleanor Roosevelt would recognize her unique characteristics.

Vada Faith picked up a silver box from the oak table nearby and handed it to Paris. "Here's the coveted crown."

The girl opened the box and lifted out the silver tiara. Her eyes grew wide as she slipped it on and smiled at herself in the hallway mirror.

Vada Faith was relieved the crown was giving Paris joy. Her thrill with it was long gone.

"My mother will love this." Tears glistened in the girl's eyes. "I don't expect you to understand. She thought if I won the crown people would accept her. She was paranoid and felt everyone in town hated her."

"Accept her? Your mom was a beauty. Why would she need to be accepted by anyone in this hick town?"

"Didn't you notice she rarely went anywhere? She didn't go to church. Nor to school. Not for anything. She didn't attend one event when I was growing up."

"Did you notice I didn't have a mother there either? I didn't have a mother at home. You were so busy feeling sorry for yourself you didn't have time to notice anyone else."

"You had a daddy!" Paris snapped. "Mine left when my mom got pregnant. He didn't want to be saddled with a kid. I can tell you something. My mom grew up in Davis Children's Shelter in Charleston, Vada Faith. An orphanage. She didn't know who she belonged to. Still doesn't. How's that for a sad tale?"

"Paris, is that why you were a jerk to me over the years, because your life wasn't perfect? Well, my baby has been kidnapped. Taken by some criminal." Vada Faith swallowed hard and said, "I may never see him again and you're groaning about your childhood."

"If I could bring your baby home, I would. I swear it, Vada Faith. I'm sorry he's gone. I never meant any harm. Me being homecoming queen meant way more to my mom than me, ever. She was sick over it. It was all she talked about when I was growing up, before I got to high school. She had it in her mind, I'd be in with the right crowd and she'd be popular too."

Vada Faith saw a tear fall onto the red blouse the girl wore, a dark spot appeared on the bright material. "My mom's sick." She whispered, "Dementia, however, she still mentions that crown at times. Now, I can put it on her night stand. She'll see it when wakes up every morning. In her mind, it's still relevant."

"Look, I'm sorry about your mother. Take the tiara. All I want is my son back."

Paris lowered her eyes. She went to the door, clutched the knob, then turned back. "I swear I hope you find James soon." She swallowed hard and then smiled. "Thank Joy Ruth for the hair cut and tell her I love it. Things are turning around for me. This afternoon hospice came. With their help and a cousin of mom's to pitch in, her care is covered. I got a job offer back in New York." Paris bit her lip and said, "I'm really sorry for the way I've acted. I lit a candle for James at church and prayed for him. I went to confession too."

Vada Faith nodded. The girl couldn't be all bad if she'd lit a candle and prayed for James.

With Paris gone, Vada Faith sunk onto the floor of the hallway and sobbed. Where in the world was her baby boy? Would he ever be found? If he was found would he be the perfect little boy that was taken? God help her, she was afraid he might not ever come home.

CHAPTER 36

"Sissy?" Birdie stood at her sister's bedside. She'd stopped on her way to get a second towel for the baby. While she'd waited for Sissy to wake, she'd given Robert a bath. She stared hard at Sissy, willing her to open her eyes. The baby's jabbering usually kept them both alert, but not today. Sissy had slept through his squeals. She'd been in bed ever since the day before, upset over the situation. She'd taken her heart pills and slept.

Birdie scooped up the baby who'd been crawling behind her and dried his fine blond hair with the air-dried towel.

Sissy didn't look well. "Sissy?" Birdie stepped closer to her sister and clutched her own chest. "Are you okay?" Birdie fidgeted with the little boy, trying to think of something to say. She didn't want to worry her sister. "If you're okay, honey," she said, leaning in to brush Sissy's gray hair off her forehead, "we can listen to the radio. That will make you better. Okay?"

"No." Sissy murmured, her breathing labored. "These chest pains will die down. I'll stay still a few more minutes."

"It's her heart!" Birdie whispered to James, carrying him to the rocking chair in the next room. She dressed him quickly. "Her heart isn't good. Mama had it. It can make you die. We have to be good. We can't cry, either." Birdie wiped away the tears running down her face. She hugged the baby. "I'm not crying, just my eyes are watering."

The baby studied Birdie and nodded as if he understood.

"See, I ironed your blue Peter Rabbit pants and your shirt. Sissy washed them. She's good, just scared of you, little buddy, and the police who might come here." Birdie sighed. "You can't live with me anymore. It's making Sissy sick."

" I don't always remember stuff," she explained to the baby, "Sissy says it's okay. Some stuff you can remember. Some you can't. That's that. Now," she placed the child on the floor after putting clean socks on him, "let's go see to Sissy."

She went to the kitchen and brought a clean cold cloth for Sissy's head. The baby crawled behind her.

"Here you go, Sissy girl. Bird will watch over you. Nothing's gonna happen to you."

"The baby," Sissy leaned over slightly and looked at James on the floor where he sat chewing on his fingers. "He's trouble, Bird, you have to take him away."

"I will, I promise. Don't you worry, honey," Birdie assured her.

"Don't take him home. It's too far. You might get caught. Oh mercy!" She fell back onto the pillow.

"Please don't die, Sissy. I'm taking him away. Today." She paused. "Now."

There was no response from Sissy. She lay so still, Birdie watched to make sure she was breathing. Finally, the woman drifted to sleep. Birdie went to talk to James.

"Sissy is resting. I'm taking you away. I don't know where. Sissy said the police will put me in jail. Maybe Sissy too. She can't go to jail, baby boy. She's too sick."

"Can you be good for Bird?" The old woman washed the baby's plastic bottle which he'd clung to all the way to Sissy's house. She added half water and half canned Carnation milk which he loved. She added a dollop of white Karo syrup to make it tasty. When he reached for it,

Birdie said, "Nope. This is for later, young man. You already ate oat-meal." She nodded down at him as if he understood.

"Baba," he said, crawling behind Birdie as she went to the closet. He watched as she pulled on her brown shawl and her orthopedic shoes. "There," she said, looking into the wall mirror and patting down her tangled gray hair.

"We're all set." She picked up her satchel and put the bottle inside. "Here you go." She lifted the baby into her arms and crept out the back door, closing it softly behind her.

A light fog hung over the tree tops and crept towards the ground as Birdie made her way through the woods. She had to avoid cars and people.

"Now here's what we have to do," she said to the baby, "Sissy wants me to take you somewhere." Birdie looked through the trees. There wasn't a place she could safely put the baby down. "You see," she said, to the baby in her arms, "I could put you down right here and I could come back to visit but you'd crawl away. Wouldn't you, big boy?" She shook her head and stared at the ground around her feet. "Uh oh, poison ivy. This isn't the place, buddy." She trudged on hugging the boy to her.

A while later, through a clearing in the trees, Birdie spotted a high-way. Down the road there was a store with red and white gas pumps. No cars moved on the highway. There wasn't a person in sight. Birdie hurried out of the woods and crossed the highway. Head tucked down, she slid through the parking lot and entered the store. No bell rang to alert anyone. Whew. She smiled at James.

Let's Make a Deal was on the wall television. Birdie loved Let's Make a Deal. The clerk, her head turned away from Birdie, clapped and hooted. A new contestant was running down from the audience in a bunny suit. Birdie wished she could have a television. If so, she'd watch Let's Make a Deal every day, like she had in the home.

She turned down the nearest aisle and slipped to the back of the store with the baby. A large cardboard candy display caught her eye. The baby smiled at the fat orange candy bars on the display. He whispered, "Baba," as if he knew he had to be silent. Birdie put him down on the floor beside the display and held her finger over her lips.

Her heart was breaking as she handed him his bottle. He clamped his little hands around it and sucked in great greedy gulps. She smiled. Karo worked every time.

While the baby concentrated on drinking the milk, Birdie kissed his cheek, pressed down her cotton dress and backed away from him. His eyes followed her. The crepe soled shoes she wore moved silently on the floor as she headed up the aisle. She slipped out the door, gently closing it behind her.

The television could be heard across the parking lot. The cheering and whistling made Birdie want to turn around and watch. She couldn't. She had to get back to Sissy. She wiped her tears and headed into the woods. It wasn't long until she picked up the path to Sissy's. If Sissy got better she would bring Robert home again. She'd go right back and get him. She would.

As an old truck backfired at the gas pumps, the clerk, Emmy Lu Ho, turned the television volume down on Let's Make a Deal. She believed her boss had someone spying on her. She'd already been warned about watching too much television. How could she ignore it when it hung on the wall behind the counter? When there were no customers she was supposed to dust the shelves. Dusting was boring.

The old truck backfired again. She went to straighten the magazine rack by the window. She could see the television and watch the truck at the pumps.

The man returned the nozzle to the pump, pulled his receipt from the machine, and hopped into his vehicle. The truck shot back onto the highway and was gone.

Yawning, Emmy Lu eyed the cigarettes on display before going back to her stool behind the counter. She'd quit smoking a few weeks earlier. Still she had the urge to light up. However, her aunt had given her an ultimatum. Quit or move out. She had no option but to quit.

Something crashed in the back of the store, startling Emmy Lu. She stood up and looked around her. She was alone in the store, she thought, but was she really? It was drilled into her head by her aunt that mini marts were perfect crime scenes. She could see that a cardboard display had fallen in back of the store.

Cautiously, she walked a few steps toward the crash.

She heard a noise. She took another step. Breathing slowly she listened and around the corner came a baby crawling as fast as his little legs would carry him. He held the nipple of a plastic baby bottle between his teeth. He moved back and forth as he crawled, a string of drool falling to the floor. He continued toward her, a lopsided grin on his face.

Emmy Lu knelt down, eye level with the baby, and spoke to him quietly. "Hey, little one. Where'd you come from? Did you come in to watch television with me? Don't tell my boss, okay?" She glanced around the store. "How'd you get in here? Was your mama with you or did you crawl in by yourself?" She put her hand out and James reached for it.

"Here you go," she said, scooping him up and taking the empty bottle from him. She wiped his face with a tissue. "What's your name, fella? You got a name? Everyone has a name. Even if it's a weird name like Emmy Lu Ho."

She went to the counter with the baby in her arms. He patted her shoulder and smiled. She remembered the flyer someone had pinned to the cork board two days earlier.

She walked over to stare at the flyer. The blond-haired baby sitting under a blue sky in a field of daisies was the little boy in her arms. The kidnapper had left the baby in her store. Oh my.

Nausea hit her. He'd been a few feet from her. He could have tied her up. Shot her even. Her aunt would see her on the evening news, dead on the floor of the mini mart. Aunt Mae would lean over the girl's dead body and tell her she'd been right all along about mini marts. They were dangerous places. Emmy Lu hugged the boy tighter.

The kidnapper might still be in the store. She walked behind the counter toward the store phone, keeping her eyes straight ahead with her knees knocking.

She punched in 9-1-1. She glanced around quickly to see everything was in order. The cakes and cookies lined on a shelf. The candy bars in boxes on the counter. Perhaps Aunt Mae was right. A convenient store might be the worst place in the world to work. She cringed and held the little boy close, comforted by his warmth. He was a cute baby and had a clean scent. He seemed not to know what danger he'd been in. Poor fellow. He smiled up at her and said, "Baba." He reached for his bottle and she let him have it. He put the nipple in his mouth and chewed on it. Then he pulled the nipple out of his mouth and said, "Baba."

"This is Emmy Lu Ho, the clerk at the new mini mart on Rt. 62," she said into the phone. "Someone abandoned a baby here in the store. It's the kidnapped baby from the flyer. I'm scared the kidnapper might still be around here. Can you get out here now?"

"Hey, Duke," the man yelled. "The kidnapped baby's been found. Hang on. Has he been hurt, miss?"

"No, not that I can see." Emmy Lu looked the baby up and down.

"Officer Cobb will be right there," the man said. "You want me to talk to you until he gets there? It can seem like a long time before an officer responds. Cobb is eager to tie this one up. Talk about a madhouse. This has been one." He coughed. "If you're scared, I'll talk to you. It's my job. I don't mind. You okay? I'm supposed to ask. That missing baby has shook things up in this office. Does the kid really look okay? You've been through a little scare too. Finding that boy in the store. What happened, anyway?"

Emmy Lu gave him a brief summary of what had happened, and said, "If you don't mind, I'll hang up now. I have to see to this baby. He's an arm load. I need to find a chair." The baby was trying to slid out of her arms. He'd eyed a basket of red and blue rubber balls on the floor by the counter. He sure was a strong little guy.

When she hung up, Emmy Lu's eyes wandered out to the gas pumps and beyond to the shadowy woods above the highway. Where on earth had the kidnapper come from? Maybe he was hiding outside right this moment?

Emmy Lu prayed the officer would hurry. She didn't want to be alone in the store. She was spooked. She lowered herself and James into a chair to wait. She kept the wooden chair behind the counter for slow times. She'd even brought a flowered pillow from home to sit on. She would read and work crossword puzzles. She glanced at the romance novel she'd left on the counter. It was good but it certainly wasn't the time for reading now.

CHAPTER 37

"EMMY LU, ISN'T it?" Duke Cobb said, when he came striding into the store, a big grin covering his face. "That's little James Waddell, yes sir. That's him, all right."

"Yes, I'm Emmy Lu, and this is James." She held the boy up for the officer to see. "I knew it was him when I checked the flyer on the board."

Had he called her by name? She didn't remember giving her name to the dispatcher but then she wasn't herself.

"Would you mind looking around?" She stared toward the back of the store, still clinging to the baby. "I'm worried the kidnapper might still be here." She pointed to a mass of lawn chairs stacked in a far corner. "Anyone could hide back there."

"Sure," Duke lowered his voice and drew his gun. Emmy Lu sat down quickly with James. She wasn't a gun lover, convinced by her aunt that they went off of their own free will.

The officer canvassed the entire store, while Emmy Lu watched from her perch behind the counter. Before coming back, he checked the dark back room where the owner stored cases of soft drinks and other supplies.

"Baba," James whispered to Emmy Lu, hugging his empty bottle tight to his chest as if he knew something was going on. She cuddled the little guy. She hadn't known a baby could offer such comfort. He was warm and soft as velvet.

"Nothing back here," Duke called. He put his gun away and came toward her and James. "Hey, kid," he said, touching the baby's cheek. "You look just like your daddy, that old John Waddell. Big football hero. You know John? He's your daddy, little fellow." He reached for the baby's hand. James put out his hand and let Duke touch it then pulled it back quickly and laughed.

"You're a friendly fellow. You take that after your mommy. Not that daddy of yours. He never was friendly to me. That may change when I bring you home. Your mama sure loves you, buddy. Your daddy, too." Duke turned serious. "How'd the little fellow get inside here, anyway?"

"I don't know. That was the strangest thing. I was watching Let's Make a Deal with the volume loud." She looked at the glass doors leading out to the parking lot and shook her head. "All I know is I heard this crash and there he was, crawling toward me smiling like he was doing a baby food commercial. Holding his bottle in his teeth. I don't know how he upended that candy bar display. He's a strong little thing, though he's not all that big."

"Someone just brought him in and left him?" The officer seemed to be looking at her a bit suspiciously.

"Well, I didn't bring him in." She pulled herself up taller, like that would lend credence to her story. "Aunt Mae wouldn't let me have a baby while I live in her home. She's strict. Puritanical, really, and if you think I kidnapped him, you got another think coming. I am not that kind of girl."

"No, I didn't mean you kidnapped him. I just can't figure who would leave a kid in a mini mart. What matters is he's safe and I can get him back to his family. Investigators will be here shortly to check things out. Look for fingerprints and that kind of thing."

"Oh dear," Emmy Lu looked at her watch. "My boss will be in soon to relieve me. I gotta clean up that mess back there. That's one thing he won't tolerate. Messes. Kidnapped kid or not."

"I'll explain to your boss. We can't clean up anything until the inspectors get here."

"Are you sure?"

"I'm sure. Now, I need to look at the security system."

"It's in the back room. I don't know much about it. Too sophisticated for me. I know we have cameras everywhere in the store."

"Take this stool with you," she offered. "In case you have to climb. I use it to reach the cigarettes overhead. I'm too short for everything."

"Don't say that," Duke said, looking her up and down. He took the stool from her. "You're not too short for many things."

"Name one." She challenged him, holding James on her hip and watching his face carefully.

"Well, you're not too short for me." He looked down at her and smiled his goofy smile.

He headed off to the back room. When he returned Emmy Lu was waiting for him with her own question.

"I'm not too short for you, is that what you said?" She blushed.

"Yep. I meant you're not too short for me to ask out. You know, like to dinner or a show." He walked over to where she stood holding James on her hip. He placed the stool against the counter. "Your boss will have to contact me with the security tape. I couldn't figure out the system." He handed her his card after underlining his number.

"All right. I'll give him your card."

"Thanks," he said. "My mother said you go to the Methodist Church and sing in the choir. Not many Asian girls in town. I figured it had to be you."

She frowned at him, moving James to her opposite hip. "Yes, I'm half-Asian."

"I didn't mean to offend you. I'm not good at conversation. With females, I mean."

"Well, I'm proud to be Asian. You got a problem with that?"

"No way. You're the prettiest girl I know." He nearly choked on his words and then he stammered, "Can I call you? Sometime, maybe, we could go out?"

"Okay," she said, not sure about the man in front of her. "You can call me." While his mother was the nicest person she knew, it didn't mean he was.

Duke caught himself staring at her white teeth. "I better go," he finally muttered. He reached for the baby and was surprised when James came to him willingly. "Whoa, little man. You're something else."

The baby smiled and patted Duke on the arm. Then he tapped Duke's shoulder with his bottle. "Baba," he said. "Baba."

Emmy Lu reached out and patted the baby's bottom. "He might be hungry. He keeps patting his bottle and its empty. I'd give him something but I don't know what he can eat." She looked around at the canned food on the shelf. "He might take a special formula. He's wet too." She sniffed the air and made a face. "He needs to be changed soon."

"I better get this boy home." He headed toward the door. "I'll be talking to you, Emmy Lu. Perfect name, too."

The baby laid his head on Duke's shoulder. The officer found himself patting the boy on the back in a soothing way as he headed outside with him.

"Okay," Emmy Lu called. It was the first male attention she'd had in a long time. Though she was a bit afraid of him, she had to admit she liked the attention.

Holding a baby wasn't bad, Duke decided as he put the boy into the borrowed baby seat and snapped him in. Not bad at all. Nothing like he had imagined. He thought he wouldn't enjoy it but he did. It was like holding a warm puppy but better, the way the baby's little arms and legs tightened around Duke as he lowered the boy into the infant seat. The kid did have a smelly diaper. He had to get him to the office quick. He wanted to notify Vada Faith and John. He checked the baby over quickly for injuries. Bruises, scratches, that kind of thing. There was nothing. He climbed into the front seat of the cruiser and started the car. He waved to Emmy Lu who stood in the front window of the mini mart.

Whoever had taken the baby did a good job looking after him. His face was clean and he smelled good. Except for the diaper. Having the boy home would put Vada Faith back on track and maybe get him in her good graces. He'd been thinking about going by and letting her cut his hair. His mother always cut his hair but lately she'd done a lousy job. Nicking his ears or cutting one side shorter than the other. Yep, it was time for a change in the hair department. Many in other areas of his life too.

Duke checked his image in the mirror and smiled at the kid in the back seat. His little head was bobbing back and forth, his eyes drooping, ready to fall asleep. He'd been through a lot. It was time to get that little fellow home to his mama and daddy.

He smiled to himself. He'd had a good day.

The officer decided instead of taking James home he needed to take him to the police station. Reporters were camped out all over the Waddell's street. He'd never break through the mob without getting his picture taken a hundred times. He liked getting his own picture taken, it wasn't that. He didn't think the baby needed all that attention right now.

"Hey, John, good news," Duke said, when the blue tooth connected his call. He turned and looked at the baby who was sleeping peacefully, holding onto his empty bottle with both hands. "I have James. Hold on, man, he's fine, I swear. Yes, I'm looking at him. He's in the back seat of the squad car. You can pick him up at my office in ten minutes. I'll explain when I see you. If those news hounds follow you, we'll stop them at the door. Yes," he nodded, "yes, Vada Faith, your boy is perfect. Just like when he left home. He smiled at me earlier. He's a little tired. You might bring him a bottle. The girl at the mini mart, Emmy Lu, thought he was hungry. Oh, he needs a diaper change. I'll explain everything when I see you."

He looked ahead at the few cars traveling Rt. 62.

The boy's parents had screamed with joy. The officer was joyful himself.

Duke wouldn't mind being in John Waddell's good graces. He'd gone by John's furniture shop and found a few pieces he was interested in. He had his own home planned right down to the furnishings if he could ever get out of his mother's house.

Who knew where a date with Miss Emmy Lu might lead. It certainly would make his mother happy if he'd settle down and start a family. Just the thought of someone to date made his heart sing. He pressed down harder on the gas pedal. His whole life was picking up speed.

CHAPTER 38

Beaming, John handed the phone to Vada Faith. "Duke has James! He's okay!"

"Thank God!" She took the phone and started to laugh. "We'll be right there!"

"Let's go get our boy!" She yelled at John, who looked dazed.

They raced through the empty house, John to get his wallet and keys and Vada Faith to pack a bag for James. Upstairs, she yelled into her prayer closet, "Thank you, Jesus! Thank you!"

She and John nearly collided on the stairs before making their way out to the driveway, giddy with excitement. Thankfully, Charity and Hope were at Louise's house learning to make her special no-bake cookies. Vada Faith sighed as she settled into the truck seat.

John revved the engine of the truck and wheeled out of the drive as his wife closed the door. She glanced back as several reporters headed to their cars.

"I'm relieved just the two of us can go get James. He doesn't need the commotion of all our family."

"Where's mom, anyway?" He asked.

"At home. Making cookies with Charity and Hope. She wanted a change of pace."

John nodded at her and parked on the street by the police station. He jumped out of the truck and went to help his wife but she'd already hopped out and grabbed the diaper bag from the floor. A few hours earlier she found herself staring at the designer bag in the nursery, wondering if she'd ever use it again. It was an overpriced shower gift from her sister. Now, she smiled and hoisted the smart-looking bag onto her shoulder.

She hurried down the sidewalk, rushing toward the glass doors of the station.

Car doors slammed on the street.

"Reporters," Vada Faith muttered, her heart pumping with excitement. Nothing could damper her spirits.

A burly officer held the door open for them. "Your baby's with Officer Cobb. He's doing great." He pointed down the hallway. As they hurried off in that direction, he locked the doors behind them.

Vada Faith could hear reporters pounding on the glass doors.

"Duke!" Vada Faith yelled, her voice echoing down the hallway. "In here!"

She stepped inside the next doorway. The minute she saw James, sleeping on the small couch, she swooped down on him. Her breath nearly stopped. He smiled in his sleep. He appeared to be fine. She smiled through her tears. She picked up the baby and sat down on the sofa with him. She unwrapped him from a furry football throw and examined him from head to toe.

"Oh, dear, thank you! Thank you, Jesus, for keeping my baby safe. He's okay, John. Look." She squeezed him with all her might as John beamed down at them.

"I covered him with the throw," Duke spoke up. "I didn't want him to be cold."

James opened his eyes and yawned. When he saw his mother he said, "Ma," and smiled. "Ma." He put his fingers in his mouth and chewed. He reached for the empty bottle beside him on the sofa and stuck it in his mouth.

"Da." His face broke into a big grin as he caught sight of John.

John let out a strangled sound and got down on his knees to pull Vada Faith and James into his arms. "Thank God."

He fought to compose himself but tears rolled down his cheeks as he turned and sat down on the sofa beside his wife. He pulled out a handkerchief and wiped his eyes without moving an inch from his son. James took John's fingers in his small hand. "Da." James drooled onto his father's hand.

It was one of the few times Vada Faith had seen her husband cry. He'd shed tears at the birth of their children, a few on their wedding day, and now.

He stuffed his handkerchief into the pocket of his khaki pants and patted his wife and son. "Daddy's happy to see you, big boy. Our little man is finally home." He reached for his son.

Vada Faith shook her head and held the baby closer. "How did you find him, Duke? Who had him? What kind of person would do such a thing?" Vada Faith kept her eyes on James. "Mommy's baby boy!" She lifted a clean bottle from the diaper bag. James grabbed it and sucked the warm milk greedily, holding it with both hands. She felt overwhelming happiness. James snuggled into her, warming the place in her body that was frozen since he went missing. She planned to stick to James like a banana to a peel for the rest of his babyhood, into his teen years, and maybe even beyond.

"We'll discuss all the details." Duke said. "Give me a minute." He tapped on his computer. "He seems to be in perfect health. That's a relief. Not just for you but for me and the whole town." He nodded at them.

"Who kidnapped our baby?" John asked, frowning at Duke. "We need some answers. Where was James for two days?" John touched the baby's silky head. "You were gone too long, buddy." The lines in John's face seemed to soften as he talked to his son. "Daddy's sure glad to see you." He rubbed the baby's head softly as he talked.

"I need Jed out in the hall to make some calls for me." Duke stood. "I'll be right back and I'll tell you all I know." He walked out and closed the door behind him.

James reached over and took his daddy's finger, holding it as he drank his bottle. Halfway through, he paused, and let milk dribble down his chin. He smiled first at John and then at Vada Faith. "Ma," he said. "Da." He patted John's hand.

Vada Faith caressed her son's soft little legs. "I don't think he's missed any meals." She wiped away her tears and smiled down at James, putting her head against his and saying softly, "Mommy's baby. This big boy is Mommy's baby." James continued drinking, his eyes fastened on her face.

"Mommy's boy needs a diaper change," she said, suddenly, holding James up and shaking her head.

"Where's the restroom?" She asked, as Duke returned. She hoisted James onto her hip and grabbed the diaper bag from the floor.

"Down the hall on the right." Duke pointed. "It's small. There's a table you can use to change him on."

The room was small, the table barely big enough for James. He seemed heavier to her as she placed him on a blanket on the table. Could he have gained weight in two days?

She handed the baby a teething toy and slid off his blue pants.

His diaper consisted of layers and layers of white cotton cloth covered with a plastic grocery bag for catching leaks. Miraculously it had worked. Who on earth would put such a makeshift diaper on a baby these days? It looked similar to the diapers Grandma Belle had described from back in her day. Minus the grocery bag. There was no plastic back then.

Vada Faith examined James carefully. There was no redness on him anywhere. Someone had taken good care of him. She was thankful but who had taken him and why? Right at the moment she didn't care. He was back. He was safe. That was the most important thing. She leaned down and kissed his chubby cheek. "Do do gah." He pointed up at her.

After she'd finished changing him, she repacked the diaper bag.

"Ma." He said. "Dada." He pointed to the hallway.

"Yes, James," she said, smoothing down his hair and picking him up. "You're daddy's right down the hall. Welcome home." She squeezed him against her.

She listened to the lightness in her husband's voice as she made her way back to Duke's office. He smiled when she walked in with the baby. John walked the length of the office, his hands in the pockets of his slacks.

"Was James okay?" He asked, as he patted his son's back.

"He's great." She put the diaper bag on the floor and shifted James in her arms.

"Want me to take him?" John beamed at the baby. "He's heavy."

"Not yet," she said, sitting down in a chair in front of Duke's desk.

"Tell Vada Faith what you just told me." John stood beside his wife.

"I got a call from the clerk out at the mini mart on Rt. 62," the officer said. "The one they put in not long ago. The clerk said someone left a baby in one of the aisles. She didn't see anyone in the store. She thought it was James, judging from the photo on the flyer. Well, I went out there and it was James, sure as anything. Smiling and talking to the clerk."

"She didn't see who brought him in?" John frowned.

"Nope. Said she didn't see a thing."

Vada Faith looked up from inspecting the baby's hands. "That's strange, don't you think?"

"I don't see how she could miss someone coming into the store." Duke twisted around in his chair. "The door does have a cheap little bell on it but the clerk said it doesn't always ring. It didn't ring when I went in. The girl was watching TV." Duke smoothed down his hair. "Name's Emmy Lu Ho. The volume on the TV was loud. She said she heard a noise, looked up, and saw James crawling down the aisle toward her, his bottle hanging from his teeth. She didn't see anyone else, just the baby. They get mostly gas customers who pay by card and drive on."

"How do you know she's not lying?" Vada Faith shook her head. "She could have kidnapped James and changed her mind? I'm not sure I believe her, Duke."

"Nah, Vada Faith. She's reliable. Sings in the choir over at the Methodist Church with my mother. She lives with her aunt. Mom knows them both. Says they're good people. Straight-laced. Her aunt is strict." He blushed. "Mom's been wanting me to ask her out on a date. Anyway, I don't see any reason not to believe her."

"We'll offer a $25,000 reward for information that leads to an arrest." John glanced at his wife who nodded. "We should have done it sooner. I can't let this happen to another baby. You need to investigate the girl at the mini mart, Duke. Make sure she's on the up and up."

"Will do," the officer said. "What seems strange to me is if the kidnapper didn't want money why did he kidnap James and then give him back. Doesn't make sense."

"No," John said, reaching for James again. The baby shook his head and buried his face in his mother's shoulder. "Makes no sense to me."

"I'll get some flyers posted about the reward." Duke jotted something on a pad of paper on his desk. "We'll distribute them around town. The best part is James is home and he's not been hurt in any way."

"Yes." John bent down and reached for James again. Vada Faith reluctantly handed him over. He hugged his son and kissed his head. James patted John's face. "You still daddy's boy?" As John nuzzled the baby against him he relaxed for the first time in days. "I'm so glad you're home, buddy." John stared down at his wife, who smiled happily.

"I'll talk to the owner of the mini mart." Duke nodded. "I'll be getting information from the security system at the store. We should get a good look at the kidnapper."

John nodded, rocking the baby back and forth as he rested on his daddy's shoulder.

Vada Faith couldn't help herself. She stood and reached for James again. The baby lunged into her arms. She smiled and cooed. "Mommy's baby boy. Yes, he is. He's my sweetheart James." He snuggled into her arms and said, "Mama."

She walked around the room with him, wanting to take him home and rock him. "We have to call everyone. Mama and Joy Ruth." She looked at her husband. "You can call your mama and your brothers. I'll call Midgy."

"I've already contacted Midgy." Duke stood up. "You should take James over to the clinic," Duke added, "just as a precaution. We have to be sure he isn't hurt in any way. I've called off the search. The guys are thrilled we got the baby. Hey, good luck at the clinic. They're expecting you."

"Thanks," she said, bending to pick up the diaper bag. John scooped it out of her reach and slung it easily over his shoulder.

"You know, Duke," John said, seriously, "James is safe but someone dangerous is still out there."

Vada Faith wrapped a blanket loosely around the baby.

"I know," Duke said. "inspectors are still at the mini mart. We'll know soon what they find. There'll be a press conference later. You'll both need to be there with James. I want the information to come from this office. Otherwise who knows what story will be told."

"Sounds good." John hovered at his wife's side in the doorway. "Let us know if you hear anything."

The officer didn't mention the video from the mini mart. He wanted to watch it first. He might solve the mystery before the press conference. Not that he wanted any glory, unless it got him a pay raise which he sure could use.

"Why would a kidnapper leave James in a mini mart?" Vada Faith asked, as she was leaving.

"I don't know." Duke extended his hand to John. "We'll find out. I guarantee it." Duke walked them to the lobby.

John pulled Duke into an embrace, surprising his wife and the officer. "We can't thank you enough, buddy." He patted a red-faced Duke Cobb on the back. "We're forever grateful. If we hadn't got James back, well, I can't think about it. You know? You ever need anything, you give us a call."

"Hey, no thanks necessary. Just doing my job and glad to do it. I'm relieved the baby is okay. You check him out good, hear?"

John led his wife and baby outside into the sunshine. He was happier than the day he'd picked Vada Faith and James up at the hospital after the baby's birth. That had been a great day for him, having his very own son to carry on the family name. When he first laid eyes on the baby in the nursery with that crop of hair and those Waddell eyes, he fell in love with him. His son looked just like him. He never said it to Vada Faith as she was positive James looked just like her family. John knew better.

Several photographers snapped their picture as Vada Faith and John stepped outside the station with the baby. She slowed her pace to let them see James in her arms. From her shoulder, James yawned, tired from the long day.

She strapped the baby into his car seat and then turned to the men. "James is fine," she called, "but he's tired. You can take pictures at the news conference later." She gave them a thumbs up, posing for them calmly for the first time since the nightmare started. "Officer Cobb will be in touch." She got into the car and strapped herself in beside her husband, who was staring into the rear view mirror watching James doze in his car seat.

When the reporters were out of sight, Vada Faith bowed her head and closed her eyes in prayer, thanking God for bringing her baby home safely.

With that, John drove away from the police station, with his wife and the son he wasn't sure he'd ever see again.

CHAPTER 39

AFTER THE SEARCH was called off, several locals loitered in the lobby of the police station, drinking coffee and rehashing the search for James Waddell.

"Okay, you guys," Duke called from his office door, "make yourself useful and get in here."

His computer was set to go with the video from the store manager. As the men crowded around his desk, he clicked the machine and the interior of the mini mart came into view, showing the dark-haired girl, Emmy Lu, behind the counter, her eyes glued to the television on the wall.

"Cute girl, huh?" Duke said, smiling, leaning back in his chair.

Lefty Parr nodded from where he sat across the desk from the officer.

A couple of customers came into the store, one to buy a newspaper, another to get a sandwich from the cooler. The clerk's eyes occasionally went to the screen beside the television that showed the gas pumps outside, but mostly she kept her eyes on Let's Make a Deal.

Then, a short pudgy woman slipped through the door of the mini mart, so quick they almost missed her. She darted down the first aisle. In one hand she held a wiggling baby and in the other a tote bag. She hurried along, her head lowered.

The clerk didn't move, her eyes still locked on the screen.

The old woman bent and set the baby on the floor. She reached into her tote and pulled out a bottle of milk. The child plucked the bottle from her hand and stuck it into his mouth.

"Look at that little guy go after that milk," one of the men said, with a chuckle. They all leaned in to get a better look. Lefty leaned in to get a closer look. "It's James all right." He smiled.

The baby patted the bottle and smiled at the woman who turned and went back the way she'd come, disappearing through the doorway.

The clerk kept her position, feet propped on a box, sipping occasionally from a bottle of Coke.

Draining his bottle, the baby leaned against the cardboard display. It went tumbling to the floor, sending candy bars flying. The baby took off crawling down the aisle toward the front of the store, holding his empty bottle in his teeth, swinging it back and forth, a big smile on his face.

"Well, I'll be." Duke shifted in his chair.

He played the tape again and they watched in silence.

"Anybody recognize the old woman?"

"Nope."

"No."

"Nah."

"Not me."

"Okay, listen," Duke said, clicking the computer off. "Someone has to know this old woman." He rubbed his hands together in frustration. "Let's get to work and find out who she is. She may be the key to this whole operation. Maybe she was keeping the baby for the kidnapper. Whatever, we have to get moving. If this woman didn't steal the baby, we have to find out who did and fast before they take another child."

"That old woman doesn't look dangerous to me." Lefty stretched as he pulled himself off the chair.

"We have to treat her as if she's dangerous." Duke rose from his chair. "I'd appreciate it if you guys would help me out with this. Just because the search for the baby is over, the search for the kidnapper isn't."

"Right, boss," Lefty said, heading down the hall with the rest of the men, as they discussed the scene at the mini mart.

A minute later, Midgy Brown stuck her head into Duke's office. "Anyone home?"

"Hey." Duke motioned her inside. He put aside a stack of papers.

"Who's supposed to be in the lobby? Someone is liable to steal that giant box of donuts on the table."

Duke stood and went to the door. "Frances," he called down the hall, "we need you out front and get everyone out of the kitchen. It's not meal time."

"What a group," Midgy said, laughing. "Thankfully we have good news about James." She seated herself across from Duke.

"Yep, James is safe," the officer said. "Now we have to find the old woman who left him in the mini mart. I want you to look at the security tape from the market, see if you know the person who left James there." Duke turned on the video.

As the tape rolled, Midgy shook her head. "I don't know her. She looks a bit like a guy, from the build, except for the dress."

The person wasn't familiar. Yet, there was something Midgy couldn't put her finger on. She shook her head after having Duke to stop the tape and let her study the woman. "No. I've never seen her."

"All the Charleston stations will be showing this footage today. Someone around here must know her. She's crazy, if you ask me. She may grab another baby."

"She doesn't look crazy, Duke. Just old and eccentric."

Duke had always loved the woman across from him. She wasn't his type, romantically, with her freckles and wild red hair. They'd hung around together, playing cowboys when they were kids, because they were neighbors. He was Roy Rogers to her Dale Evans.

"Thank God, James is okay," she said. "Do you know anything at all about this woman?"

"Not yet." He leaned back in his chair.

"Let me take another look at her." Midgy leaned toward the computer and so did Duke.

Watching the tape carefully, she finally said, "I've got it! It's her brown shawl. It belongs to Sissy Kapp, who lives on Lone Oak Road. See?" She pointed to the shawl. "It's knitted in that loopy way Sissy has with everything she makes. It's odd shaped. I doubt anyone else would wear one. It's butt ugly. Puckered in places and drooping in others."

"Does she sell those things?"

"Goodness no. Who'd buy them? This person has to be someone Sissy knows well. She's petrified of strangers. I can't even persuade her to ride the bus to the senior center."

Duke was tired of speculating. He imagined the real kidnapper out there searching for another kid to swipe, while he sat there watching an old woman on his computer. The kidnapper had to be a big dude and bad to the bone, not some broken-down old woman.

"Sissy Kapp isn't involved in this," Midgy insisted. "I'm sure of it. She barely goes outside. She never comes to town. It's not even a possibility. She's a total recluse."

"I have to question her anyway. That old woman with the shawl is our only lead. Maybe your friend, Sissy, can tell us who the woman is that's wearing the shawl." Duke rose from his chair and straightened his shirt. "I'm going to see her now. Lone Oak Road, you said?"

"Yes, and I'll ride with you." Midgy stood and pulled on her jacket. "She'll be okay if she sees me. Otherwise, you'll never get her to open the door."

"Thanks," Duke said, leading the way outside to the squad car. "I don't usually take anyone with me. Privacy, you know. She has rights, even if it turns out she's a kidnapper. I might get inside easier with you along."

"Sissy's no kidnapper, Duke, believe me, and I'd bet the old woman who dropped James in the mini mart isn't the one who took him. If the woman is Sissy's friend she's harmless." Midgy got into the car beside the officer and buckled the seat belt. "I don't know how those two women got involved but I'd put money on their innocence. You'll see when you meet Sissy. She's meek as a lamb. She'd never kidnap a child."

"We'll see," he said, pulling the squad car out onto the open highway. He pressed the gas to the floor to pass a slow moving car. He wanted to get this over with. Catch whoever was responsible for the kidnapping and get back to his life. It appeared his life might be taking a turn for the better. He had called Emmy Lu after he returned to his office earlier and asked her to lunch sometime. She said it sounded good. She would let him know. He was sure there'd been a yes in her voice.

Ten minutes later they were hiking up the hill to Sissy's house. The lane was too rough for a car.

"Sissy, it's me," Midgy called from the side porch of the cottage. "Hello. Sissy. It's Midgy. Open the door, please. It's important."

When nobody came to the door, Midgy turned the ancient knob. The door swung open. The woman stepped inside.

"Sissy?" She called, "It's Midgy."

"In here," a weak voice called from the back room.

"What on earth," Midgy said, walking into the tiny bedroom where Sissy sat in a chair covered in blankets. "What's wrong, Sissy?" The girl went to the old woman's side and took her hand. The tall woman, usually bustling with energy, was subdued and pale.

"I'm not myself today," she said. "I got the money ready for you, over there on the dresser. Thank you for the supplies you brought." She raised up to point and spotted Duke Cobb in his official uniform. She dropped back in the chair and closed her eyes. "Oh, my," she uttered, "oh my."

"It's okay." Midgy patted the old woman's hand. "Duke's a friend. He wants to ask you about your brown shawl. The one you wore when I was here. Do you know where it is right now? It's all we want, really, to look at your shawl."

"I don't know for sure," Sissy said, confused. She tried to lift herself to a standing position. She managed to get part way up then slumped back. "Look on the coat rack in the kitchen. Why do you want my shawl?"

Duke and Midgy both stepped back into the kitchen and combed through the sweaters and jackets on the rack. The brown shawl was buried among them.

"Have you worn your shawl today?" Midgy asked, putting her head back into the bedroom.

"No, I haven't been out." Sissy's voice was weak.

"Did you make more than one?" Midgy hung the shawl back on the rack.

"There's one other shawl like mine. It belongs to Birdie, my sister. She's not very well." Sissy coughed. "Why do you want to know?"

The officer stepped close to the chair. "I'm Officer Duke Cobb," he said, "with the Shady Creek Police Department. Today a woman wearing a shawl just like yours left a baby in a mini mart out on the highway. The security camera took pictures of her. You know anything about a baby or that woman with a shawl like yours?"

"No," Sissy said, too quickly, her eyes darting away from the officer. "I don't. A baby. No. I don't know anything about a baby."

"Sister!" The back door slammed and there was rustling and stomping of feet. "Sissy. I'm back."

Sissy looked up as Birdie came to stand in the doorway. Birdie's face fell when she saw the uniformed man standing over her sister.

Birdie thought she might be dreaming. Maybe Sissy had died and now they were all in heaven.

"Birdie," Sissy spoke loudly, "this is Officer Cobb from Shady Creek. This is Midgy Brown, who brings my supplies. This," she motioned to the woman standing in the door, "is my sister. Say hello, Birdie."

"Say hello Birdie," Birdie said, smiling, hoping they would laugh at her joke. They didn't. Sissy appeared to be okay with the people standing in her bedroom, though she never had company.

Birdie loved company. She clapped her hands and smiled. If Sissy was okay with visitors, she was too. They could have a party.

"Would you put the tea kettle on, little sister? Then come and help me up. We're going to sit down in the kitchen and have tea."

In the kitchen, Birdie picked up the brown shawl from the chair where she'd slung it and hung it on the coat rack. She filled the tea kettle with water and got down a box of Earl Grey tea, her favorite. She smiled. It was like a party.

Perhaps they were going to have a celebration. She chuckled and went to the cookie tin and arranged some of Sissy's sugar cookies on a blue and white enamel plate.

As Birdie sat at the table, waiting for the water to heat, and listening to the low voices in the bedroom, she remembered she might have her own visitor before the day was over. She'd taken several pieces of bread with her when she left the house with the baby. All the way home she'd dropped crumbs, hoping a child might stumble on the crumbs and follow her home. Then she would have a playmate. Someone to play paper dolls with. Sissy complained she was too busy to cut figures out of a catalogue. She wanted Birdie to grow up, to think about making dish towels or a quilt out of rags. Birdie wanted to play paper dolls. If the people left soon, Sissy might play paper dolls with her. This time she would insist on being the beautiful dark-haired bride with the red lipstick from the JC Penney catalog.

"Birdie!" Sissy called as the tea kettle whistled wildly. "Come here, please."

Birdie jumped. She stood and got out Sissy's best china cups and dessert plates before going to help her sister to the table. She would miss that little baby. He would miss her too. She would bet on it.

She had something to look forward to now. Tea with company and a new playmate.

Sissy leaned into her on their trek to the kitchen and whispered, "Little Bird, don't be scared." She patted her hand. "Everything will be all right."

Birdie had no idea what Sissy was talking about. She nodded anyway. She loved sugar cookies and the Earl Grey tea she was about to have with honey and a spoon or two of Carnation milk. Another favorite.

CHAPTER 40

AT THE CLINIC, Vada Faith and John both held onto James as though someone was tugging him from them.

"Hey, folks." A male nurse strode down the hall with an ipad. "Officer Cobb alerted us you were coming. Back this way." The man pointed down the hall. "Dr. Clem will have a look at this little guy." He led them down a long hallway to a small room with a crib.

Vada Faith hurried into the room, pleased that her own pediatrician was going to see James.

"If you'll undress him, here's a warm blanket." A female nurse handed the blanket to Vada Faith as she undressed the baby. She wrapped the blanket around him until he looked like an Eskimo baby with only his face showing.

His face turned red as he struggled to get his arms loose.

The nurse whose name tag said Tanya smiled as James fought to unwind himself.

"Honey, I think you've got him too tight." John stepped up and started loosening the blanket, giving his son room to move.

Inside the blanket the baby's legs were moving furiously. Vada Faith could see a tantrum developing.

"All right. Let his legs out too," she said, loosening the blanket, not happy that John wanted to take over.

"Good to see you folks." Dr. Clem came in, shaking hands with them. "It's good to see you, James." He put his hand out as if to shake the baby's hand and James reached out and grabbed the stethoscope around the doctor's neck.

"You look like you're in fine shape, young man." The doctor pulled the instrument from the baby. "We'll check to make sure." He listened to the baby's chest while James held tight to the stethoscope.

"Are you ready to go home, big boy? I'd say you are." He looked in the baby's mouth, into his ears and nose.

"Ba, ba. Ma, ma." James talked to the doctor as he examined him.

"I don't blame you buddy," the doctor said, "it's time to go home."

"Baba," James squealed and grabbed the stethoscope again, this time managing to unwrap it halfway from the doctor's neck.

"Ah, a doctor in the making," Dr. Clem said, retrieving his stethoscope and standing up. "He sounds good. Put him on the table here and I'll finish."

Vada Faith unwrapped James and the doctor checked his arms, legs, his bottom, as well as every inch of his little body. He was clean and smelled pleasant.

"I believe your little guy is fine." He patted James on the shoulder. "You're good to go, young man."

He turned to Vada Faith, "I'll see him in my office in a few days. I can discuss any concerns you have. For now the best thing for this boy is to go home. I bet he's missed those sisters of his. I know they've missed him."

"They have, indeed." John leaned over to help his wife lift the baby from the table.

The baby's face had turned mottled red as he worked his arms and legs wildly in protest of being held. He tried to slide down his mother's leg.

She hoisted him onto the table where she put him in a clean diaper and finished dressing him.

By the time they walked out of the clinic everyone was smiling, including James whose happy demeanor had been restored.

She couldn't wait to get James home. He needed a bath and a change of clothes. At the upcoming press conference, she would show the world her baby boy was safe.

In the back of her mind were thoughts of the kidnapper. Where was he now? Was he watching the news to see if the baby was home? The person must know where they lived. Would he return and take James again?

She planned to move out of Shady Creek. Her mind was made up. She was taking her family far away from this little town and the big family home. If a kidnapper could strike once, he could strike again. Convincing her husband wouldn't be easy. They'd always lived here, grown up here, but she intended to move and nothing John Waddell said could change her mind. She'd go with or without him.

The old Waddell place had been in John's family since the Victorian era. There was the famed porch where Eleanor Roosevelt once sat and took tea with John's Grandma Belle. The whole historic-house-worship thing seemed silly now that the baby had been abducted from that famous porch. With a kidnapper wandering around she wanted in a gated community, even if she had to build one herself. She'd move to another state. When she could get organized she was leaving.

John would have a hissy fit. The house was revered by the Waddell family. His brothers were in on the remodeling and even his mother followed the architect's drawing each step of the way inspecting the house each evening when the workers quit. The day the plaque arrived, naming the house to the National Registry of Historical Homes, his family was on hand to celebrate.

Unearthing her husband from the house and the town wouldn't be easy, but she had no choice. Her family's safety came first. She cradled James. She thought about ways she could break the news to her husband and their families. It might not be easy but she'd figure it out.

CHAPTER 41

VADA FAITH LOWERED the baby in a tub of warm water. The soap created tiny bubbles as the water continued flowing. "Bo," James said, waving at the bubbles drifting up over him. "Bo bo bo."

"That's right, baby boy. Those are bub-bles."She pronounced it slowly wanting him to remember the word. She heard the more words you said to a baby the smarter the child would be.

"Honey," her mother said, sitting down on a stool where she could watch her grandson, "I'm glad our boy is okay. God is good, that's for sure."

"He is." Vada Faith soaped the baby's tummy and his legs. "I'm so thankful, there was no harm done to him. Seems we're the only ones who suffered." She rinsed the soap off his front and then soaped the smooth skin on his back. Lifting him up, she let him stand while she washed his bottom and the backs of his chubby legs. "Ma," he said, pulling the wash cloth from her and sticking it into his mouth to chew.

"Here buddy." She tugged the soapy cloth away and gave him a clean one to chew on.

"Where's everybody?" Joy Ruth called, running up the stairs.

"Gracious girl," her mother said, when she popped inside the bathroom door. "Don't you walk anywhere?"

"Not if I can run," she said. "Move over Vada Faith," she demanded, "and let me see my precious nephew."

"Na-poo," James mimicked Joy Ruth, and tried to say nephew.

"Listen to him," she gushed. "He said nephew."

"You saw him already," Vada Faith said, trying to hold her position, kneeling over the tub. "I want to finish his bath, now go on."

"Auntie is going to finish this big boy's bath." She leaned into Vada Faith, pressing her over a few inches. "You pick out his clothes, please, Vada Faith!" She tugged the wash cloth from her sister's hand. "Vay, let me do it. Come on." She took the wash cloth and pushed her sister out of her spot on the floor.

"Oh, all right." Vada Faith stood and shook her head. "Why do you have to be so pushy?" She wiped her hands on the towel with the duck's head and went to the nursery.

Her mother followed. "That little guy is loved, that's for sure. I don't know what we'd have done without him."

"We don't have to wonder, Mama. We have him back." Vada Faith leaned over the crib and picked up the stuffed blue dog James called Blue Baby, and hugged it to her.

"I have to find James an outfit for the news conference. The investigator will handle the meeting. Duke's still on the case." She set the toy back in the crib. "I'm relieved James is home. I wasn't sure he'd ever be home again. I'm so thankful."

Her mother caught her in a hug, ignoring the tears running down her own cheeks.

"Put him in something blue," her mother advised, pulling away, and wiping her tears with the back of her hand. "I'm going downstairs to make coffee. It's been a long day."

"Right." Vada Faith looked around at the crib and all the baby's things in perfect order. She hadn't known if her baby boy would ever be in this room again or ever sleep in his crib with the Winnie the Pooh sheets. She reached over and turned on his Winnie the Pooh mobile and was serenaded by the music box.

She could hear Joy Ruth talking to James. He jabbered along with her.

She moved to the closet and pulled out a pair of tiny Old Navy jeans and a new blue shirt. He'd be the best dressed baby at the press conference. Chances were he'd be the only baby there.

Later, after meeting with the press, they gathered around the big screen television in the family room to watch.

"It was over so fast," Vada Faith said. "I don't know why I worried about what James was going to wear, even though he did look awfully cute." She'd had him in four outfits before going back to the jeans, the blue dress shirt and a tiny blue and white striped tie.

The beaming detective who'd helped Officer Cobb with the investigation held James at the beginning of the news conference while he spoke, thanking everyone who'd been involved. James continuously tried to wrest the man's glasses from his face.

"Just remember folks," the detective said, when he addressed the group, "while we're all celebrating the safe return of baby James, the kidnapper is still on the loose. Call the number at the bottom of the screen if you know anything at all. I'd like to thank all the volunteers who worked hard to find this baby. We had support from the sheriff's department, and the Shady Creek Fire Department. Those guys are the best. They'll continue to help until we can wrap up this case."

"Do you have any leads?" asked a reporter.

"Officer Cobb is following up on something right now. That's all I can say at this time."

As James climbed from lap to lap of each family member, including Charity and Hope who could barely contain him, everyone laughed. It was a time of celebration with James stealing the show when he kissed the brown bear the investigator had given him, his blue eyes sparkling for the cameras.

CHAPTER 42

As Duke sat at their kitchen table, he tried to keep his questions to the two old women friendly and casual. Midgy sat between the women.

"There's this problem," he said, as he sipped his tea. "We have a security film showing a woman wearing a brown shawl like Sissy's, abandoning a baby in a mini mart today."

"Sissy won't go to the mini market," Birdie stated, placing her pink-flowered china cup carefully on the table. She added more honey to her cup and stirred it with the silver spoon from her grandmother's set. "Sissy has a bad heart." She glanced at her sister who ignored her and looked sicker. "She gets sick and goes to bed."

After a few moments of silence, Birdie continued, "She gets sick to her stomach, too. She might get a heart attack. It could make her die, like Mama. I have to take care of Sissy. We can't leave here. Either one of us. No sir. Isn't that right, sister?"

Sissy kept her eyes down and stirred her tea with a shaky hand using one of the silver spoons.

"Well, Sissy," Duke said, "I need you and Birdie to ride into town with me. We'll look at the security tape, see if you recognize the woman with the baby in the mini mart. James Waddell, an eight-month old baby boy, was taken off his front porch two days ago. Kidnapping is a serious crime. We have to identify the person at the mini mart. She may lead us to the kidnapper or kidnappers. Midgy will take you to the clinic to see a doctor when we finish."

Midgy smiled at the two women and nodded reassuringly.

"Oh, no!" Sissy sat up straight. "I can't go. I can't leave the house." She'd turned pale as she let her teacup clatter onto its saucer. She grasped the cup with both hands and righted it on the plate.

"Please," Birdie looked at Sissy. "Can we go? Please, Sissy? Say yes. We can ride in a car. Then, we can play paper dolls when we come home. Want to?"

"I'm sorry," Duke said. "I have no choice. Your brown shawl was on the person last seen with the baby. Both of you need to come to my office for questioning."

Duke wasn't sure what role the old women played in the kidnapping but he intended to find out. This was serious, and though the child was safe now, the officer needed to know who had taken him from his home. That person needed to be locked up. They'd caused the Waddell family unimaginable pain and had created work and expense for the community. The havoc it had caused him personally was no big deal. He'd be back on track within a day or so.

Finally, Sissy nodded in agreement, her face drained of all color.

"I can promise we'll take good care of you," the officer said. "Midgy won't leave your side. Isn't that right, Midgy?"

"That's right. I'm here to help you."

Duke caught Sissy giving her younger sister a warning look. It was definitely a keep-quiet gesture. They might not be all there but they were smart, he'd give them that.

"We don't know anything about a baby," Sissy said, unconvincingly. A burden lifted from her shoulders knowing the baby was with his family.

"I don't need no doctor," she added, getting up slowly and holding onto the table. With Birdie on one side and Midgy on the other, Sissy made her way into the bathroom in the hall.

"We'll see when we get to town," Duke said.

Both women returned to the kitchen, smelling of talcum powder and dressed in clean flowered cotton dresses, each carrying a white men's handkerchief.

Duke didn't tell them they were under arrest. They weren't. Not yet, anyway.

"BIRDIE!" SISSY WHISPERED, patting her sister's arm to get her attention.

Duke Cobb pulled the squad car onto the highway.

Sissy moved closer to her sister. "We have to say we never saw that baby, do you understand?"

"I know," Birdie said, quietly. "We never saw that baby with the blue eyes."

Sissy pinched Birdie's arm. "You can't tell them about his eyes."

"Okay!" Birdie moved as far away as she could get from her sister on the back seat. She wouldn't take another pinching from her. Officer Cobb could take her to jail. Pinching wasn't good behavior.

Midgy stared straight ahead, wondering how the two women could possibly be connected to the kidnapping. Neither woman moved fast or was very sharp, but, if they hadn't taken the child, who had, and how did the two women end up with him? She hoped for the best. She just wasn't sure the women could solve this mystery. Even if they knew something, could they convey it clearly? Midgy sighed and leaned back in the seat. It had been a stressful day.

Duke Cobb smiled in the rear view mirror. He was pleased with himself. He was on his way to finding the kidnapper. He felt sure the two old women held the key piece. It wasn't long until he pulled into the parking lot behind the station, unloaded his passengers, and ushered them inside.

He could hear people talking back in the kitchen, volunteers drinking coffee and celebrating the return of the baby. Frances Green, Duke's part-time receptionist, rattled cups and talked the loudest. He could smell fresh coffee. Thankfully the phones were silent after the craziness of the last few days. The 911 dispatcher, a little woman called Tiny, had a corner office off the lobby and kept her door closed for fear someone would overhear an emergency call before she could spread the news around town.

The two old women hovered behind Midgy as Duke lead the way down the hall to his office.

Sissy watched the officer's every move. She feared he would snap handcuffs on them and throw them into a jail cell.

"Look," Duke said, turning to the women, who stopped in their tracks. "Don't be afraid. Nobody's going to hurt you." Their eyes filled with terror as he stepped closer. "I'm a good guy," he grinned, "and I'm in charge here. Okay?" He directed them into his office.

The women nodded as they looked around at the unfamiliar whirring computers. One screen showed a crashing blue ocean. The other featured toasters with wings flying across the screen.

Seeing the Waddell file on his desk reminded Duke he had to update the detective and invite Vada Faith and John down to the station. "Midgy, I need to make some calls."

"Sure. We'll freshen up." She showed the two women to the rest room. "Once we get this situation cleared up," she said, "we'll get out of here. Maybe get a sandwich."

"Oh goody," Birdie clapped. "Can we get ice cream too? I love ice cream. I really do, please, huh?"

Sissy frowned. Midgy smiled and nodded.

In the rest room, she noticed Sissy's color was better. "Are you feeling okay?" She asked, seeing the old woman staring at herself in the mirror.

"Yes, a heart pill under my tongue helped." She'd known someday her elderly aunt's pills that had been left in the cottage medicine cabinet would come in handy. Outdated but they worked.

"I'm taking you to see my own doctor after we finish here. I won't take no for an answer."

Sissy didn't say anything, just straightened her dress and stuck her handkerchief under the belt at her waist. She had no intention of going to see a doctor, with or without Midgy Brown.

When the women returned to Duke's office, he said, "We're waiting for Earl Ray Cobb, the town's attorney, to get here. He can help us figure out what happened two days ago when James Waddell went missing."

"We don't know about any baby!" Birdie blurted, her face turning dark pink, as she plopped down in the chair in front of Duke's desk.

"I'm going to show you the security tape from the mini mart," the officer said. "Let's see if you recognize anybody."

He clicked on the computer, and smiled when the dark-haired clerk came on the screen.

Birdie came into view next, opening the door of the mini mart, holding onto a wiggling James, and a tote bag. She walked to the end of the nearest aisle, placed the baby on the floor by a candy display and handed him a bottle of milk. She walked away quickly, glancing back only once.

"It's me!" Birdie screamed, unable to contain her excitement. "It's me." She clapped her hands. "I'm on television, look Sissy."

After emptying the bottle, the baby leaned against the cardboard display, knocking it to the floor, sending candy flying. The baby crawled down the aisle toward the front of the store.

Birdie laughed. "Look, Sissy. It's Robert. Remember Robert?"

Duke turned the computer off and looked at the two women. "Do you have anything to say?"

Birdie shook her head, still smiling, and Sissy looked away, her face sad.

"Okay," he said, standing to give himself more authority. "I know that's you on the tape, Birdie. I know you know something about the baby, James Waddell. I had hoped you might fill me in on what happened. The Waddell's expect answers from you. You will have to tell the attorney what you know." Duke stared at the women. "Kidnapping is a serious crime. We have to know how you got this baby."

Both women stared back at him. Silent. Birdie couldn't keep the smile off her face.

"Do you know anything about this, Sissy," Midgy asked, gently.

Sissy shook her head without looking up as Birdie continued to smile and nod.

"Our attorney is my cousin." Duke paced around the room and talked to the women. "He's a good guy. Smart, too. He'll get to the bottom of this." He sighed. "That's it then, let's head to the meeting room. It's bigger than my office. I notified the Waddell family. They'll be here shortly."

Midgy followed Duke down the hall with the two women close behind her.

The room they entered was starting to fill with people. News of the meeting had somehow spread, much to the officer's dismay.

CHAPTER 44

SOME OF THE town residents had shown up for the meeting looking as though they'd come from a nap. However, it was past dinnertime. Most wore jeans, a few had on shorts. There were four women in the front row dressed in purple dresses sporting wide-brimmed red hats.

Nobody had to tell Duke Cobb who the women were or where they'd been to eat. The smell of cat fish and hush puppies hung heavy in the air. It was the special every day at Thelma's Diner on Main. Ditzie Duncan, who was old enough to be his mother, winked at him.

"What on earth is going on?" Duke stared at the crowd. "Why are you people here? This is not a public meeting."

"Are you hiding something, Duke Cobb? We have a right to know what's going on. A kidnapping is serious business and involves the whole town." Lenny Rope's voice held contempt. He was at every town meeting and complained about everything from the landfill to roadkill.

"There's nothing to hide, Lenny. This don't have anything to do with you, or any of you for that matter." Duke glanced around the room and straightened the gun at his waist. "How'd you hear about this, anyway?"

"We live here, buddy. We hear things. We wanna make sure you do your job. You work for us, you know. Did you forget that?" Lenny stretched out his long legs in his yellow biker pants. The man was there to stay unless the town suffered an earthquake, which wasn't likely. He had his yellow biker helmet on the chair next to him. He rode around town in the middle of the road on his yellow three-wheeled bike and dared anyone to challenge him. So far, no one had.

Duke was considering giving him a citation to teach him a lesson, a public nuisance citation for annoying people, especially him. By law, he could do it too.

"Crap," Duke said under his breath, seeing more people crowding into the room. It made him nervous. "Why don't you all go home?" He yelled, waving his arms. Nobody paid attention.

When he saw his volunteers in the back of the room slapping each other on the back he knew how the news had spread. Lenny Rope, Junior, one of the volunteers, was as happy as if he'd found the baby himself, laughing and punching everyone.

"Attorney Earl Ray," Duke announced loudly, as his cousin rushed to the front of the room. "This here is Miss Sissy and Miss Birdie Kapp." They were seated at the table in front of the room, facing the audience.

Earl Ray shook hands and took a seat at the end of the table. While he and Duke whispered back and forth, Midgy patted both women on the shoulder. "All this is going to be worked out. I don't know how you got involved but I'm here to help you. Remember, I'm your friend." She glanced at the attorney. "Earl Ray is a special friend of mine."

Duke caught the look that passed between Earl Ray and Midgy and couldn't believe his eyes. How had he missed that connection? Was he so far out of the loop that he hadn't picked up on the attraction between his big-shot attorney cousin and his longtime friend, Midgy? When had that happened and how? He shook his head. He had to kick his own life into gear or he'd end up an old bachelor.

Birdie dabbed at her pink cheeks with the edge of her white handkerchief. She was sniffling loudly when sounds from the back of the room caught her attention.

People were turning to face the lobby but Birdie couldn't see where the loud noises were coming from.

"Ba ba do."

Birdie listened. It sounded like Robert. She half-rose from her seat but couldn't see the back of the room, too many people milling around talking.

"Stop it!" Sissy poked her younger sister's arm with her finger. "Don't look back there again. Not if you want to get out of this mess."

Suddenly, the baby started wailing.

Birdie strained to lean forward, not caring what Sissy said.

There at the back of the room was the blond-haired, blue-eyed baby she loved. He waved his arms in circles and smiled. Birdie waved. She couldn't see him well. Too many people.

A woman with blond shaggy hair held onto Robert. She looked as though she'd swallowed a storm cloud. Birdie sank lower in her chair. The woman was petite, cute, but if she had opened her mouth lightening would surely zip out and head straight toward Birdie, zapping her dead.

When Earl Ray banged his gavel on the table, Birdie jumped.

Sissy was right. They had to get out of this mess. Birdie wanted to go home and play paper dolls. First, she'd like to have ice cream. Vanilla. It was her favorite.

Vada Faith and John stood in the back of the room with the baby. He fidgeted and jabbered. He pulled at Vada Faith's hair and she swatted at his hand. "Stop it James!"

John smiled over at James. He wiped drool from the baby's mouth with his clean handkerchief and reached for him, but James put his head on his mother's shoulder, shaking his head at his father and saying, "No."

"Be right back," John said to Vada Faith and edged toward the front to get a better look at the people seated at the table.

Officer Cobb saw John move forward and directed him to the side of the room where they could talk in private.

"The shorter woman is named Birdie," Duke nodded toward the table. "Midgy identified her by the brown shawl she wore in the mini mart. We saw her on the security tape. Midgy knows Sissy, the taller one. They're sisters. I don't believe they took James from your porch but they haven't uttered one word." Duke's gaze took in the crowded room. "Birdie seems to be mentally challenged. The other is eccentric as heck, plus old, and possibly ill."

"Who do you think took James from the porch if they didn't," John asked, shaking his head in disbelief at the strange old women. "Could that Buck kid have lifted James from his pen?"

"We don't know yet. Earl Ray is hoping they'll open up to him and tell him exactly what happened." Duke glanced around the room. "I wish all these idiots would go home." He sighed. "You and Vada Faith need to move toward the front, so you can hear." He slapped John on the shoulder and turned back toward the table. "You folks move aside," he raised his voice to the crowd, "and let the Waddell family move closer to the front."

Vada Faith's family had arrived by then, followed by John's, and all of them surrounded James, fawning over him. He kicked and smiled but turned shy, refusing to go to anyone except his mother. John's brothers, Bruiser and Bobby Joe, crossed their muscled arms and stared at the two old women in front.

Finally, Vada Faith and John inched closer to the front with James, leaving the others behind to find chairs. Not wanting to be too close to the women, Vada Faith stopped a few rows back, finding two chairs near the aisle. If James cried she could take him out.

"Those two certainly look capable of kidnapping," she whispered to John, once she had a chance to study the two women.

"I don't know, Vay," he said, sitting down beside her. "I was expecting a couple of tough characters, not two worn-out old women who look harmless."

"They look like tough characters to me. Just think about it. They came on our porch and took our son."

"They haven't admitted to anything. The shorter one left James in the mini mart. Midgy identified her on the security tape by the shawl she had on. She knows the other one, Sissy. Duke thinks someone kidnapped James and gave him to the women to keep."

Vada Faith stood. "I'm too nervous to sit." She shifted James to her hip.

"Me too," he said, and stood, rubbing his hands together.

Up front, Duke was wondering how he was supposed to control the crowd. Town meetings were ordinarily attended by only a few residents, never a group this size. It seemed everyone in town was crammed into the room which was built for fifty or so. If the mayor was here, he'd get rid of them. His voice commanded attention. Duke's voice, not so much. He cleared his throat and wished they'd leave.

A line of people were passing by James as if paying their last respects. Most of the women reached out to touch the baby's foot or arm. James kicked and smiled, enjoying the attention. The men nodded at John and moved on. The smell of fresh coffee suddenly turned a few residents back toward the hallway in search of the coffeepot.

Sissy and Birdie kept their heads bowed, fingers working the handkerchiefs they held, ignoring the people who stared at them.

"Donuts out that way," Duke called, pointing to the side door. That caused a few more residents to vacate the meeting room.

"All right," Earl Ray pounded the gavel, "let's have some order. It's unusual to meet without the mayor." The attorney sat up straighter. "I spoke with him a few minutes ago. He asked me to preside over this meeting. I expect cooperation from you. You'll listen and stop talking. If you're questioned, you may speak. If not, keep quiet. Do you understand?"

People nodded. Someone called out, "We're not stupid, Earl Ray."

"Yeah, well, we'll see about that," he retorted, pounding the gavel.

Before the attorney could say another word, the town's only fire truck blasted its siren as it rolled past the building, its red lights reflecting in the windows.

The crowd jumped to their feet.

"Fire!" Lenny Rope yelled, slamming on his yellow helmet. "Let's go."

Men and women streamed out behind him, including the red-hatted women teetering down the aisle on purple high heels, heading for the exit. Duke watched them go with a smile. The women would ride to the fire in Ditzie Duncan's red convertible, top down, sipping Vernor's ginger ale with lemon slices in plastic wine glasses. They showed up that way at every fire, oping to appear worldly when they were nothing but small town girls, aging not so gracefully.

"What luck," Duke muttered, filled with relief. The townspeople loved a fire more than a town meeting. The volunteers and reporters were gone before the siren faded. One fledgling reporter was left in the back leaning against the wall. He'd badgered Duke all day to give him an exclusive on the kidnapping story when the officer wasn't even sure there was a story. The kid moved up to the front row now that a space had opened up.

"John," Bruiser touched his brother's shoulder from behind. "Old man Isaac's barn is on fire. Just got a text. I need to go. Only hay in the building but they can't find the old guy. I'm taking off with Bobby Joe. You okay?"

"Sure." John nodded toward Bruiser. "Be careful."

After the room cleared, Earl Ray wielded the gavel again. John settled into his chair as did Vada Faith.

"I'm taking Miss Birdie Kapp and Miss Sissy Kapp into the conference room for their statements," the attorney said. "Officer Cobb and

Ms. Brown will accompany us. Ms. Brown will act on behalf of these two women. Is that right, Ms. Brown?"

"Yes," Midgy nodded. "I know Sissy through my work at the senior center."

"If the rest of you people want to leave, please do. If you're waiting for information about this case, you may have a long wait. We have to sort this all out." Earl Ray coughed. "Might be easier to watch the news later tonight and get the story. Also, the donuts in the kitchen were donated by Friends of the Library. I understand there are some left and plenty of coffee. There's a cigar box on the table by the donuts for your donation. The money goes toward the new library." He glanced around the room. "Thanks for coming."

"Joy Ruth has to leave, too," Vada Faith whispered to John, "to check in at the shop. She passed me a note. She's worried about the new girl she left in charge. Also, our folks are all going out to get something to eat. Mama says Earl Ray is slow as molasses. She says they'll be back before he comes back in the room."

John nodded.

Earl Ray directed everyone into the conference room next door and closed the door behind him.

CHAPTER 45

DURING THE BREAK, Vada Faith took James to the restroom for a diaper change. As she finished with the baby, he chortled happily and grabbed for the ear rings that dangled from her ears. She hugged him tight and lifted him from the table. The last two days were a nightmare of the lowest lows and the highest highs. Just when she should be feeling relief that the kidnappers may have been found, she felt nothing but defeat. How could those old women have taken James? How could they have set off the chain of events that blew her world apart? Was there some horrible monster-person still loose on the streets?

"What can they be saying in the conference room that we can't hear?" John asked, when she returned and sat down beside him. He stood to stretch his legs and arms. "Cobb should be out on the streets finding the real kidnappers. It was premature to call off the search. Even with the baby safe, Duke has no clue who kidnapped him. Someone had to give James to that old woman. What are we doing here, anyway? Is this another one of his crazy ideas?"

"Aren't you and Duke reconciled? You told him earlier today, he could call on you anytime, for anything. Remember?"

John ignored her. "He's losing time while a real kidnapper goes free. I bet these two old women had nothing to do with taking James. We haven't seen one shred of evidence. Did you see those two limp out of here? They could barely walk. I know they can't run. Whoever took James had to get away fast or a neighbor would have seen what happened."

While Vada Faith played peek-a-boo with James to keep him busy, John crossed his arms and stared straight ahead. What could be taking them so long?

When the conference door opened, Duke lead the group back to the table. After they'd seated themselves, Earl Ray pounded his gavel.

Birdie glanced back at James and smiled.

Sissy elbowed her sister. Birdie frowned and lowered her head.

The baby, in his father's arms, was above the crowd, and he could easily see the table in front of the room. He yelled and waved his arms like a windmill.

Birdie smiled at the baby and gave a little wave when Sissy wasn't looking.

"Do you see that woman smiling at James?" Vada Faith pulled James from his father's arms. She tried to put his head down on her shoulder but James was having none of it. He stretched himself as far as he could to stare at the woman.

"Stop it, James." Vada Faith faced the baby toward the back of the room. He screeched, his face turning red. Exasperated, she turned him to face the front of the room. He waved and squealed. She sat him down, hoping to occupy him with toys from the diaper bag. Finally, he settled on her lap and chewed contentedly on his rubber duck.

"The baby saw me!" Birdie blurted above the crowd and half-stood. "Sissy, did you see him? He knows me."

Sissy put her arm around Birdie's shoulder and pushed her back into her seat. She shushed her as the attorney began to speak.

"We're after the truth here today. The truth of what happened the day James Waddell disappeared from his front porch. Sissy and Birdie have signed a statement and now they are going to tell you what they told us. This will clear up some of the mystery."

The two women pushed themselves down into their seats.

"Who would like to start?" Earl Ray asked.

"I will," Sissy spoke softly, "I'm Sissy Kapp, the oldest. Birdie is my baby sister." She reached over and took Birdie's hand. "My sister's not exactly right."

"I am right," Birdie blurted and grabbed her hand away from Sissy. She smacked her sister on the arm. "I am. You said I am." She turned and smiled at Earl Ray. "You can call me Bird, Mr. Attorney."

"Yes, you are right, Bird." Sissy ignored Birdie's outburst. "However, Birdie must have someone to take care of her. She can't make decisions on her own. She ran away from the home where she lived. She rode a bus back to Shady Creek. They mistreated her, it seems."

"They pinched my cheeks," Birdie chimed in. "They stole my Cinderella watch. They didn't let me watch Let's Make a deal."

"Bird!" James said, with excitement, hearing the woman's voice. He threw his rubber duck on the floor. "Bird!" He tried to stand on Vada Faith's lap.

"Oh, no, John!" Vada Faith hissed and looked over at John. "Good grief. He said Bird." She tried to make him sit on her lap but he wouldn't budge from his standing position.

"I heard." John groaned.

"Bird," James said, louder now. "Bird." His arms stretched toward the front of the room.

"He knows me," Birdie screamed, throwing a kiss toward James and waving. "Did you hear, Sissy? He said Bird. The baby said Bird."

"I heard." Sissy refused to look toward the Waddell family or their son.

"Now, listen," Earl Ray said, "we have to move on and get to the bottom of this. You were saying, Miss Sissy."

"I was saying Birdie took the baby," Sissy spoke so low Vada Faith had to strain to hear her. "She didn't mean any harm. He resembles

Robert, our baby brother, who's deceased. Birdie found the baby on the sidewalk in front of his house. We both swear that is true. She brought him home two days ago. I was too scared to bring him back. Then I got sick. Birdie didn't know how to get him home."

"Was this kidnapping planned? Did Birdie take James intentionally?"

"No! She was searching for my house. She rode past my stop. She thought the Waddell home was our old farm house." Sissy's body shook. "None of this was planned."

"Did you or your sister intend to harm James?"

"Goodness, no. We love every living thing. I wanted to take him home right away. I just couldn't. I'm sick and Bird can't take care of him or herself." She blushed a bright red. "I did threaten Bird I would drop him off somewhere if she didn't take him away. Of course, I wouldn't."

"Birdie," Earl Ray smiled at her, "can you tell us what happened that day when you saw the baby on the sidewalk in front of the house?"

Birdie didn't move a muscle nor did she speak.

Sissy pushed at Birdie, causing her to lurch forward. "Go ahead, Little Bird. Tell them how you got the baby."

"Stop touching me, Sissy!" Birdie clamped her mouth shut and edged her chair away from Sissy. Finally Birdie began, hesitantly, to tell her story. "I rode on the bus a long way through the mountains." She stared off into space as she talked. "I fell asleep. The bus stopped. Everyone got off. I did too. Only I couldn't find Sissy's house. I walked and walked. Then there was the big white house where we used to live with our mama." Birdie grew excited now. "Robert, our baby brother, sat on the sidewalk playing with his bottle. He called me mama." Birdie puffed with pride. "Robert always called me mama. Sissy said that baby there is not Robert." She pointed to James who was again chewing on his rubber duck. "I thought the boy beside Robert was going to put him in his cage. I gathered the baby up and got out of there fast."

"There was a boy on the sidewalk? Did you know him?"

"No, but he had a bird's nest in his hand. I was afraid he'd put Robert in his cage. I ran fast as I could away." She stopped and breathed in deeply. "Are you mad, Earl Ray?"

"I'm not mad," he said. "Did anything else happen? Was anyone else on the street? Why did you stop at that house?"

"It was mama's big house. I could smell her baking."

Sissy frowned at Birdie.

"Sissy says it isn't mama's house. It only smelled like our house. When I saw the baby, I remembered Mama saying we should always take care of our baby brother. He knew me. He did." She frowned. "Sissy got sick with her heart. Mama died with her heart. I don't want Sissy to die. She said she can't go to jail. I took that little baby. Back there. That's him." She pointed in the direction of James who still sat on his mother's lap, now stretching his head to see the woman. "My heart isn't sick. I can go to jail."

Midgy put her arm around Birdie who looked up at Midgy and said. "Do you like paper dolls? Can we play paper dolls? Please?" Midgy nodded and patted Birdie's hand.

"Let me get this straight," Earl Ray said, "one last time, Birdie. Did you pick the baby up off the sidewalk and take him home because you thought he was Robert, your brother?"

Birdie nodded as tears began rolling down her face. She wiped at them with her hands until Sissy took her own handkerchief and dabbed at Birdie's eyes.

Earl Ray frowned. "Is your receptionist here, Duke?"

In the front row, Frances Green raised her hand.

"Would you take Miss Sissy and Miss Birdie to the kitchen? Fix them a cup of tea while I meet with Officer Cobb and Ms. Brown in private."

"Sure," Frances said. She rose and directed the two women out of the room and down the hall.

Officer Cobb and Midgy followed Earl Ray into the conference room and closed the door.

"HAVE DUKE COBB and Earl Ray lost their minds?" Vada Faith didn't care if her voice was above a whisper. "Those two women are criminals, John. Of course they'd like a cup of tea! Why not serve them a hot meal too?" Her face burned. "Well, I could use a cup of tea." She blew her wispy blond bangs off her forehead in exasperation. "They should be in shackles! Hauled out of here in chains! Instead they're being coddled because they're old and decrepit. I'm done with Duke Cobb and this meeting!"

"I don't know what to think, honey." John shook his head and frowned. "After the day we've had I'm dead on my feet, almost too tired to think. You have to admit someone gave James great care while he was gone and he likes Birdie." John put his arm around his wife and son. "Do you think the Buck kid could have taken James out of his play pen for some reason? I don't believe the old woman came onto the porch."

The baby had settled on his mother's shoulder and his eyes were slowly closing.

"It's possible," she said. "Why isn't George here? Duke doesn't know a thing about being a law officer. I'm just thankful James is okay. I can't bear to think about those two women having their hands on him." Vada Faith looked down at her son, trying to calm herself for his sake. She touched his soft blond hair. "Those old women shouldn't have been taking care of him. They stole him. I'm sick over it, John. I don't know if I'll ever recover."

A door slammed behind them. Vada Faith jerked around to see George entering the room with his mother, Carrie.

Carrie nodded solemnly on her way to the front of the room. George followed keeping his head low. He dragged the cage with him, placing it on the table.

Opening the door to the conference room, Duke said, "We've been waiting for you." He shook Carrie's hand and ushered the two into the other room, closing the door firmly, but not before Vada Faith noticed the boy's drawing in Duke's hand.

"Give me the baby, honey," John said. "You get up and walk around. This may take awhile. I know this is tough on you."

Vada Faith slid the baby onto John's lap without waking him and straightened her clothes. She was warm and wrinkled from holding James. She smiled down at her son. He was growing overnight. It seemed he'd grown an inch the two days he was gone. Those old women had robbed her of time with James that she couldn't get back. She'd never forgive them. Never.

"I'll be right back." She patted John's arm.

She hurried out of the room. She wanted to look into the eyes of those batty old women to judge for herself if they were capable of telling the truth. Mostly she wanted to scratch their eyes out of their heads and stomp on them. Another part of her wanted to sit them down and listen to what they had to say about their time with her baby. What did he do for all those hours? Another part of her, a very tiny part, wanted to pray for them.

The kitchen was empty except for Duke's receptionist, Frances, who was washing cups at the sink. "Hey, Vada Faith," she said, turning to greet her. "Want something to drink? Coffee or tea?"

"Where are those crazy old women?" Vada Faith pulled out a chair and plopped down, letting out a long breath she hadn't known she was holding.

"They went back into the conference room. Duke went to his office to get his laptop. He collected them as he passed by. He said something about an old obituary. Those women followed him like little pups. They're a bit off, but not crazy, in my opinion."

"They're more than a bit off, Frances. Did they talk to you about stealing my baby?" She asked, biting her lip and fighting tears.

"Not a word. The one, Birdie, rambled on some about Robert, her baby brother. She kept wanting to play paper dolls. That made her sister steamy. They fussed some. They said nothing incriminating if that's what you're asking."

"George Buck drew a picture of the day James was kidnapped. He was there when the old woman came along. I saw George myself, outside before I went into the house. If the old woman picked up James from the sidewalk then George had to take James out of his play pen. Why would he put the baby on the sidewalk? I can't figure it out."

"I'm no mind reader, honey. If I was, I'd hang out a sign." She laughed. "Then I wouldn't have to work with Cobb. You know kids don't think things through, honey. Birdie Kapp is like a little kid. She doesn't think things through either. That old woman doesn't know right from wrong, or up from down." She chuckled and winked at Vada Faith. "She's living in her own world."

"She can live in her own world in jail." Vada Faith got up and paced around the kitchen, noting the countertop wasn't all that clean. "They can throw away the key to that cell too. I can't wait. I hope she enjoyed James because she won't ever get her hands on him again."

"Earl Ray will do what's right. You can trust him. I've seen him represent people in court a few times." Frances finished her cup of coffee and put the cup in the sink. "He might not seem like the brightest rock in the pile but he knows the law. He got my sister a divorce from that druggie Inky Rollins. Tattoos all over that boy. He got her a tidy sum of money too. Inky thought his drug money was hidden from the world. He should have taken it somewhere other than his mama's shack in the mountains. My sis bought herself a fancy house in that subdivision of Crystal Springs and a cute little cottage in Myrtle Beach. I'm going down to visit next month."

Frances smiled and looked at the wall clock. "I better get back to the front desk. Cobb will have a conniption if I'm back here enjoying myself." She waved with her little finger as she disappeared into the hallway.

Vada Faith found John sleeping soundly in the folding chair, his head resting on his chin, a sleeping James locked in his arms. She sat down next to him. James was making sucking noises. She noticed that her mother and Alfred were seated behind her along with her mother-in-law, Louise. She put her finger to her lips to indicate that James was asleep. Otherwise they'd be wanting him.

As she leaned back, her chair squeaked loudly. John opened his eyes and stretched his legs in front of him.

The door of the conference room opened suddenly and Earl Ray breezed in with the others following him like a line of ducks. Carrie took a seat beside Earl Ray with George on the other side of her.

"Anyone not involved in this case is dismissed." He looked around the room at the few remaining people. "That would be right now." He stood and crossed his arms, waiting.

The few men left on the back row sauntered out the door.

Sitting in front, the young reporter raised his hand.

"What?" Earl Ray asked as he sat down. "Wasn't I clear enough?"

"Yeah, it was clear. Come on, Earl Ray. Let me stay? Please? My story won't go in the paper until tomorrow. I swear I won't leak anything. How about it? You can read every word of my story before it's printed. I'll fax it to you by midnight. What do you say? Give me a break, will you?"

Earl Ray sighed and gave the young man a do-what-you-want dismissal with his hand.

"I'm not leaving," Helena Warfield, called from behind her daughter. "I want to hear what happened to my grandson. I have grandmother rights."

"I'm not leaving either," Louse spoke from Helena's side. "He's my grandson too."

"Great," the attorney said, "let's move on. This meeting has already taken more time than I anticipated. We've finally pieced together what happened two days ago. George," he looked at the boy, "will you tell us what happened when you went to visit James. Was his mother on the porch?"

"No," George said quietly shaking his head. "She went inside."

Helena called out again, "FYI, Earl Ray, my boyfriend Albert isn't leaving either."

The attorney turned to stare at Helena.

Vada Faith looked back to see her mother flashing her diamond ring for Earl Ray to see. "We're engaged. Albert will soon be the baby's grandfather."

"If you folks want to spend the night here," Earl Ray said, angrily, "go right on talking." He leafed through the papers on the table in front of him, finally pulling out George's drawing.

"Now, I'll continue." He scowled at Helena. "George drew us a picture of the sidewalk." The attorney stood and held the drawing up for everyone to see. "George wasn't able to speak that day to explain what happened. Thus the picture. He's regaining his speech slowly. Is that right, Mrs. Buck?"

"Yes," Carrie said, "he's speaking better every day. He's less stressed about it."

"Thank you." Earl Ray held a pointer toward the drawing. "Here, George drew a baby on the sidewalk, baby James with blond hair." He walked over to show the picture to Vada Faith and John, then to the reporter.

As he went back to the table he said, "You probably noticed the big tree near the sidewalk and a bird's nest in the corner. Of course, George is pictured with his cage on the sidewalk. It's the cage he uses to transport injured birds and small animals back to his home where he and his mother nurse them back to health. Then they're released. Is that right?"

"Yes, sir," the boy said, and his mother nodded.

"Now," Earl Ray pointed to the picture he held up, "here in the middle of the picture is an adult wearing a brown garment with brown fringe. Am I to understand, Sissy, that you made this brown garment for Birdie?"

"Yes, I made Birdie's brown shawl."

"All right." Earl Ray took his seat and dropped the drawing onto the table.

"Now, George, tell us what you saw when you went onto Vada Faith's porch."

The boy started in a low voice. "Baby James was in his cage. He plays there with his toys, but when he sees me he wants out. He reaches for me and wants to be picked up. That day he kept reaching. I didn't mean to take him out of his cage." He stopped for a minute to take a deep breath and his voice became stronger. "I always lift James high in the air but I put him right back. He likes it. That day when I lifted James, he held onto my shirt with his little fist and he wouldn't let go. No matter how hard I tried, I couldn't pry his hand from my shirt. I got scared I might drop him. I picked him up to get a better hold on him. Then I saw a bird fall out of the big tree in the yard. A nest tumbled down behind the bird."

"All right." Earl Ray cleared his throat. "What did you do then?"

"I ran off the porch with James in my arms. He was holding his bottle with one hand and my shirt with the other. I wanted to see if the bird was injured and if there were eggs in the nest. There weren't any. I put James down in the grass to investigate the bird's injured leg."

"What happened next?" Earl Ray ran his finger around his shirt collar and smiled at Midgy who blushed.

"James crawled quickly to the sidewalk. He plopped down and grinned back at me."

"Did you pick James up again or did he crawl anymore?"

"No. I didn't pick him up and he didn't crawl anymore." George looked at his mother. "The woman in the brown sweater hurried to him. She wore big black shoes. She picked up James, looked at me, and ran away with him."

"Can you point to that woman?"

The boy pointed to Birdie.

Birdie glared at the boy and sniffed into her handkerchief.

"Anything else?"

"No, except I put the nest in my cage with the bird and went to show my mother his injury."

"Do you believe that was the right thing to do to leave the yard after you saw James being taken away by a stranger?"

"No." George swallowed hard. "My mother said it wasn't."

"What should you have done?"

"Knocked on the door to show his mother James was gone."

"That's right. You will do the right thing if that ever happens again."

George nodded. "Yes, sir." His mother reached over and took the boy's hand.

"Yes," Earl Ray said, when John raised his hand.

"Shouldn't George know the difference between a play pen and a cage? Does he think we would put James in a cage?"

"I'll answer that, John," Carrie Buck said. "George didn't know the correct term for play pen. That's my fault for keeping him too close to my side and to home. I explained that the purpose of a play pen was to keep a baby safe, not to cage him in. We decided, George's father and I, after this incident George needs to have more social interactions with kids his age and with other people." Carrie looked as though she would cry. "He's enrolled in a private school starting next semester. He's fully recovered from the lightening strike with no permanent damage. We're thankful." Carrie looked at George. He smiled up at her. It was the first time John had seen the child smile. "George is excited about going to school and hopes he can still visit James."

John nodded. That was fine with him. He looked at Vada Faith and she nodded at the boy and his mother. Vada Faith wasn't sure how that would work but she'd try to be civil to the boy.

Earl Ray turned to Officer Cobb. "You had something to show Vada Faith and her family."

The officer picked up his computer and walked back to the couple. As they stood James came wide awake and yawned. He smiled at his grandmothers, Helena and Louise, who'd come to stand beside them. "I managed to pull up the obituary for Sissy and Birdie's brother, Robert Kapp," Duke said, "he was almost two when he died in the house fire. There's an obituary for their mother who died in the same fire. Check out the photo of the baby."

Chills ran down Vada Faith's arms. The child on the screen could pass for James or be his identical twin. Though the photo was grainy and black and white, the child had the same beautiful eyes as James, the same long eyelashes and hair so light and soft it could belong to James.

Without meaning to, Vada Faith started to cry. She took James from John's arms and sat down. She pulled a cloth from his diaper bag and wiped her eyes. Her mother and John's mother had gone back to their seats quietly after reading the obituary. Nobody had said a word.

Vada Faith held onto James with all her strength. The old women had lost their baby brother to a terrible death. She still held her baby in her arms.

The officer seated himself back at the table. A hush fell over the room for the first time since the meeting started.

Birdie and Sissy wiped fresh tears as the officer closed his computer and they could no longer see the photo of their baby brother.

CHAPTER 47

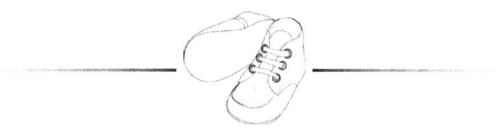

"Wow," JOHN SAID, sitting down beside his wife after Duke took his computer away. "That kid in the obituary looked so much like James, it's scary. It gave me chills. That old photo could be of James. I can see why the old woman thought James was her brother." He pulled Vada Faith into his arms and buried his head on her shoulder to hide his tears. James sat on his mother's lap patting her arm. "Thank God, we have him back."

She hugged him as he wiped tears with the back of his hand.

"All right," Earl Ray said pounding the gavel heartily. "I've reached my decision, after consulting with Officer Cobb and Ms. Brown. We have agreed, that is, Ms. Brown has agreed to petition the court to become the legal guardian of Birdie and Sissy Kapp. The women have agreed."

Vada Faith's face went white. "Midgy? Their guardian? I can't believe it, John. She's such a good friend. Why would she do that?"

"Because that's Midgy. She's a caregiver. Always has been. It's her calling."

"I know, but why those two? They're the ones who took James from us!"

"No, honey, they aren't. Birdie is, and she didn't do it on purpose. You saw the picture in that obituary. In her mind, James was her baby brother and she wanted to take care of him. Look, she's mentally

239

challenged, Vada Faith. Midgy knows Sissy and cares about her well-being. We don't have to understand. Someday you might do that for someone."

"No way. Not someone who stole a baby," she hissed, patting James firmly on his butt. The baby frowned at her. She blew out a long breath. "I can't believe you'd agree. This is craziness. I don't know anyone that unhinged!"

"Sure you do. Your mama. Remember Helena?" John grinned at her. "She's somewhat unhinged."

She punched him on his muscled arm. "Stop! My mama is not unhinged and you know it. Not really."

"How many times has she been engaged to poor old Albert? Five at least. He keeps giving her more jewelry hoping she'll set a date. When they disagree over the television remote, she breaks up with him. Poor old guy. He gives her a week or two to cool off and they're back together."

"That doesn't make her unhinged." She punched him again but this time not as hard. She smiled. "She's fickle, that's all."

"Nah," he said, "she's unhinged." He grinned and shushed her as the attorney started speaking. "But I like her anyway," he whispered.

"I find these two women innocent of kidnapping James Waddell," Earl Ray said. "They're guilty of wrong doing, yes, but they've committed no crime. They've agreed to move to Shadybrook Care Center. They'll spend tonight there. After they're settled in, they'll undergo mental and physical exams. I've assured Miss Birdie she'll have plenty of friends. Some might even play paper dolls with her." Earl Ray smiled across the table at the two women.

Birdie clapped loudly until Sissy took both her hands and held them tightly.

Earl Ray continued, "Miss Birdie will have her own television provided by myself and Ms. Brown."

"I want to clap, Sissy." Birdie cried, trying to free her hands.

"No!" Sissy shook her head.

"Mr. Earl Ray, can I watch Let's Make a Deal?" A red-faced Birdie inquired.

"Every day," he said. "Okay, now, Vada Faith and John, Sissy has written a letter to you. I don't believe she's able to read it. Therefore, I will." He unfolded the note and started to read.

"Mr. and Mrs. Waddell, we're sorry about Birdie's misguided actions the day she took James thinking he was our baby brother, Robert. She meant no harm. She thought she was protecting our baby by bringing him home. She wants you to know how much we loved Robert. He was a beautiful boy. He looked like your boy, James. I'm to blame for not returning your baby. It was my responsibility to look after my sister and I failed." Sissy sniffed at the attorney's words. *"I hope you will accept my apology and Birdie's. Please forgive us. Sincerely, Sissy and Birdie Kapp."*

"Well," the attorney said, folding the letter and holding it toward John, "this is yours." John went to the table and retrieved the letter.

James squealed and in his excitement thumped Vada Faith in the head with his rubber duck. "Bird," he said, waving his arms, "Bird."

When James thumped her head a second time Vada Faith took the toy from his hand and pushed him toward John. James smiled as he landed on his father's lap.

"All right," Earl Ray looked at them. "Do either of you want to speak?"

John stood with James. "Yes," he looked at the sadness on his wife's face. "Will we forgive these women? Maybe, someday." He hesitated and held onto his son. "Will we forget? Doubtful. What happened to us should never happen to anyone. When a baby or child disappears no matter what the reason, a parent is left with hellish thoughts and nightmares every second until he's back in their arms. We visualized all sorts of awful scenarios. Do we hate these women? No, it's not our place to hate them or to judge them. Somehow we'll move on with our lives. Right now we just simply don't know how."

John sat down and James protested by letting out a loud howl. John handed him a teething ring from the diaper bag and he latched onto it and chewed furiously.

"Anyone else?"

"One other thing," John said, staying seated as the baby happily chewed on his toy. "What about George? I don't expect the boy to be punished but shouldn't he have to do something to show regret for taking James from his play pen that day and putting him down in the yard? That was a careless act."

"Yes," Officer Cobb said. "We have settled with George. He will work for two weeks after school at the police station. Frances will teach him to file paperwork. He'll shelve our stack of law books. He's volunteered to clean the squad car. That's a big job. I believe that's fair. What do you think, John?"

"That's fair," John said.

Vada Faith looked unconvinced.

She whispered something to her husband.

"My wife and I want to thank everyone," John said. "Officer Cobb, and Earl Ray and Midgy. You gave up your time to help sort out this mess. We appreciate the support of our families, the churches, the firefighters and the community."

"Let's finish up then," the attorney said. "Sissy and Birdie will move to the care center tomorrow. As you know this isn't a formal hearing. However, I'd like to end it with everyone in favor of the findings and in favor of ending this meeting, to please say aye. Those who are opposed to ending the meeting and opposed to our findings, please say nay, and to all of those thinking of saying nay, meet me outside in the parking lot." He ended with a goofy grin aimed at Midgy, who smiled like a school girl until her face turned pink.

A resounding, "Aye," could be heard from everyone in the meeting room except Vada Faith and John. They were trying to contain James. He stood on his father's lap, jabbering and drooling, flapping his arms as if he might fly to the front of the room.

Vada Faith let out a weary sigh as she turned to pack the diaper bag. There'd been no restitution and there was no one to blame.

Everyone started talking at once.

John stood and handed James to Vada Faith.

"How's my baby boy?" She stepped past John to stand closer to the aisle. She hoped to have a word with Midgy.

"Ba ba do," he said, waving the bottle of milk she'd handed him.

Realizing he wasn't hungry, she took the bottle before he threw it and handed him a pacifier. He stuck it in his mouth and sucked happily, running one hand through her hair as he drooled onto her shirt. He'd usually have nothing to do with the pacifier.

"Every bone in my body aches," John said.

Vada Faith yawned. They were drained. They'd faced the trauma of James being gone, the elation of getting him back, the worry over his health, topped with the press conference, and ending with this emotional meeting. It was all too much. All she wanted was to take her family home and close the door on the world.

As people in front started down the aisle, Vada Faith nudged John who was still sitting down. "I can't get up, Vay. My leg's asleep." He stretched his leg out in front of him and worked his ankle in circles.

"Crazy turn of events, huh?" Duke Cobb said, walking up to them and tweaking James on the shoulder. "Who would have thought it would end this way?" He looked at his watch. "I've got to finish a report before I go home." He patted James on the back. "Gotta run, see you all later."

Thankfully, their families had already left. Vada Faith didn't want to discuss the outcome of the meeting with them. They were unhappy but she couldn't change anything.

Earl Ray rushed toward them with his briefcase in tow. "Sorry, folks, I'm late for a meeting."

Midgy followed Earl Ray at a much slower pace. The two old women dallied along behind her.

Vada Faith tried to shield James from their view. She pushed his head down on her shoulder.

"I'll call you tonight," Midgy said, barely glancing at Vada Faith.

"Sure," Vada Faith frowned. What could Midgy say? She'd made her choice. It was her or them. Obviously, she'd chosen the old women over her.

Birdie and Sissy kept their heads down. Birdie stopped when she came to Vada Faith and James.

James lifted himself from his mother's shoulder and flung himself at Birdie. She smiled sheepishly at him.

Vada Faith hung on to the baby and tried to reign him in.

"Bird," he called, and waved his arms. "Bird."

In a split second he'd lunged out of his mother's arms and into Birdie's. "James!" Vada Faith screamed, watching with horror as he left her arms.

The old woman grabbed him just before he hit the floor.

"No, James!" John jumped from his seat but he was too late.

"Oh, baby boy," Birdie said, scooping him into her arms, "you gonna hurt yourself. Now don't do that again. Look at those blue eyes, Sissy. Did you ever see such eyes?"

"Not since Robert," Sissy said, "he had beautiful eyes."

"Bird," James said laying his head on Birdie's ample shoulder and resisting his mother's efforts to pull him away.

Sissy, who'd moved on, turned back, and pulled Birdie by the arm. "We have to go, Bird. Give him back."

Vada Faith and John stared at James. He sighed contentedly on the old woman's shoulder.

"Well, buddy, here's your family." Birdie kissed James on the cheek and held him toward his father. She ignored Vada Faith, whose frown scared the old woman. "I love you, baby boy." She touched his head and glanced at Sissy. "I know, sister, he's not Robert. He's James."

James went into his father's arms willingly. He waved when Birdie said, "Bye, James." He squealed and kicked his legs happily as they departed.

Vada Faith stared after the women until they were out of sight. She never wanted to see those two again. Ever.

CHAPTER 48

AFTER THE MEETING, news of what had happened to baby James spread through town quickly. People were relieved. They said it wasn't a kidnapping but a case of mistaken identity.

If it wasn't a kidnapping, Vada Faith wondered, why was her family so shattered? Mistaken identity, indeed!

The couple tried to return to normal. They resumed work part-time. Vada Faith made dinner and the family ate together every evening. They spent time with the girls and laughed at the antics of James. He'd devised a new game, throwing his plush football from his high chair and hitting the nearby wall.

His football game was fine until the day he threw a hard plastic truck instead, leaving a small dent in the wall.

"No!" John said, pointing his finger at his son. "No!"

"No," James repeated, laughing, and pointing his finger at John. "No!"

"James, throwing the truck is a no." John tossed the soft football at the wall. His sister handed the ball back to James.

"See," John said, holding up the plastic truck, "this is no, no!"

He gave James the soft football. The baby frowned and reached for the plastic truck. John said a stern, "No."

James whined and pushed against the straps that held him in his chair. His face grew red. When he didn't attract any attention he settled into throwing the soft football for his sister to retrieve.

The night after the town meeting, Vada Faith got a call from Midgy. Her friend wasn't able to adequately explain her feelings for the two old women or why she chose to be their guardian. Her apology hung in the air. Why apologize? Midgy intended to take care of the two women who had kept James away from his family and turned their world upside down. Vada Faith didn't get it.

John tried to convince her that the best decision was made under the circumstances. Yet it brought no comfort.

They gave thanks every day that James was home, every morning, every meal, every evening.

One night late, Vada Faith and John collapsed on their bed.

"Finally," he said, "the three children are asleep and it's just us." He hugged her against him.

"I'm so happy." She yawned.

"Can we talk, if you're not too tired?" He motioned to a package on her dresser. "That's for you." He hesitated, looked embarrassed, and then continued, "There's something I want to say first."

"Should I be nervous?" She smiled and sat up as he stood to hand her the package.

"Nope." He smiled. "All is good."

He opened the dresser drawer and pulled out the tiny baby shoes she'd bought for the surrogate baby, the baby she'd miscarried. He sat down beside her holding the lacy white shoes in his hands, rubbing the soft satin toes.

"When you lost that baby," John began, "I wasn't there for you in the way I should have been. I was ticked off." He petted the shoes like he might pet a puppy. "I didn't get it, why you felt so hurt. The baby wasn't even ours. That's what I thought." He cleared his throat. "I forgot one thing, honey. The baby was yours. The minute James went missing, I got it. I realized the hurt you must have felt when you lost that child. I had no idea, Vay. My pride was hurt. I didn't understand what you were going through. I know now that baby truly was yours. You had every right to feel what you were feeling and to grieve when you lost the baby. I'm so sorry. Can you forgive me for being a jerk?"

"I already have," she said, and pulled him close. She didn't tell him she'd spent two years praying for this moment. They both shed a few tears and then she asked, "Can I unwrap the package?" She had no idea what was under the wrapping.

"Here, let me help." He pulled the string from the roughly wrapped package and the paper fell away.

"What's this?" She held up an exquisitely carved wooden box with engraving on top.

"This is for the baby's shoes, the baby you didn't get to hold." He swallowed a lump in his throat. "I just finished it today. I started on it while James was gone."

"That's why you were in your shop so much." She wiped her tears and looked at the engraving. "John," she said, "it's engraved Baby Waddell."

"That's right. That child was mine too. You know why? Because it was yours. It took me awhile to figure that out."

"Oh John," she said, opening the lid to reveal a blue velvet lining. "It's perfect." She placed the little shoes inside. Closing the lid she placed the box on the dresser and went into his arms. "I love you, John Waddell."

"I love you too, Mrs. Waddell." He kissed her on the lips.

CHAPTER 49

Four months later, Vada Faith mailed invitations for the baby's first birthday party. She couldn't believe her little guy would be one year old in two weeks, on Valentine's Day.

Christmas had brought the little boy so many gifts John had banned gifts for his first birthday. Their families, the churches, and the townspeople had given James enough toys and clothes to last him through his entire childhood. Not to mention the toys her father, Delbert, brought the children from Alaska. Each loved their Eskimo dolls best. She'd put aside a few toys for the baby's birthday and she'd donated the duplicates.

Instead of gifts for the party, she requested canned goods be brought for the local food pantry. She had to reiterate to her mother that the gift ban meant her too. John finally relented and agreed to let Helena buy spring outfits for the three children. He gave strict orders they had to be saved until spring.

A few days before the party, Vada Faith received a package in the mail. Ripping off the wrapping she found a shoe box full of tissue paper. Inside the layers of paper she found a little boy's brown knitted cap that tied under the chin. It wasn't the best knitting she'd ever seen, but it was cute. She handed the cap to James who was clinging to her leg trying to walk. Immediately, he fell to the floor and pulled the cap onto his head like a toboggan. She read the note. Then she looked at her son. "James, give mommy the hat. Thank you," she said sweetly, which sometimes worked. She reached for the cap but James crawled away. "No, no, James, you can't keep it." She moved to grab the cap but he grasped it tightly and refused to let go. His face went from red to purple. "Stop it, James," she said, "stop it now." He hung on to the cap for dear life.

When she let go, he turned and crawled away with the hat barely sitting on top of his head. He plopped down in a corner of the kitchen where he thought he was out of reach.

She ignored him and read the note again, this time aloud. *"Dear James, we hope this hat will keep you warm this winter. It's to remind you of us. It's made from the same yarn as Birdie's shawl that you liked so much. We hope you have good memories of us like we do of you, dear little boy. It's an early present. Happy Birthday. Love, Sissy and Birdie."* It was Midgy's handwriting.

Vada Faith tried to grab the cap from James again. It was going straight into a donation bag when she got her hands on it.

James screeched, "No! No! No!" He held onto the cap with both hands. His face screwed up and he started crying, big tears rolled down his cheeks.

"Oh, stop it right now. You can't keep the hat. It's from that old woman named Bird or Birdie. Silly name anyway."

"Bird." James smiled and sucked on his two middle fingers, a few stray tears rolled down his cheeks, the cap now perched on his head lopsided.

She rushed to grab the hat but he was too fast. He grasped it tightly and screamed, "No, Mama! No!"

She walked away from him and shoved the box and papers into the kitchen bin. She left the note on the table for John to read. She covered her smile. Every day James responded with more words. Not always cute ones but still, they were words.

Accepting the cap would be accepting the old woman who had taken James. She couldn't do that. That was asking too much. She didn't want James connected to her in any way.

John would be home from work soon. He'd help her figure out what to do about the cap. Unlike her, he'd gone back to work full-time. She was happy going in every other day. The girl they hired was working out well. Helena and Louise enjoyed sharing James when she went to the salon. Louise had never kept James before but couldn't seem to get enough of him. He was a delight to be around. Always laughing and making new discoveries, although he did have his moments, like now with the hat. He stared at her from the hallway where he'd crawled, out of her immediate reach, the hat still on his head. She couldn't help it. She smiled at him.

Also in the mail was a catalog of gated communities. At the time she'd ordered it, she thought it was the only way to keep her children safe. Now she knew living behind bars wouldn't work. She had no more control in a gated community than on her own street. She couldn't dictate who lived there anymore than she could here in Shady Creek. At least she knew her neighbors here, many of them all her life. There would be no moving from the old Victorian house. Her family was as safe here as anywhere in the country. Maybe more so.

The phone rang when Vada Faith was giving James lunch. He was engrossed in finger painting spaghetti sauce on his tray. For her benefit, he dabbed it on his face and into his blond hair, his blue eyes filled with mischief as he watched her reaction.

"No, no," he said, looking at her and pointing his finger. "No," he repeated, putting a noodle into his mouth.

"Hello," Vada Faith said, grabbing the phone.

"Hey." It was Midgy. "Thanks for the party invitation. I'd love to help celebrate that little guy's birthday."

"Great!" Relief sounded in Vada Faith's voice. She was happy to hear her friend's voice.

"How are you these days, Vay?" Midgy used her high school nickname.

"I'm good." Vada Faith took in a deep breath. It felt good to talk to her old friend. "You?"

"Okay." Midgy paused and then said, "I was wondering if you'd do me a favor?"

"Sure. What?"

"Would you bring James to the senior center for a visit tomorrow afternoon? Most people who come here don't have family. They miss seeing children. I've told them how adorable James is. He's a bit of a celebrity since I brought in the newspaper clipping with his picture. We'd be thrilled if you could bring him in. It would be a treat."

"Let me ask James." Vada Faith held the phone close to the baby. "Midgy has invited us to come visit her and her friends tomorrow. What do you think, James?"

"Ba ba ba," he said, offering the phone a smear of spaghetti. Instead a noodle fell to the floor. James pointed down at the spaghetti and said, "Lalala!"

"I believe that was a yes, Midgy." Vada Faith laughed and moved the phone out of his reach. "How's tomorrow after lunch, say one?"

Vada Faith hummed all through the baby's bath. She put him down to play and later she thanked God for Midgy's call. She hoped it was the first step to mending their relationship.

At the senior center the next day, James was a hit. The women put their chairs in a circle and passed him around. They hugged him and tickled him under the chin. He babbled and pulled on their beads and ear rings. Midgy had bought him a fuzzy dog which he loved. He chewed on its ear while Midgy gushed over his new red football jersey and jeans. The number one was printed on the front of his shirt, with Waddell printed on the back like a real football player.

Even the secretary came out of her office to admire the baby then carried him off to meet other staff members. By then, the women were heading for Bingo leaving Vada Faith and Midgy alone.

The two collapsed on a sofa in the sitting area.

"I've wanted to talk to you, Vay," Midgy said. "I wasn't sure how to start the conversation."

"I didn't either. I've missed you, Midgy. This is the longest we've gone without being together."

"I know. I've missed you at the beauty shop. Look at this mess." She shook her curls. "Joy Ruth isn't you, honey, I'm sorry." She ran her fingers through the tangle of red hair that had escaped from the clip at the back of her head.

Vada Faith chuckled. "I can see. I bet your hair missed me more than you did."

"Could be," Midgy said, and laughed. "I want to explain why I decided to be a guardian for Sissy and Birdie. It's taken me some time to be able to talk about this. Believe me when I say it's helped me more than them, I promise."

Vada Faith settled in to listen. "Okay."

"Earl Ray knows this and of course my mother. Volunteering is my life, even more so the last year."

"I know. I'm happy for you."

"I don't want to belabor what I have to say." Midgy smiled and looked out the front window. "I can't have children, Vada Faith. Ever."

Shocked, Vada Faith reached out and took her hand. "I'm sorry."

"Don't be. Not at all. I'm okay with it." Midgy shook her head. "I've come to terms with it. I have a tube abnormality. I'm all right otherwise. I've spend time thinking about it. I'm fine with it. I have other things I want to pursue. I'm unhappy with the way senior issues are being addressed or I should say, not being addressed at the state level. I believe I can make a difference. I've decided to run for State Representative. Earl Ray supports my decision. He'll help me and he has influence where it matters. I'm really happy. I hope you'll be happy for me, too."

"Of course. Why didn't you tell me about Earl Ray? That's great news, Midgy. I thought we were good friends. Has our friendship been replaced with these other people in your life?"

"No. I've had issues to deal with regarding Earl Ray. I've been coming to grips with our relationship. I love him but he's older by twelve years. My mom is having fits. We kept it quiet to give her time to accept it. Well, she hasn't and won't. I'm too old to keep secrets anymore. My mom doesn't have to approve of my guy, and that's that. I'm relieved the news is out. We're getting engaged soon. I love him so much, Vay. I didn't think I'd ever love someone this much and have the love returned. He's as interested in the well-being of seniors as I am. I love that about him."

"I'm so happy for you." She hugged Midgy. "Congratulations! I mean it."

Vada Faith's thoughts were interrupted by the baby's jabbering nearby. "I can't stay much longer. James will be needing a nap."

CHAPTER 50

As the secretary brought James over and handed him to his mother, the senior bus pulled up to the glass doors. An elderly group streamed into the lobby.

Birdie Kapp walked in, dragging her brown shawl behind her. She held the hand of a women in an orange sweat shirt. Shadybrook Nursing Center was lettered in black across the woman's front. Birdie smiled when she saw Midgy.

"Bird!" James squealed. Birdie noticed Vada Faith and lowered her head.

"Birdie," Midgy called and went to take Birdie's hand. "Birdie, this is Vada Faith." Birdie nodded and put out her hand as the women drew near. "Vada Faith, this is Birdie. I don't think you have formally met."

Vada Faith dreaded the old woman's touch but she held out her hand. James leaned in and grabbed the old woman's hand first. Birdie shook his hand and giggled.

"Hello, baby boy," she said, touching James on his cheek.

"No, Mama. No, Bird." James looked up at his mother and stuck his fingers in his mouth and grinned.

"Birdie, come join us." Midgy pointed to a chair across from them.

Uncomfortable, Vada Faith shifted her weight on the sofa. Why would Midgy invite the woman to join them? Seeing her was enough. Inviting her to sit was going too far.

She sighed and hoped the woman went away soon. At least a glass table was between them.

"You girls go on to the game room," Midgy called to the women waiting by the water cooler for their friend. "Birdie will be there shortly." The women went on down the hall. The aide from the nursing center leaned against the wall and opened a paperback, apparently waiting on Birdie.

"Wanda's kind, isn't she Birdie." Midgy waved and the woman nodded. Birdie smiled and waved her arms in the air. "I love Wanda."

Vada Faith thought of what her pastor had said during church on Sunday. *Do unto others as you want them to do unto you.* Later he said, *judge not lest you be judged.* Pastor Pinwheel looked straight at her as he spoke those words. He didn't have to make it so obvious that he was speaking to her. Had he heard how mean she was and how unforgiving? She'd left church early to get away from his words.

Now, looking at Birdie, she made a vow to rein in her mean spirit. Besides, the old woman looked as though she'd had a rough day.

"Would it be possible for Birdie to hold the baby, Vada Faith?"

Vada Faith scowled, unintentionally.

"Only if you approve, of course," Midgy hastened to add. "Birdie knows she's caused you heartache. Isn't that right, Birdie?" The old woman nodded. "I'm going to get us a cup of tea." With that Midgy left the two alone.

Birdie made noises in her throat and smoothed down her dress, keeping her eyes on the floor.

Vada Faith brushed off the legs of the baby's pants. What was Midgy going to ask next? To let the old woman move in with her? It was all too much. She held onto James as if he might escape her arms.

The baby struggled to break free. He didn't like confinement. His face was turning red. She pulled his rubber duck from the diaper bag. He sent it sailing across the floor. "Baba, duck," he screamed, "no, baba, duck!"

"We do not throw our toys!" She bent to get the toy, clinging onto James. "He said duck," she said, amazed. His vocabulary was growing in spite of the disruption he'd had in his life.

"Yes," Birdie said, clapping, "duck." James smiled at Birdie and clapped. Birdie clapped.

"Enough with the clapping." The moment the words were out, Vada Faith was sorry. She sounded mean and vindictive. So much for her good intentions.

Birdie looked ready to burst into tears.

Vada Faith prayed Birdie would get hold of herself. She'd cried copious tears during the meeting with Earl Ray. It hadn't bothered Vada Faith then but now it made her nervous.

"Bird," James said and clapped. "Bird, Bird," he repeated.

Birdie smiled and clapped back.

James clapped.

Birdie clapped. They stopped clapping and smiled at each other.

James tried to shimmy off his mother's lap but she held onto his little body and refused to loosen her grip

Birdie held out her wrinkled hands to James.

James lunged toward Birdie, causing his mother to hit her hand on the wooden arm of the chair trying to hold onto him. "Ouch," she said, loosening her grip on him. She was tired of wrestling. She put her son on the floor. He could make his own decision. He was strong-willed, just like his father. She frowned at him and rubbed her hand.

He crawled straight to Birdie, grinning from ear to ear. She picked him up and crooned to him. He buried his head in her shoulder. "Bird," he said. She sang quietly, "Lullaby and goodnight in the sky stars are bright."

"Well." Vada looked over at Birdie holding her son. What could she say? The two didn't know she was in the room or care. "Guess I'm on my own here," she muttered.

She watched James watching Birdie as she sang to him, the words to the song jumbled now.

Vada Faith knew a decision had to be made. She could either carry her anger to her grave and let it continue to bore a hole in the lining of her stomach or she could choose to forgive the old bird, as Grandma Belle referred to old people. Unfortunately, she was already on a prescription to heal a small ulcer and right now the spot in her stomach burned like fire. What was she going to do?

The answer bounced into her head. Forgive her. Isn't that what the Bible said to do? Wasn't forgiveness next to Godliness? She wasn't sure that's what the Bible said but it was something like that. She had some brushing up to do on her Bible verses, especially if she was going to quote them. "Lord," she prayed silently while Birdie rocked James, "give me some help here. I'm depending on you and not myself to get me through this situation."

"Here we go, girls. Tea time," Midgy interrupted, putting a tray on the table between them and leaning toward Birdie. James yawned. "You're sleepy little one." Midgy patted his arm.

The baby lifted his head and stared at Midgy with his big blue eyes. He yawned and put his head back down.

Vada Faith saw that James was utterly at ease. She had to admit she wasn't as uncomfortable as she thought she'd be with the woman holding him. Her anger was beginning to fade.

For the first time in ages, she enjoyed the cup of tea. Honey and cream made it the best she'd had. "Good tea," she remarked to Midgy.

"Birdie and Sissy's recipe," she said. "It's got Carnation milk in it. Now I'm hooked on the stuff."

Vada Faith smiled and took another sip.

James had fallen asleep on the old woman's shoulder. She was surprised the woman was so immaculate. Sitting there quietly, Birdie wasn't at all what Vada Faith imagined. She smiled often and nodded at James.

After they'd finished their tea, Midgy sent Birdie off to the game room. The old woman handed a sleeping James to his mother. She looked at Vada Faith, really looked at her for the first time and her weathered face softened. She patted Vada Faith's arm.

This was the first time Vada Faith hadn't been uneasy around the old woman. She couldn't bring herself to smile at her but she didn't frown either.

"She's like a young child," Midgy commented, sipping her tea. "If she isn't with Sissy locked in their apartment, she has a sitter. She's scared to be alone and tends to wander if she is. I'm shocked at how rude people in town treat her. Birdie's not accepted anywhere Vada Faith, except the care center and here at the senior center. She's shunned when I take her in a store. People whisper about her. Birdie doesn't get it but she will eventually. I'm hurt by their behavior, even my good friends ignore her. They think if they're kind to Birdie, they're betraying you and John."

"I'm not her friend, Midgy, you know that, but I won't treat her badly."

"I know. The thing is you're the only one who can change how the others treat Birdie. I'm not asking you be her friend. All I'm asking is, if you see her in public, treat her well. Others will follow your lead." Midgy lifted her eyebrows. "Would you, please?"

"Of course." It was all she could say. She wasn't going overboard for the old woman.

"I just thought of something," her friend said, a twinkle in her eye. "I have a big favor to ask you."

Vada Faith was elated. Midgy was about to ask her to be a brides-maid. She'd be delighted, of course. Most likely, she'd ask Joy Ruth too. The three of them together again. How fun would that be?

Midgy smiled and ran her fingers through her hair.

"Come on, ask me! What is it? I can't wait!"

"Okay. Here goes. Maybe if I brought Birdie to the birthday party for James, people would accept her. They'd see that you have. I know it's a big step for you but Earl Ray would help me with her. What do you think, Vay, please say yes?"

By then, Vada Faith was standing with James on her hip and the diaper bag on her shoulder ready to leave. She didn't know what to say. She could only manage a nod. "I'll talk to John," she whispered so low she doubted her friend heard her.

How could Midgy expect her to invite the woman who kidnapped her son to his birthday party?

CHAPTER 51

ON VALENTINE'S DAY, it was sunny and warmer than usual. It was the baby's first birthday and his party was in full swing at the community center.

James was quite the celebrity. He held the record for being the only person in Shady Creek to be kidnapped and the only baby with a birthday on Valentine's Day. Two reasons to celebrate.

Nearly everyone the Waddell's knew had phoned to say they'd be there, whether they were invited or not. John had rented the community center at the last minute to hold the crowd.

A few people even showed up who hadn't bothered to call. It seemed any event held at the community center was considered open to the public, even if a fee was paid to use the facility. The residents of Shady Creek had elevated James to celebrity status and were there to celebrate.

James couldn't take his eyes off the birthday cake. It rested on a table in the middle of the room, a huge white and blue five-tiered confection with race cars on the top and circling the cake. Each layer of the donated cake was a different flavor, frosted with thick white and blue fondant. James had clapped when he first saw it and while his attention was drawn away periodically, his eyes kept going back to the dessert.

Charity and Hope, the junior welcoming committee, went to every table and thanked people for coming. The two got plenty of attention as they spun around the room in their frilly pink party dresses and black patent leather shoes, the bows in their hair shimmering with sparkles.

"Wedding cake," John said, with a grin when he saw the birthday cake. Vada Faith punched his arm playfully. "It was free," she said, "so don't complain." Balloons and streamers hung from the ceiling and danced above them as the ceiling fans stirred the air.

Seated in his high chair, the birthday boy feasted on bits of potato-chip chicken, sliding each piece across his tray until he could corner it with his fingers and push it into his mouth. Several pieces of macaroni and cheese stuck to his cheek and his blond hair was slicked back with something other than hair gel.

Vada Faith hadn't intended the party to be a luncheon but Mertie and Ditzie had other ideas. They'd gathered the Kitchen Angels from church and had transported everything needed for a full meal including all the essentials. Their friends from the red hat club assisted. The main item was Ditzie's famous Potato Chip Chicken.

"For he's a jolly good fellow," played in the background. James clapped with the song when his focus wasn't on the cake or the bits of food in his hands.

The baby squealed when Ralph, Doreen Moon's date, walked past with a three-foot tall bear with a happy birthday balloon tied to its hand. James held out his sticky hands but Ralph sidestepped the boy and hurried to the gift table.

John's gift ban was forgotten. The gift table held an assortment of presents and the cardboard box nearby was filled to capacity with canned goods for the food pantry.

Duke Cobb and Emmy Lu Ho came in with a toy police car, a red bow on its top. The two made a grand entrance. Duke saluted the crowd and announced Emmy Lu's name as if she were royalty.

James clapped along with everyone else and yelled appropriately.

"Thanks for taking care of James in the mini mart," Vada Faith said, shaking Emmy Lu's hand. "There's plenty of food so help yourself and there's dessert." She pointed to the birthday cake. "It's hard to miss," she said, laughing.

James was getting impatient to get out of his chair. When he caught sight of the cake he held out his hand and beckoned, as if calling it to him. His baby sitter, Cindy Sue, washed his face and hands and turned him loose on the floor.

It wasn't exactly the party Vada Faith had planned. However, James was thrilled and his vote was all that counted.

George sat across the room with his mom and dad, a gift clasped in his hands. He refused Vada Faith's offer to put his gift on the table with the others.

Vada Faith's frustration with George had dissipated. After four months, she was able to look at the boy and not want to throttle him for taking James out of his pen.

"Presents," Joy Ruth called, "time for opening presents."

Charity and Hope ran to help their aunt distribute the packages.

Vada Faith placed James in the middle of the circle of chairs and couches and the girls piled presents around him. Someone had brought over the giant teddy bear. The baby fell onto it and gave it a slobbery kiss.

His mother sat him back up and handed him the police car. She was thankful it didn't have batteries. James was flipping the on and off switch which operated a siren and lights.

"Thank you, Officer Cobb and Emmy Lu. James throw Duke and Emmy Lu a kiss."

He puckered up, kissed his hand, and threw it in the air. Then he fell back onto the fat bear, squealing in delight.

Helena and Louise sat together on the couch with Albert standing behind Helena, a glass of punch in his hand. The three of them were now best friends. Vada Faith wasn't sure if that was good or not, her mother and mother-in-law friends. Who could she gossip to about her mother-in-law now. Whoops. She'd forgotten. She was no longer gossiping. Well, that was a work in progress.

Charity and Hope placed themselves on the other side of the bear. "We'll help you unwrap gifts, James, okay?"

The baby frowned at them and waved his arms.

"Can I give my gift to James?" George asked shyly, coming up to Vada Faith who sat on the floor with the baby.

"Of course," she said. "Look James, here's your buddy, George."

George sprawled on the floor in front of James and handed him a package wrapped with brown paper. "I wrapped it myself. You're gonna like this, James. It kinda belongs to both of us."

Vada Faith was curious to see what it was.

James turned the box over and then raised it in his hands as if to throw it. "No," George said and grabbed the baby's arm.

"Could you open it for him, please?" Vada Faith asked. "He doesn't have the hang of unwrapping gifts yet. I'm sure that will soon change."

"Sure." George ripped off the wrapping and held up a shadow box for everyone to see. "My dad helped me make it. Inside is the bird's nest me and James found that day in your yard. There's also a feather from the bird. I thought you could keep this for James, maybe hang it on his wall as a reminder that things do turn out all right. My mom thought of that. She said everything with James turned out all right, just like with that bird. He healed and I let him fly away. Now, I'm better too."

Vada Faith hugged George, embarrassing him. He turned and gave James a high-five before hurrying to sit down.

"Here we are," Midgy called from the doorway. "Hello everyone. Sorry we're late." Midgy waved at different tables around the room, seeing people she recognized. Earl Ray had his arm on Birdie's and helped her into the room. He found a chair for her and Midgy helped her out of the plastic boots she wore over her shoes.

Midgy helped Birdie to where James sat on the floor rolling around on the bear and drooling onto his bib. His eyes lit up when he saw the old woman.

"Bird," he said, crawling to her feet. "Bird. Hi, Bird."

The old woman had been directed to a nearby folding chair and Earl Ray sat down beside her.

"Happy Birthday, little fellow." Birdie reached out and touched his shoulder but she didn't reach for him. James tried to climb onto her lap but she didn't assist him. She kept her hands on the package in her lap.

Everyone in the room had stopped talking when Birdie arrived.

At John's urging, Vada Faith had invited the old woman. However, she wasn't convinced it was the right thing to do.

"Sissy said to thank you for inviting Birdie," Midgy said to Vada Faith, then sat down beside Earl Ray.

Vada Faith nodded.

"Do you have something for James?" Midgy nudged Birdie.

"Yes," the woman said, as James continued to pull on her dress and try to climb her leg.

"You can pick him up, Birdie, it's okay." Vada Faith felt herself blush.

The crowd murmured and shuffled around restlessly as they stared at Birdie.

Charity and Hope watched with curiosity. They weren't sure it was a good idea to let Birdie hold their baby, even in the crowd of people. The woman might grab him and run. "We'll keep our eyes on her," Charity whispered to Hope. "We'll be spies until she leaves."

Birdie picked up the baby. She watched the baby's mother until the woman nodded again. James patted the old woman's arm and said, "Hi, Bird!"

Vada Faith felt the crowd relax. They were ready to move on. She had to show them she was ready too.

"It's me, old Birdie," Birdie said, and positioned James on her lap, giving him a squeeze. "This is for you." She handed him her package. Not sure what to do with it, he stuck it into his mouth. "Oh no," she said. "Here," she pulled off a piece of paper. "It's for you."

James gave a jerk and a pair of knitted brown mittens on a string flew out of the package and dropped to the floor. "Uh oh," James said, looking down at the mittens below him. "Uh oh."

Vada Faith beamed. "John, did you hear what James said? He's learning new words, honey." She leaned down and picked up the brown mittens and handed them to her son.

"I heard him." John sat on the sofa between his mother and his mother-in-law. "He's smart like his daddy."

"Uh oh." The baby smiled. Then he clapped as everyone turned to stare at him.

Vada Faith went to the coat rack by the door and took the brown cap from the pocket of her coat. They couldn't find the hat the baby usually wore so she'd brought this one. He'd need a hat on the way home if it was windy.

James grabbed the hat when she handed it to him. He jammed it on his head. She handed him the mittens and he worked to get his hand inside. The way he was working it would take a while.

"He likes them, Birdie, thank you." Vada Faith gave the woman a half smile. Maybe someday she'd give her a whole one. Just not now.

"Let's have cake," John said, coming up to kiss his wife on the cheek. "That was the right thing to do, honey." He whispered, "I'm proud of you."

"I know," she said, "but because it's the right thing, doesn't mean it's the easiest."

"I know, but you did it. That's what matters. You did it for our boy."

John went to his son and tried to help him with his mittens. "No, da, no." The baby pulled his mittens out of his father's hands.

Vada Faith stood in the middle of the room near the cake and held up her hand. "Can I have your attention?"

It took a few minutes for the crowd to settle down.

"Thank you for coming," she said. "We're thankful for each of you. We appreciate the gifts and the food. I don't know how to tell you what you mean to us. If you ever have an emergency and can't find Officer Cobb, James now owns the second police car in town." Everyone laughed.

"This is a blessed day," she added. "All our family and friends are here to help us celebrate our baby's first birthday."

She picked up James who was crawling on the floor now with his hat sideways on his head and the mitten string around his neck. She held him high in the air.

"Let's sing Happy Birthday to James," Joy Ruth said, starting the song.

Everyone joined in as James smiled and clapped from his mother's arms.

Vada Faith lit the giant candle on top of the cake and held James down to blow it out. "Make a wish, baby boy."

"Weesh. Weesh," James said. His mother moved him away quickly before he drooled on the cake and blew out the candle herself.

Mertie and Ditzie came forward to cut the cake and place it on race car plates.

"Help yourselves to cupcakes, too," Joy Ruth called, "the baker sent several dozen along with the cake. Take some home. Come on, folks, help yourself."

"Yes," Vada Faith said, adding, "let's all have cake and coffee. Then we can head home to our own Valentine celebration." James was squealing, holding his plastic fork in the air. His mother put him in his high chair and handed him a blue cupcake.

"This concludes the party," John announced, balancing a piece of cake on a plate, "thanks everyone for coming."

"Wait, John," Joy Ruth rushed toward the couple. "I have something to announce before anyone leaves. Don't leave yet, folks." She clapped her hands. "We're not finished."

Helena yelled from the sofa. "I have something to say, too, Joy Ruth. Where's Albert? Where are you, Albert?"

"Right behind you, honey bun, right behind you." Albert helped Helena off the sofa. She said, "We have something to add to today's celebration." Albert blushed and took Helena's hand.

"Okay," Vada Faith said, "Hurry it up, Mama. What's your news?"

"We're getting married in June!" Helena blushed, coming to stand beside her daughter in the center of the room. "The whole town is invited."

The crowd clapped. Several men wolf-whistled.

"Oh, Mama. Congratulations." Vada Faith hugged her mother. "James would love to be your ring bearer." James joined in by squealing, "No! No! Baba."

"Will it be big?" Her daughter asked.

"Of course, it will be big," Helena said. "Look at the size of this diamond." She held out her hand and people gathered around to check out the ring.

"Can I be a flower girl?" Charity asked, from the cake table where she was helping herself to a blue cupcake.

"Me too!" Hope seconded, standing behind her sister. "I wanna be a flower girl, too, Nanny. Can I? Please?"

"Yes," their grandmother called, "goodness, yes."

"Mama, you interrupted me," Joy Ruth said, cupping her hands around her mouth so her voice would carry, "like always, you hog the spotlight."

"Joy Ruth, that isn't true. I never hog the spotlight."

"You do too, Mama. I don't have time to fuss with you. I have something important to say." Joy Ruth beamed.

"What's this about, anyway?" Vada Faith looked at her watch. "I have to clean up here, Joy Ruth. James has to rest or he'll be cranky when Cindy Sue comes to baby sit. John and I are going out to celebrate lover's day."

"Where's my husband? Bruiser, where are you?" Joy Ruth looked around the room. "Where is he?"

"What on earth is going on?" Vada Faith put her face close to her sister's to look into her eyes." Are you sick?" She stared hard at her twin. "Are you and Bruiser having problems?"

Joy Ruth laughed, her face turning red. "Are you insane? I love that guy more than ever."

"Well, you must be adopting a baby, then?" Her sister had talked about adoption, just not recently. Vada Faith knew she'd overstepped when she saw the look on Joy Ruth's face.

"Stop it, right now! It's none of those things. You're being rude."

"I'm sorry." Vada Faith sighed. "We're just tired of waiting, honey. Say what you have to say, already."

A red-faced Bruiser made his way to the center of the room and took his wife's hand. "Okay, tell them, honey." He towered over Joy Ruth.

"No, you tell them." She squeezed his hand and pushed against him. Bruiser started sweating.

James began to whine. "Baba, baba."

"If one of you doesn't tell soon, I'm going to blow." Vada Faith unbuckled a whining James from his high chair. She handed him to Cindy Sue who gladly bounced him in her arms.

"Okay," Bruiser yelled, "we're having a baby!" He lifted Joy Ruth held her in the air. She screamed, "Put me down. Are you crazy?"

The room erupted in cheers. James squealed with delight and clapped.

"Put me down," Joy Ruth repeated. "You might drop me, silly."

"I'm three months," she called to the noisy crowd, "due in August."

Bruiser lowered her to the floor, "We're over the moon," he said, his face redder than ever.

"We are! We are!" Joy Ruth hugged everyone around her.

"Oh, honey," Louise rushed up to her daughter-in-law and grabbed her in a hug. "Being around James has been such a joy I can't wait for your little guy to get here. A mini Bruiser."

"It might be a girl," Vada Faith offered, as she wiped blue frosting from the baby's chair.

"Might be twins," John said, coming up to give his brother a bear hug.

"John!" Joy Ruth threatened him with her small fist. "Don't say that, ever. I remember your babies. They were a handful!"

"Don't say never, girl," Vada Faith said, "look back there. I said never too." She pointed to her girls sitting on the floor playing with the baby's toys. Thankfully, James hadn't noticed. When he did there would be wailing.

People were everywhere now. Talking. Laughing. Shaking Bruiser's hand. Hugging Joy Ruth. Gazing at Helena's diamond. Punching Albert in the arm. Patting John on the shoulder. Passing James around from person to person. James loved every moment of it, especially now that he had a bottle of milk in his hand.

Earl Ray had left with Midgy and Birdie, along with a plate of cupcakes for Sissy.

Vada Faith had wanted no connection between her family and the two women. She'd wanted to keep them as far apart as possible. However, it came to her that afternoon when she saw Birdie with James that the day the old woman took James from the sidewalk of their home, their lives had become entwined. Not for the two days James had been gone, and not for the few months that had passed since his return, but for all eternity. They shared an experience that couldn't be erased or forgotten. Yet, she realized, it could be forgiven.

She knew she could either make peace with what had happened or let it torment her the rest of her life. It wasn't worth the physical and mental anguish to hold on to her anger. She'd had to pray about it many times. She'd had to push forward through it. Somehow she had come to terms with what had happened the day Birdie walked down their street.

Vada Faith had resolved to move on and not let that one day ruin all the days she had left.

James and Birdie had a connection. She didn't like it anymore than she liked that warm weather wouldn't be back until June. She couldn't change either fact.

She would never forget the last few months. It was the worst and best of times. They'd all changed and grown, her more than the rest, and she knew for sure that God was in charge.

A burden was lifted from her shoulders.

She had a wedding to look forward to and a new baby on the way for her to love.

Her family was happy and safe.

She needed nothing more than what she had right this moment.

The end

Ditzie Duncan's Never-Fail Potato Chip Chicken

1 cup sour cream
Dash garlic salt
Dash onion salt
Dash paprika
1/8 teaspoon pepper
12 ounces of crushed plain potato chips
2 lb. boneless, skinless chicken breasts, if desired cut into one inch strips
1/2 c. melted butter
Parmesan cheese, optional

In bowl combine seasonings with sour cream. Dip chicken strips in sour cream mixture then into separate bowl of crushed chips. Use 15x10x1 inch baking dish, covered with oil. Drizzle strips with butter. A few sprinkles of parmesan can be used to top strips. Bake in a pre-heated 400 degree oven. Bake for 30 minutes. Check for doneness. Ten more minutes may be necessary, depending on how big the strips are cut. Serve warm with your choice of sauce. Barbecue, ranch, or honey mustard. Recipe makes approximately 10 servings.

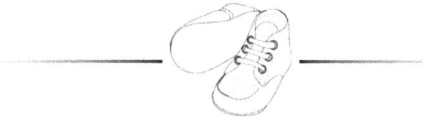

Other Books
By Barbara

A novel by
Barbara A. Whittington

THE BEST TIME of Vada Faith's life was growing up in the small town of Shady Creek and playing in the creek with her twin, Joy Ruth, and her friend, John "Wasper" Waddell, and his brothers. Yet, her adult life isn't much fun. Marriage to her high school sweetheart, John Wasper, owning her own beauty shop, and mothering their twin girls leaves her wanting more. Her dream is to have a big home in the beautiful new subdivision of Crystal Springs and get rid of their old Victorian house, which belonged to her husband's family.

When she sees an ad to be a surrogate mother for Roy and Dottie Kilgore, a new couple in town, she goes for it. She'll have money for the downpayment on the Queen Anne model home and be known as the first surrogate mother in town. She isn't fully honest with her husband when she explains her role as a surrogate.

Once she's pregnant, she learns the childless couple are smalltime criminals. Then, real heartache strikes and Vada Faith has to rethink her entire life: past, present, and future.

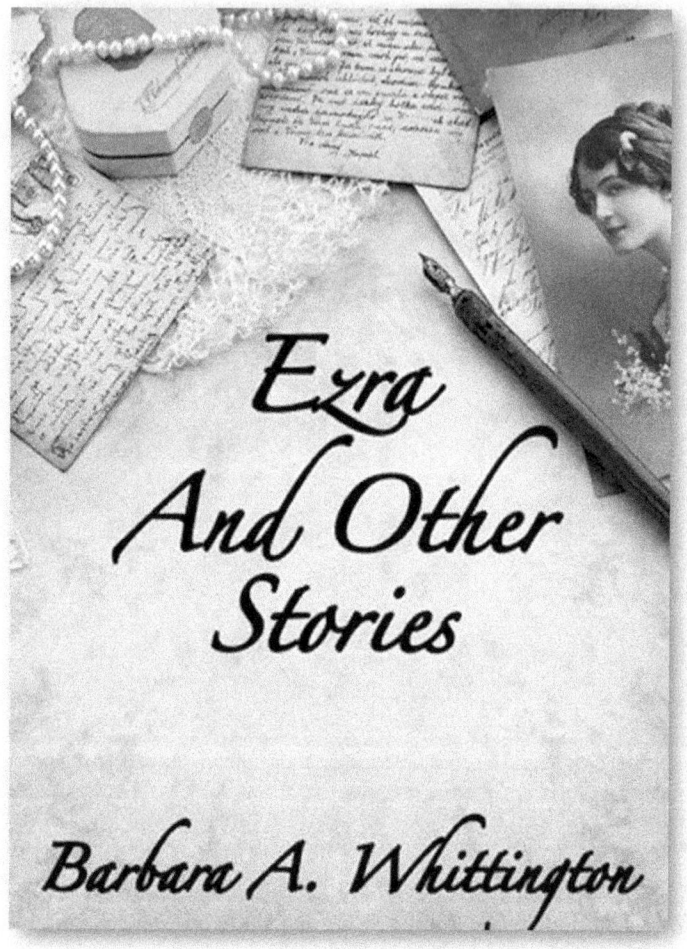

Enjoy the romance, suspense, and humor in this collection of eleven short stories. The title story, *Ezra*, poses the question, "Can only the young find the kind of love that makes your pulse race and your palms sweat?" *Ezra* offers hope for those who feel they may have missed the love boat early in life. *Joy Ruth* and *Minnie Hendrix* first appeared in The Writer's Magazine Issue #4 UK. *Mabel and the Garage Sale* was dramatized by British Broadcasting Corporation for National Public Radio and aired worldwide.

In this story, Barbara Whittington takes us back to a wartime era, in a foreign land, where distance is bridged by newlywed love. This sweet love story is over-shadowed by the horror of fighting in war, loss, and longing to be back home with his loves. From the first, you feel the soldier's internal turmoil as he deals with external danger. The Dear Anne: Love Letters from Nam were addictive to me. I looked forward to returning to them each time, and I plan on reading them again.

Five star review by Teresa C. on Amazon